Lindsey Love Loves

LLL Book 1

Sophie Sinclair

To my sister Allisson, thank you for always putting the Band-Aid on my knees when I fall.

When I saw you I fell in love,
and you smiled because you knew.

– Arrigo Boito

Dear Reader,

Music plays a big part in my life and my writing. I post the playlists on Spotify for all my books under their titles. I've included songs for certain chapters in this book that were either mentioned or fit well with the chapter. You don't have to listen along with the book, but sometimes it adds an extra element if you love music while you read. Enjoy!

Chapter 1: *Crazy Little Thing Called Love* – Queen

Chapter 3: *Break My Stride* – Matthew Wilder

Chapter 4: *When She Was My Girl* – Four Tops

Chapter 6: *What Are You Listening To?* – Chris Stapleton

Chapter 8: *Manic Monday* – The Bangles & *How Will I Know* – Whitney Houston

Chapter 9: *That's All* – Genesisx

Chapter 14: *Head Over Heels* – The Go-Go's

Chapter 15: *You Shook Me All Night Long* – AC/DC

Chapter 16: *Every Little Thing She Does Is Magic* – The Police

Chapter 20: *Under Pressure* – Queen

Chapter 23: *Everywhere* – Fleetwood Mac

Chapter 27: *Never Have I Ever* – Danielle Bradbery

Chapter 31: *One More Night* – Phil Collins

Chapter 34: *Volare* – Gypsy Kings

Prologue

SMOKE BILLOWS UP blurring my vision as I gasp for fresh air. Bullets ricochet off the table above me and I scream Nick's name, shooting my hand out as I try to grasp his shirt, but I just grab air. Patrons are screaming as I curl into myself blocking out the sounds and the carnage around me. I can't breathe. Please God, I don't want to die alone under a café table. I hear Nick shout but there's just too much smoke.

Another loud bomb goes off as more people scream. I wrap my arms tightly around my knees and bury my head into them. I know I'm crying but I can't feel anything except for a fiery heat in my ankle as I rock back and forth.

"Nick, please help me. Nick! Nick Elliot, please be alive. Please help me," I chant as I cry.

I can't see anything because of the smoke, but I'll never forget the sound of people shouting, glass breaking, bullets lodging themselves into the café walls around me as sirens roar in the distance. I pray that Nick and Patrick are alive. I don't want to survive this if they aren't.

I feel like hours have gone by, but in reality, it's only been minutes. A woman at a table next to me starts wailing. Please God, make it stop. I need Nick. I need him to hold me and tell me it's going to be all right. I need him to make it all stop. Tears blur my vision as I rock. Suddenly a hand grabs my arm and I shriek. "Please don't kill me!"

"Shh, Lindsey, it's me. I've got you. Come on, we have to get out of here. Quick," Nick whispers in my ear as he pulls me into his hard chest. I sob in relief against him. "Shh, I've got you. You're safe. Come on, I need you to move your feet."

"I can't," I cry back. "It hurts. I think I've sprained my ankle."

Strong arms quickly lift me as I bury myself into his chest, gripping his t-shirt.

"Whatever you do, keep your head down and your eyes closed." His breath tickles my ear as we start to move.

I disobey him and look up and see the lifeless body of a man in body armor I can't ever unsee. "Oh my God, oh my God…" I mumble hysterically. "Where's Patrick?"

"Goddammit woman, do you ever listen to me? Close your eyes! He's safe."

I immediately close my eyes and say a prayer thanking God that both my men are safe. Nick stops jogging as someone speaks to him harshly in French. He answers back, his tone just as severe, and then he continues to jog. If I weren't freaking the fuck out I would have commented on how flawlessly the French language rolled off his tongue. But I can't think about that. I don't want to think about anything. I whimper and Nick's arms tighten around me.

"I've got you Lindsey, you're safe now. I've got you."

Chapter 1

Lindsey

Mrs. Bixby

Eight weeks earlier

IT'S SOUPY HOT as I trudge down the cobblestone street carrying my messenger bag and unsweet tea. The ice has already melted in the five-minute walk from the coffee shop to King Street where I am currently wilting like a magnolia flower left out in the sun. I turn the corner and sigh in relief as my apartment comes into view.

I live in a little two-bedroom apartment on the second floor of an old brick walk-up. Apparently it's the original structure since the Civil War. It's beautiful in its old grandeur, but it definitely needs some updating. My kitchen sink faucet leaks, the floorboards creak like crazy, and the air conditioning is always on the fritz. Why do I continue to live in this ancient, creaky old place, one might ask? Because it has an incredible screened-in porch that overlooks the most glorious gardens with a pool tended by my landlord's wretched elderly grandmother, Mrs. Bixby. It's also dirt cheap.

Mrs. Bixby lives below me and I keep waiting for the day she keels over or moves into a retirement home. I know, I know, *shame on, you Lindsey Love for thinking such horrible thoughts*, but Mrs. Bixby is…

"Well it's about time."

I sigh as I look up at the crusty old bat I just summoned from hell by thinking about her in my head. She's standing in her doorway with her nose in the air, her snow-white hair perfectly coiffed. Her blouse is starched to perfection and her floral skirt is the appropriate length. Her pantyhose from 1965 have never seen a run in them and to top it off she's wearing her pearls and heels, even though I know she hasn't left her apartment. She looks like the grandmother that would greet you at the door with a tin full of freshly baked chocolate chip cookies. Trust me, she's not.

"Good afternoon, Dinah."

She clucks her tongue. "Didn't your mama teach you any manners? It's *Mrs. Bixby*. Stop making such a racket! I can't hear *Jeopardy*."

Did I mention she used to be a third-grade teacher? She probably used a ruler across knuckles and made kids pee in their pants with her vapid stare when they got the answer wrong. I imagine Mrs. Bixby was never on anyone's most-favorite list.

"Um…I was just turning my key in the lock, Mrs. Bixby."

"Never you mind! Are you going out like a harlot again tonight? All that makeup caked on your face. Why back in my day a woman looked pure, her skin dewy like a cool spring morning." She eyes me up and down. "You look like you just went for a swim. A lady never shows that she perspires. She carries herself with grace and dignity, no matter the temperature."

She wrinkles her nose in revulsion as I try to picture her playing shuffleboard at *Seasons by the Bay*, a local retirement community. It's my go-to daydream whenever she opens her mouth. I seriously don't want to listen to her midcentury lessons on how a woman should be. "Mrs. Bixby, is there a reason you stopped me? Do you need something?" *Like a muzzle?*

She crosses her arms over her thin body. "I told Richie that you make too much noise coming home at night. All the floors creaking. Bringing home different men at all hours. Moaning and groaning against my door. And I heard your cat meowing again like it was in heat."

What on earth is she talking about? Add delusional to her list of attributes. My cheeks heat as I push open my door. "I think you've been watching too many soap operas, Mrs. Bixby. I haven't brought a man home in quite a while, not that it's any of your business. I come home late because I *work* late. And my cat isn't in heat. He's neutered. And male. Tell Rich to fix the stairs if it bothers you so much or better yet, move out!"

"Why I never!" she gasps just like Scarlett Ohara in *Gone with the Wind*. "I'm gonna report you to Richie!" She steps back in her apartment and slams her door. For being such a feeble old Southern woman, she sure can make that door rattle.

"You do that, ye old bag," I mumble as I trudge up the narrow flight of stairs. I'm not afraid of her. I'm always on time with my rent and Rich is a good friend of mine. He hates his grandmother, but he lets her live here rent-free because she's family. Secretly I think he just wants her inheritance, but he's never voiced that out loud.

I open my door at the top of the stairs and breathe a sigh of relief as cool air washes over me. Thank goodness the A/C is working today. The humidity is so thick outside you could cut it with a knife. My cat Mac meows from the couch.

"Don't get up." I reach over to pet his head when I pass the couch and he tries to bite me. Mac and I have a love-hate relationship…he loves to hate me. He was my parents' cat before they decided they wanted to sail around the world on a cruise. So now Mac lives with me.

I'm his servant who feeds him and changes his litterbox and I think he appreciates me…okay, he doesn't appreciate me. But one of these days I know I'll win him over.

I drink the rest of my tea and then change into a tank top and shorts as I sink back on to the couch and turn on the television. I flip to the Food Network and watch a new episode of Bobby Flint. My eyes start to close just as my phone vibrates on the coffee table. It's my sister Shannon.

"Hello?"

"You sound awful, are you okay?"

"Yeah, just tired. I must have dozed off."

"Are you packed?"

"Not yet."

"Lindsey, do I need to come over there and pack your bag for you? You should be excited! It's not every day a food critic gets asked to do a show for *Food and Travel*."

"I know, I know. I *am* excited, I'm just nervous. I wish you could go to the meeting with me."

Shannon sighs. "I know, me too. Don't worry, it will be

a snap and you have Margot there to help pave the way. You've got this. I'm really proud of you, little sister!"

"Thanks Shanny, I'll get up and pack right now so you don't call me every fifteen minutes."

"Don't forget to pack that sexy red dress we talked about!"

"Yeah, yeah. Call you later."

"You got this! Byeee!"

I look up at my TV and fall back against my pillows. I'll pack later…one more Bobby Flint episode won't hurt. I wonder if they're going to air the Paul's Balls episode again. Head out of the gutter, I'm referring to his risotto balls. My guest spot on that show is what spun me into mass public appeal. My giggling over Paul's balls caught a TV executive's eye for *Food and Travel* and six months later, here I am flying out to New York City tomorrow to meet with executive producer Simon Blake and my agent Margot Andrews. My sister is right, this is the chance of a lifetime.

My phone buzzes again. It's Margot.

"Hey Margot." I try to sound chipper but fail miserably.

"Are you sick? What's wrong?"

"Nothing, just groggy. My sister woke me up from a nap right before you called."

"Oh, okay. Are you ready for tomorrow night?"

"I think so?"

"Lindsey, Lindsey, Lindsey…where is the confident feisty persona I know and adore? You need to *woo* Simon Blake with your charm. He wants to meet you and see what all the fuss is about when it comes to Lindsey Love."

"There's no fuss—"

"Lindsey, stop being modest. Your followers adore you, and now millions will fall in love with you. Okay, so listen, I've got to run. I'll send you your flight info and itinerary and I'll see you in New York tomorrow night!"

"Okay, Margot, I promise I'll turn this frown upside down! See you tomorrow."

I started a food blog in college called "Lindsey Love Loves." It started out simple, critiquing the dorm food and local restaurants in the area. I started posting live videos on social media and YouTube. It was an instant hit. My blog and YouTube channel blew up and I started getting advertisers which meant I was getting paid. The best part? I can live anywhere and travel around to local eats. Kind of like "Diners and Drive Ins" but I don't have Guy Fieri's crazy hair or annoying loud voice.

One of my videos caught the eye of a producer on Bobby Flint's show and they asked me to be a guest judge on the show. What a train wreck that turned out to be. One of the contestants going up against Chef Bobby went absolutely ballistic when he lost and security ended up having to taser him to the ground. Viewers took to social media and thought my reactions and comments to Paul's balls were pure gold. I even have a meme, *bless it.*

Everything I've worked my butt off for is finally coming to fruition.

I get up off the couch and stretch. Margot is right, I need to get my head in the game. Simon Blake, prepare to be dazzled!

Chapter 2

Nick

Scar

"NICK ELLIOT, IT'S good to see you."

I look up from the desk and curse Cherise for letting this self-righteous asshole into my office.

"Whatever it is, my answer is no."

"Aw, c'mon, man. You don't even know what I'm going to ask."

I arch an eyebrow and fold my arms over my chest. "I bet I can guess. You have some new awful show you want me to produce. My answer is no."

Simon chuckles and shakes his head. "How long have we gone back?"

"I'm not going backward or forward with you. Now get out."

"Scar, we need you on this. Europe has gotten unpredictable. I need someone who has a sense for danger and knows the lay of the land. Besides, you're used to the hustle-bustle of getting projects done on time and under budget." He smiles cheekily at me. "It's totally different than *Naked in the Wild*. This time there will be a cute little brunette eating at fancy restaurants, not a hairy naked guy eating worms in the wild."

I sit back in my chair and arch an eyebrow at Simon. "I told myself after *Naked in the Wild* I would never put myself through your bullshit again. What on earth makes you think I want to globetrot, babysitting a snotty little food critic, and produce her show?"

Simon quickly sits down in the seat across from me, getting way too comfortable for my liking. I'm pretty sure I just said no to his offer. "Okay, so *Naked in the Wild* was a little much, even I'll admit that, but the show itself was a huge hit!"

I growl out, "Not with me." The last show Simon asked me to produce and provide security for was pretty much like the show with Bear Grylls, except I had some pansy-ass British model who pretended to do daring stunts, naked, in the Colombian rainforest. The only thing was, he usually chickened out right before the stunt and I ended up having to fill in for him. All those naked scenes of a guy jumping off a cliff? Yeah, that was me. Never again.

"Remember when you got caught in a mudslide on the side of the mountain? That was fucking epic! You won an Emmy for that!"

"Remember when I had to shoot my way out of a drug lord's backyard? I'm pretty sure my wanted poster is still all over Cartagena. You left me hanging out in the wind to fend for myself." I grimace at the memory of nearly losing my life as we were trying to leave the country. And I thought being a Navy SEAL had been intense.

"Eh, you got to the American Embassy in the nick of time." Simon grins as he snaps his fingers.

"Get out."

His grin slides off his face. "Scar, please. I'll owe you one for this. I'll get you whatever you want while on location. First-class airfare, five-star hotels, private drivers, fancy restaurants. Anything you want, it will be yours."

"Don't call me Scar... I told you, I'm done. And if you knew me, you'd know that shit doesn't impress me."

Simon sits back in his chair and steeples his fingers. "Nick, you're the best at this. You already have the tie-in with *Food and Travel*." He takes his phone out and pulls up a video, sliding the phone toward me. "She has a huge following. This will blow up her career and be a huge hit for the network."

"So basically, this will make you look good."

Simon turns serious. "And *you*. I wouldn't be here if this wasn't important. I'll never bother you again after this, I swear."

I close my eyes and heave a sigh, shaking my head.

Chapter 3

Lindsey

Seth Rogan and Sliders

I WALK INTO the swanky bar in Manhattan. I'm feeling good in a tight red dress that hits right below my knees. Shannon insisted I wear it because she said it looked killer on me and it's a power color. My chestnut-brown hair is down, soft waves curled into it. I nervously tuck my black clutch under my arm as I look around the crowded room for Margot. I quickly scan the patrons by the bar, my eyes connecting with a pair of direct brown ones.

The man eyes me unswervingly as he bites into a slider. He chews it sensuously as his gaze rakes over me. He's eyeing me like he knows me…intimately, and it leaves me feeling exposed. *Damn you Shannon for making me wear this tight dress if it attracts creeps like this guy.* A glob of sauce drops down on his shirt, but he doesn't notice. My finger automatically goes to my chest as I point to the spot where the sauce is dripping down his front. He misinterprets this regrettable move as an invitation. He smirks and gives me a wink as he chews and then takes a drink of beer before swallowing his food. I grimace in revulsion.

The guy gives me a nod but I don't return it, because I

don't want to encourage him, yet I can't look away from this car wreck. He has bushy curly hair, a beard, and black horn-rimmed glasses. The whole hipster Seth Rogen vibe he's got kicking doesn't do a thing for me. He bites into the slider while blatantly staring at me, taking another drink of beer while he chews. That right there would be my dealbreaker. Who eats and drinks at the same time? I frown at him as I turn and direct my attention elsewhere. This girl is *not* interested. Out of the corner of my eye I can see him start to get up out of his stool and I know he's coming for me. I panic as I quickly turn in circles looking for Margot.

"Lindsey Love, there you are!" Margot waves from the back of the bar as she makes her way over to me. *Oh, thank you Lord Jesus.*

"Hi Margot, it's so good to see you! You look gorgeous!"

Margot has been my agent for the last two years. She's very New York chic, her shiny black hair cut into a sleek bob, her Chanel suit fitting her like a glove. She's in her fifties, on her fourth marriage, and looks like a million bucks. If anyone were to play her in a movie, Bebe Neuwirth comes to mind. Margot's a hoot, but a shark when it comes to business deals. I'm so lucky to have her in my corner. She's been working her tail off to get me a television deal for the past year.

"Darling, you're too kind." She air-kisses my cheek in greeting. "How's my favorite food critic? Love this dress, perfect for our meeting. Come on, let's get you a drink and meet Simon, he's over by the bar. He's a handsome devil. If I were ten years younger…" She laughs as she steers me toward the bar—to the guy eating the slider.

Oh no…oh god no, Simon Blake is the slider guy? How am I going to schmooze with him and tell him how badly I want this deal when he's leering at my boobs?

"Margot, maybe this isn't such a good idea—"

"What? Shush, you're just nervous. Simon! Hello, darling! I want you to meet Lindsey Love."

The slider-eating, beer-drinking, hipster-wannabe turns around and my stomach drops. Particles of food are stuck in his beard as he licks his lips. I'm seriously questioning Margot's judgment in men when he speaks.

"Finally, Lindsey Love… I've been wondering when you would arrive."

I'm staring at him, but his lips aren't moving. Movement to my left causes my eyes to flicker over to a tall handsome blond man who's smiling at me with a twinkle in his eye and his hand outstretched towards me. *Oh, thank God.* Relief shutters through my body as I realize my mistake.

Margot clears her throat and laughs nervously. "Oh, she must still be jetlagged from her trip. Lindsey dear, *this* is Simon Blake from *Food and Travel.*"

I turn my back on fake Seth Rogen and put my hand in Simon's. His strong warm hand engulfs mine. I give him my megawatt smile and shake it firmly.

"It's so nice to finally meet you."

"The pleasure is mine. I've been following your blog and your YouTube channel for a while and I think your next step should be television. Margot didn't mention how exquisite you are in person."

I blush at his compliment, totally falling apart under his hot gaze. "Oh, um thank you. I'm very excited that *Food and*

Travel is even considering me."

"I see someone I need to introduce myself to. Simon, I assume Lindsey is in good hands?"

"Kid gloves, Margot."

Margot winks at me as she waves to someone across the room. Simon leans in and his scent makes me want to lick his neck. "I'm going to let you in on a little secret."

Is it dirty, Simon? I'll be your dirty little secret. Oh for God's sake Lindsey, get a hold of yourself. I wonder if he can tell that his voice turns me into a limp noodle, a puddle of goo, a simpering idiot. "Oh? What's that?" I ask breathily.

"You're not being considered. You've got the show."

My mouth drops open and he chuckles at my reaction. "For real?"

"For real." He smiles a full-blown movie-star grin and my knees tremble. "I'll need to meet with Margot and iron out the details, but if you want it, the show is yours, Lindsey Love."

I do fist-pumps in my head, I'm so excited. "Yes! Yes, of course I want it. Thank you so much," I gush. "Um, Mr. Blake...I—"

"Please, call me Simon."

"Oh, okay, Simon. I know it's kind of ballsy to ask for this up front, and I may kick myself later for asking, but I can't...no I *won't* do it unless my friend Patrick can do the filming and editing."

Simon blows out a woosh of air. "Oh...I don't know...I think we have someone already."

"Please, Simon, he's amazing. He's been with me from the very beginning and knows my style. He's super easy to

15

work with and just an all-around likable guy."

"I'll have to run it by the producer and director. *Food and Travel Network* isn't giving us a big budget for this project, so I was only going to have the producer travel with you and whoever he picks to film, but maybe he'll be open to Patrick." He smiles genuinely at me. "I like ballsy by the way." He lightly touches his finger to my nose. "You're adorable. I think the ratings are going to go through the roof."

I smile at him. "Don't worry, I'm going to wow the pants off of *Food and Travel*."

Someone from behind bumps into me, causing me to stumble into Simon's arms. He catches me easily as he looks down into my eyes. "I'm counting on it," he murmurs.

I'm lost in his ice-blue eyes as they lock onto mine. I gently push myself away from him. As handsome as he is and as easily as I could get lost in his sexy smile, he's my executive producer. I can't get involved and screw up my one opportunity. He smiles knowingly.

"Should we celebrate with some bubbly?" Simon tips his finger at the bartender and orders three glasses of Moet.

"Yes, that would be great."

"So! Have we made a deal, Mr. Blake?" Margot steps into our circle as Simon hands her a glass of champagne. He gently places his hand on my back, his touch searing through my dress. He winks at me as I beam back at him.

"I believe we have, Margot. Cheers, ladies, to the next chapter of *Lindsey Love Loves...*" He takes a sip and looks down at his watch. "Shoot, I have another party I need to get to. Margot, I'll call you tomorrow to iron out the details.

Lindsey, I'm going to say yes to Patrick, so that's a done deal." My smile splits my face as he leans in to kiss my cheek. "I look forward to getting to know you better, Miss Love," he whispers in my ear causing me to shiver, my skin breaking out in goosebumps.

Simon Blake is going to be hard to resist, that's for sure.

He shakes Margot's hand and turns to leave. "Oh, right, I almost forgot. Lindsey, can you meet with the producer tomorrow morning for coffee? I'll try to make it as well."

I look over at Margot and her eyes are dancing with excitement as she nods at me. "Yes, of course I can."

"Great, let me get your number." He whips out his cell phone and we exchange numbers. "I'll text you a time and location in the morning. Ladies, it was a pleasure."

I sigh as he steps away.

"Well, congratulations Lindsey, you definitely worked your magic!" Margot hugs me as I'm left in a daze.

"I can't believe it. Lindsey Love is going national!"

"Honey, Lindsey Love is going *international*. Buckle up, because you're going on the ride of your life."

Chapter 4

Nick

There's Always the Subway

I LOOK AT my watch as I put the sports section of the newspaper down on the table in the coffee shop. She's late. This does not bode well. This whole production is making me uneasy. After I retired as a SEAL I wanted to pursue my love for directing documentaries and wildlife. But then Simon, a former Navy SEAL who served in my company, called me up and gave me the opportunity to start knocking down some doors that would have otherwise taken me years to open. I couldn't pass it up. *Naked in the Wild* was a pain-in-the-ass show, but we did receive three Emmys for it, so I can't complain too much. It gave me the credibility I was so desperately seeking in the directing world.

I text Simon that she's late. Tardiness makes me grumpy. It's the years of military training, but it's also common courtesy. I have to head up to my family's cabin this afternoon in the Catskills, and I don't want to spend my morning waiting on some princess who overslept.

I'm facing the door when it slams open and a petite brunette comes in shaking the rain off her broken umbrella. She looks like a drowned rat as she looks around the coffee shop, her eyes landing on me. I arch an eyebrow at her and she mimics my expression. She tosses the useless umbrella by the newspaper stand at the door, rolls her shoulders back and strides towards me, a dazzling smile replacing the scowl she was wearing. My initial reaction to her punches me in the gut. She's breathtaking.

"Mr. Elliot? Hi, I'm Lindsey Love." She stands in front of me with her hand outstretched dripping water on my newspaper. I move the paper away from her.

"Is that your real name?" I ask rudely. Sounds like a porn star name to me, not a food critic.

She looks affronted before she quickly recovers, flashing me a brilliant smile. "Yep, the name my mama gave me on my birth certificate." She glances down and notices the water pooling on the table. "Oh, sorry, I got a little wet. Rain, who knew?" She chuckles as she wrings out her shirt with her other hand.

"People who listen to the weather report."

"Right." She giggles nervously. Her hair is plastered to her head, strands stuck to her cheek. Mascara has made little smudges under her eyes where the rain has melted her makeup. Her jacket and jeans are drenched.

"You're late." I hand her a napkin, ignoring her wet outstretched hand as I indicate for her to sit in the booth across from me.

She quickly grabs the napkin and wipes her hands, peeling off her jacket, the smile sliding off her face. "Yes, and I do apologize. I'm not usually late, but it started to rain on my walk here, so I had to stop and buy an umbrella, but the cheap thing fell apart after one gust of wind. So then I tried to hail a cab, but some jerk jumped into the one that stopped for me and so I just schlepped it the rest of the way here."

Her Southern drawl is like honey drizzled over buttered biscuits. She lifts a finger, signaling for the waitress.

"There's always the subway," I say gruffly.

She looks at me irritably. "Well, yes, and I'll probably take that on the way home if I can figure it out. Thank you for that helpful advice," she replies testily as she quickly peruses the menu. "Are you eating?"

"No."

She stares at me for a beat. I know I'm being an asshole, but I can't help myself. This whole project rubs me the wrong way. I should have listened to my gut and turned Simon down, but now the ball is in motion and I have to follow through.

The waitress appears and she quickly jots down Lindsey's order.

"So Mr. Elliot, it appears that we will be working together." She assesses me as she drums her fingers on the table.

"You can call me Nick. Yes, I'll be your producer and director on this assignment. I will also be your security."

She laughs and it's the prettiest sound I've heard in…forever. My jaw clenches as I grind my teeth.

"Oh, I won't need security, but thank you for the offer. I'm just a country-bumpkin food critic from South Carolina, no one will look twice at me." She winks at me which makes me scowl.

When she walked in, all heads turned in her direction, not because of her being drenched, but because she's a natural beauty. There's a sweet innocence about her that makes you look once and let your eyes linger appreciatively.

"I disagree. I think you're savvier than that, Ms. Love, so you can leave the 'country-bumpkin' innocent act at the door."

She arches an eyebrow at me as the waitress sets her coffee down on the table with a huge plate of eggs, bacon, hash browns, and a slice of sourdough toast. She dives into her food with gusto.

"New York seriously has the best diner food," she mumbles around a mouthful. I watch her lips as they wrap around her fork and I imagine it wrapping around my... *Jesus Christ, Elliot, get a handle on yourself.*

I clear my throat and shift in my seat trying to regain my composure. "So, I've looked at your blog. Why don't you tell me the direction you see the show going."

She shrugs and takes a sip of her drink. "I don't really know. I assumed it was up to *Food and Travel*. My style is to just go somewhere new, a place that hasn't been done before. I kind of like little off-the-beaten-path hole-in-the-walls. I mean anyone can find the trendy new restaurant that just opened up around the corner, right? I like the little mom-and-pop places that are the town's best-kept secrets."

I run my hand along my jaw as I stare at her. She looks like a wet dog that just came out of the rain, but her skin is smooth and creamy, her mossy green eyes bright and beautiful. She's bouncy and cute and ridiculously likable, and every cell in my body is pinging signals of want and need off of her. What I *need* is to ignore this gut response to her appealing beauty if I'm going to be taking this project on.

I focus my attention on her coffee cup. "Have you been

to Europe before?"

"Only to London, which I think is one of the places F and T wants us to go to, right?"

I nod. "Okay, so how are you planning to research finding little holes in the walls over in Europe? You should have come to this meeting with a prepared list."

Her jaw flexes as she grinds her molars. "Considering I was just offered the deal last night I haven't had much time to prepare. My friend Patrick who will be filming with us—"

"Wait, who? What do you mean filming with us?"

"Oh, Simon didn't tell you?"

My skin feels suddenly itchy with annoyance. "No, Simon didn't tell me."

"I didn't tell you what?" Simon approaches our booth and smiles down at Lindsey. "Hello again, Ms. Love. I see you two have gotten acquainted."

Lindsey smiles up at him and scoots over in the booth bringing her coffee and plate with her so that Simon can sit next to her. I don't like the way she's smiling at him, like he's fucking dessert.

I clear my throat. "You didn't tell me about…"

"Patrick," Lindsey supplies.

"Oh that. Right, so part of Lindsey's contract is to bring on her partner Patrick Healy to film the project. I figure you'd be okay with it."

"Well a heads-up would have been nice before a decision was made. Does Patrick even know what he's doing?" I give Simon a pointed look.

Lindsey bristles across from me. "Of course he does. He graduated as a film major and has worked with me for the last three years."

Simon puts an arm around Lindsey and squeezes her shoulder. "This one here is a tough nut to crack, I had to make a decision on the spot. Trust me, Scar, I've seen his work, he'll get the job done right."

I want to break Simon's arm off at his shoulder and hit him over the head with it.

"Scar?" Lindsey looks over at me, raising a perfectly manicured eyebrow. I ignore her as I pick up my pen and start a list on my tablet next to me.

"So Simon, what does the network need from us? Are we starting any shows in the United States or is it all Europe?"

Simon looks over at Lindsey and smiles. "I think the majority will be over in Europe. The network wants one or two here in the States. Maybe a region Lindsey has never covered before to give you guys some practice working together before going overseas."

Why is he looking at her like he wants to eat her? I flex my fingers so that I don't reach out and strangle him. An absurd idea suddenly pops into my head and it comes tumbling out of my mouth before I can think through my plan.

"I know a good hole-in-the-wall about two hours from here in Upstate New York near my fishing cabin. We could head out there tomorrow."

"Fantastic!" Simon starts typing on his phone.

"Tomorrow?" Lindsey chimes. "Oh, I don't know..."

"Why not? You have something better to do? When do you head back?" I challenge.

"I um...I don't have Patrick!" she shouts as if she's down

to the last second on a game show.

Simon smiles at her. "It's just a practice run, Lindsey. It will be good for you and Sca…Nick to get to know each other. You have a few days, right?"

Lindsey visibly swallows as she looks up at me.

"Good, it's settled." I smirk. "I'll text you the address."

"Oh, we're not driving up together?"

"No, I have to head out this afternoon."

"No worries, I'll have the hotel arrange something for you."

"Okay, thank you, Simon."

Is that relief I see flash across her face? I run my hand across my two-day-old scruff and curl my lip up at her. "Well, I've got to head out. Simon, I'll call you later."

He waggles his eyebrows at me and it takes superhuman strength not to pop him in the mouth. I give him a warning glare. If he lays one finger on this woman…

"Lindsey, it was nice to meet you and I'll see you tomorrow." I drop a few bills on the table. "Please don't be late."

Her lips purse in annoyance. Why do I love trying to get under this woman's skin so much? And why do I want to beat Simon to a pulp as I watch him squeeze her shoulder? I gather my things before I do something I'll regret and leave without a backward glance.

Chapter 5

Lindsey

He's Not a Nice Guy

WHAT THE HELL was that? I stare down at my half-eaten plate of food. I feel like I just got kicked in the stomach.

"Lindsey, are you okay?"

"Oh, I'm sorry Simon, did you say something?"

"I said I know he's a lot to take, but he's the best I've ever worked with, trust me on this one."

"Hmm, is he always so surly?"

Simon laughs. "Yeah, pretty much. Don't take it personally. He really does know his stuff. Listen I've got to run too. I'll see you this afternoon to sign the paperwork. Maybe we could have dinner after? A little celebration."

I smile shyly up at Simon. "Sure, I'd love that."

Nope. No ma'am. You are *not* getting involved with him…but he's so damn cute and appealing! No girl, he is *off limits*. He's your executive producer for fuck's sake. I must remain professional. I tamp down my inner hussy that wants to jump Simon's bones as he stands to leave.

"See you this afternoon." He winks as my ovaries flutter in anticipation.

I smile at him as he exits the restaurant. Simon Blake is

kind and charming, the complete opposite of that snarly asshole that was just sitting across from me. I mean I'd be rude too if I had a nickname like Scar. More like Scab.

I can't *believe* he had the audacity to tell me I was late and then he refused to shake my hand! Granted, they were wet with rain, but still! And then to ask if that was really my name? Like I haven't had kids making fun of my name my whole life! I felt like I was transported back to high school when Billy Doogan spread rumors that I was a porn star after I turned him down for homecoming. I turned him down because he was eighteen and would pick his nose and wipe the boogers on his jeans...said it was a guy thing. It was gross is what it was.

I pull my phone out and quickly text Patrick.

Me: *Any way you can quickly get up to New York City by tomorrow morning?*
Trick: *Uh, no can do Lovie. Trouble?*

I sigh in defeat.

Me: *I met our Director/Producer today. He's a real gem.*
Trick: *Well, this should be interesting! At least you have me.*
Me: *At least I have you. Xo*

I type Nick Elliot's name into Google. Several images of him show up with a tall blonde on his arm. Curiosity sparks inside of me to know more about this strange, surly man.

He does look super sexy dressed in a tuxedo, I begrudgingly admit to myself. But just because he has a killer body, muscular arms that could kill a man with just a twitch of muscle, a broad chest that makes his t-shirt groan in protest, and a butt that fits his Levi's perfectly...does not mean he's a nice guy.

And just because his perfect Roman nose, dark sapphire-blue eyes, and hold-onto-me-while-I-screw-your-brains-out sexily styled chocolate-brown hair makes my body hum in pleasure...*does not indeed* indicate that he is a nice guy.

And just because he has a dimple when I saw a half-smile form across his perfectly shaped lips that would even make Mrs. Bixby's almost-dead black heart flutter, most definitely *does not* indicate that he is a nice guy.

He's an asshat is what he is.

And now I have to drive out of New York City, which scares the hell out of me, because *he* deemed it necessary. Taking a taxi is terrifying enough, but to have to get behind the wheel with all the crazies in the city and drive? Pure suicide. All to meet Mr. Congeniality at some remote cabin in the woods. It makes my stomach roll just thinking about it.

I quickly read his Wikipedia page as I stab at a piece of scrambled egg on my plate. It says that he's thirty-three years old from Ithaca, New York and that he is a retired Navy SEAL. Interesting. Explains the incredible physique and military-like attitude, but how on earth does a Navy SEAL become a producer at a Food Network? He's single, except for the pictures he's in with a gorgeous blonde named Whitney Moreau, a former swimsuit model...shocker. And he won a few Emmys for some show called *Naked in the Wild*. Interesting title.

And now this guy, Nick Elliot, is directing and producing my show, *Lindsey Love Loves.* I mean, I'm proud of what I do, but I imagine it's a bit of a low blow for his career. He should be paragliding off rugged mountains and wrestling alligators in the Amazon. Do they even have alligators in the Amazon? Whatever, it doesn't matter.

What matters is that I'm the new chip on his shoulder and I'm going to have to find a way to make him my friend. I also don't want to embarrass him, or ruin his career.

Man up, Lindsey, you got this girl. You are going to drive like Mario Andretti to that cabin tomorrow and be *so* awesome that Nick Elliot will be begging you to be his best friend.

With my new plan and renewed energy I pay my tab, grab my broken umbrella, and walk the eight blocks back to the hotel. Screw the rain, screw the subway, and screw Nick Elliot's gorgeous face!

Chapter 6

Lindsey

Chocolate Cake

I MANEUVER THE cute little Fiat onto the highway after sweating bullets driving through Manhattan. Talk about a clusterfuck of scary-ass drivers and pedestrians who will just walk off the sidewalk into traffic. One had the audacity to step out in front of my car and then bang on my hood when I almost ran him over. I'm pretty sure I peed in my pants a little. I call my sister to catch her up on the last couple of days.

"Dr. Mason's office."

"Oh, hi Carol, it's Lindsey. I meant to dial Shannon's cell phone, I must have accidentally dialed the office."

"No worries, I'll patch you through!"

"Thanks."

"Hey Linds, everything okay?"

"Yeah, sorry, I must have pressed the wrong button while driving."

"You shouldn't be driving and talking, it's illegal."

"I've got you on Bluetooth. Anyway, do you have a minute? I want to tell you about my dinner last night." I sigh dreamily as I think of Simon.

"Dinner? Aren't you there to be signing important contracts?"

"Yeah, got that all done. I went to dinner with the executive producer of the show last night. Oh my god Shannon, I am seriously swooning."

"What? Did you have sex with him? That's not very professional, Lindsey. I mean I'm all for a healthy sex life but...I hope you're using protection, and not just the Pill. Do you need me to give you more condoms and a safe-sex packet?"

I groan. "Please don't go all Dr. Shannon on me. I'm thirty years old, I think I know about safe sex. And I don't need any more protection, I have a ten-year supply thanks to you." I look over my shoulder as I zip into another lane. My sister is an OB/GYN and constantly badgering me about safe sex. "Sadly, we did not have sex because he *is* the executive producer of my show and I kept it professional. Besides, Margo was there too, that might have gotten a little awkward." I sigh thinking back to our dinner. "He's so sweet and charming though."

"He's also your new boss. Where are you headed to now?"

"Ugh, I'm going to some remote part of Upstate New York to have a trial-run dinner with my new director-slash-producer. I met him yesterday morning. He's a total jerk."

"Oh no, this is the guy that you and Patrick will be traveling with? Why is he a jerk?"

"He's an ex-Navy SEAL and he doesn't crack a smile. He got mad at me for being late to a breakfast meeting when I got caught in a downpour. He...he's just so...ugh! He's so damn frustrating!"

"Is he hot?"

"I mean, if you consider Oscar the Grouch hot…"

Shannon chuckles. "Well this should be good."

"What did you say? The car must have gone through a dead zone."

"I said have a good time. Oh, my next appointment is here. Have safe sex with the grouch!"

"Wait, what? I'm *not* having sex!" I yell, but she's already hung up on me.

She must have misunderstood me. I don't want to have sex with Nick Elliot. That would be…just probably be…pretty damn good to be honest. I picture his hooded sapphire-blue eyes as I trail my fingers down hard muscle…his dimples popping out with a satisfied smirk. *Oh, yes.*

No, Lindsey, he's a jerk! You aren't allowed to think that way about him. Think about Simon. Safe, sexy, charming, Simon Blake. *No, no, you can't think about him either, he's off limits.* Better yet? Think of chocolate fudge layer cake, that's safe and won't bite your head off or shoot daggers at you. It may make you gain a pound or five, but it's oh so worth it.

Damn it, now I'm craving chocolate. I turn the radio up to drown out thoughts of Nick, Simon, and chocolate as I blast down the highway.

TWO HOURS LATER I pull down a gravel drive to a beautiful

wood house jutting over a serene lake. Wow, this isn't what I was picturing. I double-check the address to make sure I didn't make a wrong turn, but the address is correct. Weeping willows gently blow in the breeze near the wraparound deck. I cut the engine and take a deep breath. It's four p.m.—ha, I'm actually early, take that Nick Elliot! But I'm also tired and hungry, not really wanting to get back in the car and find some hole-in-the-wall fish camp. I grab my purse and my suitcase and wheel it up to the front door. All the bushes around the house are meticulously trimmed, the green grass recently cut.

I ring the doorbell and Nick opens the heavy oak door. Oh sweet Jesus, he's even better looking today. He's wearing a fitted blue T-shirt that shows off his spectacular upper body with athletic shorts. The color turns his eyes into a brilliant blue. They're stunning.

"Hi." I smile uneasily as he steps aside for me to come in.

"Hi," he says gruffly.

I swallow past my unease as I look around. I'm not going to lie, I'm nervous as hell. I just met this man for about an hour yesterday. It's so strange that I'm now having a sleepover at his house in the middle of nowhere, New York.

I look around pleasantly surprised by my surroundings. I was expecting some dingy hunting camp with overgrown weeds and a couple metal cots thrown in the middle of a poorly lit room with an old cracked linoleum floor. What I find is honey-brown glossy hardwood floors with a sunken living room that opens up to a large back deck overlooking the magnificent lake. The views are incredible. The suede sectional couch looks so cozy positioned in front of a large working fireplace and television. A football game is currently playing on the giant mounted screen and logs crackle in the heat of the fire. It's September, the days have been warm, but the nights have started to get chilly.

"You can put your bag in this room." He walks down a darkened hallway. I quietly follow him wheeling my suitcase. He flips on a light. "I hope this is okay." He shrugs as he turns around.

The room is beautiful with a queen-sized sleigh bed, a matching nightstand and chest of drawers. The duvet looks like a cloud I want to sink into. The sliding glass doors open up to a small deck and another amazing view. I meet Nick's eyes.

"It's perfect, thank you. Listen, I know we're supposed to go to dinner tonight—"

"I'm grilling fish if that's okay with you."

"Oh! Yes, that would be perfect, thank you. I'm a little tired so I'm just going to freshen up if you don't mind?"

Nick nods and leaves the room just as quickly as he came in. I close the door behind him and sink down on the bed. It's amazing, but the awkward feeling of staying in this house alone with him rushes right back. I mean, he's practically a stranger. He could be a serial killer for all I know, who lures his victims out to the middle of nowhere, seducing them with his movie-star looks and then quickly snuffs their life out. He's an ex-Navy SEAL after all. He could probably push his thumb to some part of my neck and I'd be dead before I could even blink. They have skills like that. Killer skills.

I quickly text my sister and send her the address, and

some possible places they could find my body...like the lake or a hidden cutout in the floorboards just in case. Jesus, I need to stop listening to the *True Crime Chronicles* podcast. I'm not going to sleep a wink tonight.

I use the ensuite bathroom and quickly wash my hands, check my teeth for spinach or poppy seeds, or whatever may have gotten stuck in there from my lunch, and run a brush through my hair. If I'm gonna die, I'm gonna die looking put-together. I crack open my bedroom door and look out into the darkened hallway. My heartbeat picks up thinking he might be hiding right around the corner ready to pounce on me, but then I hear pots clanking in the kitchen and music playing.

I grab a magazine to read in case he gives me the cold shoulder and creep slowly out of my room, trailing my fingertips along the hallway wall like the cops do on your car in case they need to find fingerprint evidence that I was here earlier. *Okay Lindsey, get a grip.* I'm really freaking myself out.

I enter the living room that opens up into the beautiful spacious kitchen when I spot him. Oh *mamacita*, he's got a body like Henry Cavill! Okay, so maybe this guy isn't a serial killer. He is one-hundred-percent sex on a stick as he stands with his back to me at the island, without a shirt on, as he cuts vegetables. Didn't he have a shirt on earlier? Does chopping vegetables mandate a no-shirt policy? If so, I'm making sure I eat veggies around this guy every night. No, no, no, you can't lust after the serial killer. Chocolate cake, Lindsey! You can only have chocolate cake!

I'm frozen in place as I watch his back muscles bunch

with every chop he makes, wanting to run my fingertips over his shoulder blades and down his spine. I want to trace the tattoo he has on his side with my tongue, dip my hands down into his athletic shorts and squeeze that rock-hard ass. I unconsciously moan causing him to turn around and arch an eyebrow.

"Are you okay?"

I slowly drag my eyes up to his, silently cursing my brain for letting my gaze remain glued to his butt five seconds longer than necessary. "Yes, why?"

"You're leaning against the column fanning yourself with a magazine." He smirks.

I immediately straighten up, chucking the magazine across the room. I tuck my traitorous hands into the back pockets of my denim cutoffs. "I'm fine...what happened to the shirt you were wearing ten minutes ago?" *Chocolate fucking cake.*

He smirks as he turns back around. "I got hot...apparently you did too."

I sputter as comebacks zing through my brain but die a quick death on my tongue. "I...I wasn't hot, I was feel-ing...nauseous," I say primly.

"Do you need some Dramamine?"

"Some drama what?"

He turns to me as I approach him at the island. "Drama-mean," he says slowly, making my blood boil.

"You're mean," I blurt out before I can stop myself. I clear my throat as heat crawls up my cheeks as I try to recover. "Meaning...me...being drama...oh Jesus, what are we even talking about again?"

His shoulders rise and fall as he takes a deep breath. "If having my shirt off offends you, then too bad."

Wow, this guy is a class-A jerk. He *is* mean! Didn't his mama teach him any manners? Oh god, now he's making me sound like Mrs. Bixby, which makes me hate him even more. No one should sound like her. It's on the tip of my tongue to give him a piece of my mind, but I swallow down my contempt. Be polite, Lindsey. You are a guest in his home and you don't want him killing you in it.

I take a deep breath and plaster on a smile. "Can I help?"

"Do you like to cook?"

I smile ruefully. "Not really. I like to eat more than I like to cook, but I can find my way around the kitchen." I pick up a lemon as he continues to chop veggies. Dammit, he smells just as good as he looks. I notice a long puckered scar that runs along his side underneath his frog skeleton tattoo. I want to reach out and run my finger along it, curious to know what story lies beneath it.

He glances down at me. "Great, you can make the lemon butter sauce for the fish."

I fumble the lemon I'm holding, dropping it on the floor. "Uh, so when I said I can find my way around the kitchen, I meant I won't burn the toast to a blackened crisp...on a good day."

He snorts and smiles. Holy shit did I just make Severus Snape smile? I wink at him as I pick up the lemon and he resumes chopping the vegetables. "There's wine or beer if you want a glass. I'll finish cooking if you want to take a look around." He nods toward the back deck. I'm itching to go sit out there with a glass of red wine, so I take him up on his offer and pour myself some.

"Is this your house?"

"It's my parents' house, but my sisters and I are free to use it whenever we want. They're in Europe right now on a cruise."

"It's beautiful. What's this area called?"

"You're in Sullivan County."

"What's this lake called?" I stand up on my tippy toes to look out the kitchen window over the sink. Every view from this house is incredible.

"It's the Toronto Reservoir."

Not much of a conversationalist, is he? Chris Stapleton plays from hidden speakers. "I love this song, but it reminds me of the time my—"

"Are you always this chatty?" he rudely interrupts.

"Yup." I fake a dazzling smile as I look at him over my shoulder.

Jerkface.

"Figures," he grunts as he steps next to me to wash his hands. Silence hangs in the air as I decide whether I should annoy him further and ask more questions or if I should just make my escape with my wine. I walk toward the back door choosing the more favorable option when a big black dog with pointed ears jumps on the screen scaring the shit out of me.

"Oh my god, there's a dog out there!"

I hear Nick chuckle behind me. "Sorry, I forgot to tell you my parents have a dog. That's Sasha. Are you allergic or afraid of dogs?"

I look over at Sasha as she stands with her paws on the

door, her tongue lolling out the side of her mouth. She looks so soft...like a grizzly bear. "No, we had a beagle growing up. She's just so...big. Is she friendly?"

"Yes, but she used to work over in Afghanistan as a bomb-sniffing dog. Let her smell you first before reaching out to her, okay?"

I nod as I step away from the door. Nick opens it and Sasha comes bounding in. She turns toward me and immediately sticks her long muzzle right in my crotch. Jesus, why do dogs do that? I gently nudge her away, scared she might take my hands off.

"Sasha, no," Nick chastises which means he saw. My cheeks heat up as Sasha immediately sits at Nick's command. Her big brown eyes track my every movement.

"Why is she just staring at me?" I look up at Nick as I realize I'm plastered against the kitchen wall, my heart thudding fast in my chest. I slowly ease away from the wall.

"She's sizing you up. Just hold out your hand to let her get to know you." He says a command in a foreign language and she gets up and circles me as she sniffs my shoe, my hand, then my hip. She suddenly barks causing me to come unglued.

"Oh god, don't take my arm off! I don't have any drugs on me! I smoked pot once in college, but I didn't like it. It made me feel out of control and I didn't do it again. I swear I don't do drugs! Okay maybe there was the one time I tried mushrooms, but I think they were just shiitake because nothing happened to me or my roommate, but I swear that's it!"

Nick arches an eyebrow at me as he fights a smile. He

rubs a hand across his sharp jaw. "Lindsey, she's a bomb-sniffing dog...not drug-sniffing."

"Oh..." *Someone shoot me now.* "Yeah...you mentioned that, didn't you?"

Nick? Now is the time to use your ninja skills on me and put me out of my misery. Please.

"She's barking at you because she wants you to throw her the ball."

I look around and notice a slobbery lime green tennis ball at my feet. "Right." I huff out an embarrassed laugh as I run a hand over her soft black pelt. She practically mows me down as she excitedly barks. She lunges for the ball tossing it back at my feet. "I'll just go outside with her then." I gingerly pick the disgusting ball back up.

"Be careful, she can get boisterous with that thing." He eyes the tennis ball in my hand. Sasha barks as she follows me outside. I throw the tennis ball off to the side and she jumps down the steps and disappears. I sit down in a lounger and wipe my hand on my shorts. Weeping willows hang gracefully around the left of the deck with dogwoods interspersed turning ruby red in the crisp fall evening. I bet this place is amazing in the spring when they bloom. The setting sun glints off of the water as I watch a sailboat float by in the distance.

It's so quiet and peaceful compared to the city. It reminds me of Charleston, and for just a second, I feel a twinge of homesickness. This house is beautiful, but the company sadly is not. I breathe in a lungful of fresh air as I try to figure out how I'm going to get through the next two days with *Mr. I don't like to wear shirts or talk.* Oh who am I kidding? I have to survive forty-five days in his company! He's so rude and unpleasant. He's got to have *some* nice qualities, right? I'll have to dig deep to expose them.

I sigh as I realize I have nothing to read since I threw my magazine somewhere in the living room. I'm about to get up when the screen door creaks open and he comes to stand over me.

"Dinner will be ready in five minutes."

Direct, to the point. He's got that going for him.

I peer up at him as I take a drink of my cabernet. He's put his shirt back on which strangely makes me sad. Well, at least I won't have to stare at his bare chest all through dinner. It's chiseled and smooth—an amazing work of art if I'm being honest, but I'd probably start drooling. The last thing I want is for him to see how much he affects me.

"Do you need me to help set the table? Or maybe we could eat out here? It's a beautiful evening."

"This isn't a date."

I have to pick my jaw up off the ground as my neck and ears heat up in embarrassment. Mama, I'm sorry, but screw being nice. I get up out of my chair and face off with him.

"Well, no shit, Sherlock, because I'd never date someone like you. You are rude and condescending. You're, you're…"

"I'm what?" He bites down on his lip.

Is he fucking smirking?

I pause as I try to make my boiling blood simmer down to at least a two. I drag in fresh lake air as I pretend he isn't standing two feet away from me smelling incredible. "I've got news for you…you're stuck with me whether you like it or not. You can't have a show without me." I blow out a breath and soften my voice, willing myself to calm down. "Listen, I get it, I really do…you don't want to work with me. And well, I'd really like for you not to be a total jerkface jackass, but neither is going to happen is it? So, we're going to buck up and make the best of it."

He stares at me like I've grown two heads. "I don't think you heard me correctly. I said this isn't great…meaning dinner." He gestures to the plate I never noticed in his hands. "I burnt the lemon sauce, so we're just going to have to eat it without."

Wait…what? Oh god no. I swear he said *This isn't a date.* Not *this isn't great.* Didn't he? Jesus lord, I just went off on him like crazy Kanye and he's telling me dinner won't be great? Did I really just call my new producer a jerkface jackass? Can lakes produce waves? Because I need a big wave to come off the water and swallow me whole, or for Sasha to take me down and place me in a sleep hold. I close my eyes and count to ten, trying to regain some semblance of composure.

"I owe you an apology, Nick. I misunderstood you," I say quietly.

"Are you Irish?"

"Uh…a little Irish mixed with some Italian, why?"

He smiles, even white teeth and perfect lips, the sexiest dimples. "Well, that explains your temper."

I cross my arms over my chest. "And how would you know?"

"Because I'm Irish and my sisters are just as crazy."

"Are you calling me crazy?"

He shrugs and moves to the table and sets the platter of

fish down.

"That's smart. Don't answer that question."

He smirks as he heads back in to grab the rest of dinner while I circle and pace wanting to throw myself off this deck and end my misery.

Chapter 7

Nick

Rude Egomaniac Asshole Serial Killer

I WALK BACK into the kitchen and smile to myself. I don't know why I like tormenting this woman so much, but something about her drives me crazy. I burnt the lemon sauce because I couldn't stop staring at her ass in those cutoffs. When she came up to stand beside me while I was chopping veggies for dinner, I almost sliced my finger off with how good she smelled. Like vanilla and sugar cookies. I wanted to reach over and pull her into my arms and kiss the smirk right off her face.

But I can't do that. I have to remain professional. I can't get involved with her; my heart and my head don't need that kind of drama. This is a means to an end. Get in, do your fucking job, Elliot, and get out. No strings, no attachments, and above all else, no sex. Be coldhearted if you have to…make her despise you. It will make things easier in the long run.

I grab silverware, napkins, two plates and the side dish and make my way out to the back deck. The sunset is incredible tonight as orange and pink hues melt from the sky into the water. It casts pink hues off of Lindsey's rich brown hair as she leans against the deck railing. Her shoulders are hunched as she mutters to herself while absentmindedly petting Sasha.

"Ready for dinner?"

She shakes her head no, but doesn't turn around. Jesus, women are so freaking finicky. Didn't she just want to eat outside?

"Would you rather eat inside now? Whatever you want—"

"No, it's fine."

Warning bells go off in my head. Being the only male among four sisters growing up has taught me the valuable lesson that when a woman says she's fine it means everything is most definitely *not* fine. "Is something wrong?"

She lifts her shoulders in a shrug, but still doesn't turn around. I set everything down on the table and walk over to her. "Are you okay?"

She quickly wipes her face. Aw, shit, I made her cry. Something in my heart rips open telling me to go easier on her.

"Yes. No. I don't know. It's just allergies."

I drag a hand down my face. Crap, I'm not equipped to handle an emotional woman right now. I just wanted a quiet night to watch football and drink some beer. "Lindsey…"

She quickly wipes her eyes again and turns toward me, her hands automatically landing on my chest. Her touch burns through my shirt making my skin hot. Her red-rimmed eyes widen in surprise. I take a step back from her and her hands drop. She swiftly picks up her wineglass and takes a large gulp.

"Sorry. Jesus, I'm a mess, aren't I? I'm so embarrassed about earlier. I just went off on you, and you've been nothing but...accommodating. I mean, in my head I've made you out to be an egomaniacal asshole serial killer, but you're not, you're just rude. But that's probably not your fault, probably just the result of being in the military, but dammit it's completely unnerving...it makes me crazy because I can get along with anyone, but not with you. It's like there's this permanent stick up your...oh my god I'm doing it again! Forget what I just said." She waves her glass in the air as her cheeks stain a pretty shade of rose pink. "I don't know, you just make me insane! And I'm...I'm still fucking this all up, aren't I?" She scrubs her hand down her face as I arch an eyebrow, crossing my arms over my chest.

"You think I'm a rude egomaniac asshole serial killer?"

"Gah, it sounds really bad when you say it like that." She peers up at me through her fingers covering her eyes. Goddamn, she's so adorable.

I nod my head and grunt. "Let's eat. The Giants are playing in twenty minutes and I don't want to miss it."

"Okay, okay." Lindsey sinks into her seat. "This looks so good. I'm famished."

We sit quietly as she takes a bite of her fish. She moans in appreciation and my dick gets instantly hard. I look up at her watching her savor the bite, her eyes closed, her lips tilted up into a little smile. It's no wonder people like to watch her eat.

"Dang, Nick, this is amazing! Have you ever taken cooking classes? Seriously, this is like Bobby Flint good."

I look down at my own plate thinking to myself it's

nothing special, but her compliment makes warm heat spread through my chest. "My mom and sisters love to cook, so I guess I just picked it up."

"Are you the oldest?"

I smile thinking about my crazy sisters. "No, I'm the baby. Four older sisters."

She winces. "I'm sorry. I just have one older sister and if I'd multiply her by four, I'd go insane."

I chuckle. "She a lot to take?"

"Shannon is like my mom, my best friend, my annoying sister and my significant other all rolled into one. Basically, I love her to death, but she's a meddler and drives me crazy."

I smile because my sisters are the exact same. "Try being fourteen and going on a date to the high school football game and your older sisters all show up and sit in the bleachers right behind you. One put gum in my hair, the other kneed me in the back every time I'd try to talk to my date, the third oldest took pictures, and the fourth talked to my date the whole night about my bedwetting problem when I was eight. They haven't gotten much better as we've gotten older."

She laughs, making my heart stutter. "Seriously? That's pretty bad."

Shit, I can't believe I just told her all that. She makes me want to make her smile every minute of the day. I let my guard slip *again*. Be professional, Elliot. She is not your friend. You don't like her. I sit back and drink my beer, eyeing her over the bottle. She's lost in thought as she looks out over the lake.

"So why does Simon call you Scar?"

I don't answer her because I'm mesmerized by her delicate features and her full lips. Her eyes are a soft bottle green. Her olive skin dewy with a slight tinge of rose at her cheeks. Her hair a rich brown with honey-gold highlights. I'm struck senseless by my intense physical attraction to her. I've never had a visceral reaction like this to a woman before, not even to my ex.

I can't get involved. Strike that, I don't *want* to get involved. I get up and collect our plates, shutting her out. "Going inside to watch the football game."

Lindsey's smile slips a little before she recovers. "Oh, okay!"

I get to the kitchen door when her voice stops me.

"Hey, Nick, can I have a do-over? I mean, can we pretend that whatever I vomited out of my mouth tonight can just be forgotten?"

I nod curtly because the hope in her voice nearly has me dropping to my knees wanting to give her whatever her heart desires.

Chapter 8

Lindsey

How Will I Know?

I SLIDE OPEN the glass doors leading out to my deck overlooking the lake. The crisp clean air cleanses my face as I take a deep breath. I stretch on my toes feeling like a million bucks after sleeping a dreamless deep sleep. I need that bed in my life for the rest of my life.

Movement down on the shore directs my attention to a shirtless man taking off his running shorts, standing only in his black boxer briefs down on the dock. Hello, Marky Mark, when did you get in town? This man is built like a Greek god, his muscles bunching as he twists in his Calvins. His thighs are thick and muscular, his waist tapering down into a tight ass, not an ounce of fat anywhere on him.

"Dang it, Nick Elliot, why do you have to be such a good-looking dickweed?" My eyes track his movement like a hawk preying on its next meal as he dives into the water, barely making a wave. His arms slice through the water in clean even strokes.

I'll admit, I watched a couple episodes of *Naked in the Wild* last night on my laptop just to get a taste of what Nick has been through before this. Trevor, the moronic model hosting the show, couldn't rub two sticks together, but he did love prancing naked through the jungle every chance he got. And I'm not going to lie, I might have paused the video when he jumped naked off a waterfall, because it was clear as day to me that it was Nick jumping and not Trevor. But even though his body is sinful, he's still a dick.

I watch him for a minute longer then decide to go in search of coffee.

I throw a sweatshirt on over my cami and sleep shorts and pull my hair up into a ponytail as I wander into the bright kitchen. Sasha jumps off the couch and comes to greet me. I'm momentarily alarmed until I remember how sweet she is and rub my hand down her soft coat.

"Ili, sweet girl, got any coffee in here?"

I see a small black Alexa speaker in the corner. Nick's out swimming, so I'll enjoy my morning like I normally do.

"Alexa, play some eighties music."

The speakers start piping out Manic Monday. "Good tune, Alexa." I pour some coffee and look in the fridge for some cream. I spot the half and half and also spy some eggs and tomatoes. I open the cheese drawer and find some herbed goat cheese. I may not be a great cook, but I can make a killer omelet.

My mind drifts to last night. Nick Elliot doesn't deserve my kindness after he barely acknowledged my presence the rest of the night, but to be honest it's probably a good thing. I was a complete train wreck. Did I really call him an egotistical psychopath? I giggle to myself as I mix the ingredients in a bowl. I bite my lip as I pour the egg into a frying pan. Probably didn't win any points with him, but I'll be the bigger person and be kind since I have to travel internationally with this guy for a couple weeks.

Whitney Houston's "How Will I Know" starts to play and I ask Alexa to turn it up. I grab a spatula as I start bouncing around the kitchen to the beat. Sasha's prancing at my heels as I sing along with Whitney. Well, maybe singing isn't quite accurate. I have a terrible voice, so it's more like shouting. I flip the omelet and throw myself back against the counter as I belt out the refrain using the spatula as my microphone. *Get it, Whitney!* I sing the tune as I make up my own version.

"How will I know if I'm just horny? I say a prayer with every butt cheek. I fall in lust whenever we meet. I'm asking you because you think he wants to kill me. How will I know if he wants to kiss me? I try to talk but he's too hot, mercy me. Falling in love is so bittersweet—"

"What the fuck?"

I spin around and immediately throw the spatula in the sink as if I wasn't just performing Whitney's greatest hits with it. Nope, not me. I'm just standing here making an omelet. Nothing to see here, folks.

Nick stands in the kitchen doorway with water dripping down his naked tanned chest. You want to know how I know if he's really thinking of me, Whitney? Because his *I want to murder you* eyes tell me so.

"I heard screaming while I was down at the lake, so I ran up here."

"Oh,   um...yeah,   not   screaming, just...me...uh...singing." I stare up at the ceiling. My cheeks feel like they're on fire. I can even smell smoke, I'm blushing *that* hard.

"Your omelet's burning."

Not my cheeks, just my omelet.

"Shit, shit…thanks." I immediately move the pan and turn off the burner. Why do I keep getting caught by this guy and why does it make me want to throw myself off a tall building every time? I shouldn't care what Nick Elliot thinks of me. I shouldn't care that he just watched me belt out Whitney with a spatula and I shouldn't care that his beautiful blue eyes were burning with some uncontrolled emotion when I turned around. I shouldn't care, but I do, and that pisses me off even more.

"Alexa, stop!" I yell shakily over the music as I turn back around to face him. He's moved into the kitchen and he's rubbing his t-shirt over his head. His dark hair sticking up in spikes and damn if he doesn't look completely edible. I walk over to the counter and lean my hip against it. "So! What's our plan today?" I pick up my mug of coffee and take a long gulp.

"I need to get some things done around here first and then we can head out."

I eye him over my mug. "Oh, okay, sounds good."

"I would like you to think about what places you want to visit so we can narrow down our locations and investigate restaurants in the area."

Uh-huh. Whatever you say, blah, blah, blah. My gaze travels down his bare chest, past the washboard abs to the little happy trail going into his black athletic shorts.

"Lindsey, are you listening to me?"

My eyes immediately shoot to his. He's arching an eyebrow and the slight smirk on his face makes me want to kiss it right off. "Yup, got it." I nod curtly as I turn around and slide my omelet into the trash can. My stomach grumbles and I sigh.

"Would you like me to make you an omelet?" he says.

Flustered, I start scrubbing the pan vigorously. "No, I'm fine. I'll just eat a banana."

"Suit yourself. Don't forget to shut the door to your room. Sasha likes to snoop."

"Oh, okay. I'm just going to finish my coffee, get dressed, maybe I'll walk Sasha..."

He walks down the hall to his bedroom and shuts the door.

"Right. Good talk." Guess he doesn't give a shit what my plans are. I finish cleaning the pan, then grab a banana and my coffee and head out to the back porch. Ugh that man frustrates the hell out of me. I pull my phone out to text my sister.

Me: I'm in hell. It's beautiful here, but Satan is definitely managing it.

Shannon: Well that's a wee bit dramatic for a Saturday morning don't ya think? Drink some coffee.

Me: I'm serious. He's such a jerk.

Shannon: Well, the good news is you're alive.

I snort out a laugh.

Me: I think it will be me that ends up killing him.

Shannon: Dan says to just have sex with him already and get it over with.

Me: *Totally disgusted by that comment. Tell my brother-in-law I'm sorely disappointed in him.*

Shannon: *Hmm. We'll see.*

Me: *What? Nothing to see here. If I'm having sex with anyone it's going to be that James Bond Simon Blake.*

Shannon: *Is he British?*

Me: *No, he's American.*

Shannon: *Then he's not James Bond.*

Me: *You're annoying me right now.*

Shannon: *Maybe Dan's right. Gotta run, Sadie has a soccer game. Luvs ya! Stay alive!*

I throw my phone on my chair and eat my banana as I watch some rowers glide across the lake. I might as well go take a shower and get dressed. The sooner this day ends, the sooner I can get back to New York and then skip, hop, and jump back to Charleston.

Chapter 9

Nick

Betty's Fish Camp

"YOU'RE NOT SERIOUS."

"What?"

I look from Lindsey to the clown car parked in my driveway. "I'm not driving that."

"Well, it's a good thing I'll be driving then."

I fold my arms over my chest. "Lindsey," I say gruffly, "I can't even fit in that."

She smirks at me. "I love a good challenge."

"Lindsey…"

"It gets great gas mileage. I filled it up right before I got here."

I'm about to tell her no, but the words die on my tongue. She's got me right where she wants me. I forgot to fuel up the truck. I could drive twenty minutes in the opposite direction and get gas, but it's already dusk and by the time we get gas and get to the fish camp, they'll be slammed and we'll have to wait forever to get a table.

"Fine, but I'm driving," I grit out. How the hell am I going to fit in this thing with my wide shoulders and long legs?

"Oh, sorry friend." She doesn't look sorry in the least. "My rental agreement says only I can drive it. Ready?"

Irritation tightens my chest. "Hold on, let me grab a bag from my truck." I walk into the garage and grab a supplies bag in case of an emergency and my phone charger. "Let's roll."

She unlocks the Fiat and I nearly fall on my ass as I try to fold myself into the passenger seat. I have to move the seat as far back as it will possibly go. "This car is ridiculous."

"It was actually really convenient in the city." She bites her lip, trying not to laugh as she looks over at me. I punch the address into the navigation system trying my damndest to ignore her, but her soft vanilla fragrance wafts over me, causing my senses to go into overdrive. I roll down my window all the way to get some fresh air in this small space as she pulls onto the main road.

What I really want to do is recline my seat, reach over and have her straddle my lap. I groan out of frustration and need. I thought I took care of that frustration in the shower this morning when I pictured her in her tight little sleep shorts, but no such luck.

She looks over at me worriedly. "Are you okay? Is my driving making you sick?"

"No," I bite out as I turn the radio on to ease the tension in the car.

She turns the music down. "So, I've been jotting down some notes. We have five episodes we need to film. London, Paris, Germany, Italy, and Greece."

"You're not up for Asia?"

She shrugs. "I mean I know there are amazing places in

Asia, but according to Simon, it's not in the budget."

My hackles rise at the mention of Simon. "He's missing out on the mass appeal of Asia. Greece doesn't make sense."

She looks affronted. "Greece was my idea. No one has a clue how to find the best hole-in-the-wall there."

"Why not Spain? It seems more budget-friendly than Greece, plus more people from the States are likely to travel to Spain over Greece."

"I feel like you're arguing with me on purpose. Greece is beautiful, it's exotic—"

"So is Spain. We're going to Spain."

"See? Right there is what I'm talking about. It's really frustrat—oh shit!" She swerves the car to the right. The wheels hit gravel and we fishtail.

"Pump the brakes! Turn the wheel to the left!" I reach over and grab the wheel.

"Stop yelling at me!" she screams as she does the opposite as we fight for control of the wheel. The car lurches to a stop. "Shit." She undoes her seat belt and gets out of the car.

"Lindsey!" I shout, afraid she'll get hit by a car. I get out, not speedily because of the low seats, and watch her pick up a turtle and move it to the side of the road. "Are you fucking kidding me right now?" I mutter angrily as I stand watching her with my hands on my hips. She trots back over to the car and holds her hand up at me.

"Don't give me that pissy look. I almost flattened that poor turtle. The next car along would have, so I had to move him. If I hadn't, I would have been miserable thinking about him the rest of the evening."

Is she fucking for real? "You could have killed us! You

could have gotten hit on the road trying to move it! All for what? A fucking turtle?"

"Nick," she sighs as she buckles herself back into her seat. "I don't expect you to understand, but I can't let an innocent animal get hurt. It's my thing."

"It's her thing…" I say under my breath as I strap back in. She hits the gas and we veer back onto the two-lane highway. "Did you even look in your mirror before you merged?"

She blows out a breath, clearly annoyed with me. "Of course, I did. It's not like this road is bumper-to-bumper."

"I just don't want to die in this tin can."

"Are you always so dramatic?"

I glare at her as I turn the radio up drowning her out. This lady is infuriating. How the hell am I going to survive over a month in Europe with her? I look at the navigation system and see that we only have about ten minutes until we reach the fish camp, *thank God*. I reluctantly turn the radio back down as I plan how tonight will go in my head.

"So for tonight, I figure we'll kind of do a dry run-through…what's that noise?" I strain my ears hearing a *thump thump* coming from outside. "Lindsey, pull over."

She eases the car over to the side of the road. "I don't hear anything."

I get out and stretch as I stand up and crack my neck. I look down at the front tire and then squat in front of it. This day could not get any worse. I scrub my face with my hands and lean down into the passenger window. "You must have gotten a nail in the tire or something, it's shredded. We're going to have to change the tire."

She looks at me as she chews her bottom lip. "I don't know how to change a tire, but I have Triple A."

"I can change a tire. Did they show you where the spare was when you rented this?"

"Uh, no. The lady barely looked at me. She just gave me paperwork and the number stall my car was in."

"Open up the back," I say tersely. She pops the lift gate and I look around the tiny space in back. No spare tire. Of course not. All for a fucking turtle. I knew we should have taken my truck. "Lindsey, please call Triple A, there isn't a spare in this thing."

"Um…I don't have service," she says quietly, an edge of panic lacing her voice. I look around at our surroundings. It's getting close to dark and we're in the middle of nowhere. We're going to have to hike to the fish camp to get service.

"Come on, grab your stuff and lock the car up. We'll have service farther up."

"You mean we have to leave the car and walk?" she whines.

"Yes, Driving Miss Daisy, you blew the tire when you ran us off the road to save a turtle."

I swear I hear her mutter *kiss my grits* as she locks up the car. I sling my backpack over my shoulder and start walking north.

"Wait for me!" she yells as she jogs up next to me. "Do you know where we're going?"

I nod and move her to the right side of me, away from the cars passing us. "Walk on this side of me."

We walk in silence for a few minutes. She blows a breath out. "I'm sorry I blew the tire. Can you slow down? My legs are about half the size of yours."

I chance a glance at her and she's jogging to keep up with me. I slow my steps. "It was just an accident," I concede. We walk in silence as I keep checking my phone for a signal.

"So, tell me something weird about yourself that no one else knows."

"Something weird?"

"Yeah, I'm just trying to get to know the *real* Nick Elliot. You know, I'm weird because…"

"There's a lot of weird things about you."

She thwacks my arm with hers. "I'll start. I'm weird because I can't stand sweet tea."

"Of all the weird things about you, that's the one you're going with?"

"It's *weird* because I grew up in the South. Mamas give their babies sweet tea as soon as they're off the boob."

"Off the boob?" I side-eye her.

She clears her throat as we trudge along. "Anyway, can't stand the stuff. It makes me un-Southern."

"What the hell is un-Southern?"

She rolls her eyes. "You know un-American…un-Southern, not a true Southerner."

"I do not know."

She groans in frustration. "Just tell me something weird about you! Jesus, are you always this difficult?"

"Yes."

She glares at me, and I have to bite back a smile.

"Okay, let me think…um, yeah no…not that either." I look over at her and smile. "I've got nothing."

"You suck at this game. *That's* your weirdness."

I smirk as I steer her off the road. "Turn down this road."

"This looks creepy." Lindsey looks around at the woods surrounding the old gravel road. "*Ms. Betty's Fish Camp*," she reads the old wooden sign as we pass it. "This is like the bad start to a horror flick."

"I promise, it's good. Ms. Betty has run this place for forty years. It's comfort food. It's just over this hill."

"So why do they call it a fish camp if it's comfort food? I never understood that. I feel like a fish camp should just be fish and that's it, right? There's this fish camp in Hilton Head and oh my god it has the most amazing menu. 'Fish Camp' doesn't do it justice. Anyway, she should call it like Betty's Comfort Eats, or Betty's Place."

"Do you always ramble?"

"I'm not rambling, just trying to make conversation. Sorry for being friendly," she scoffs. "Not to mention walking down a dark gravelly road in the middle of the woods is making me an eensy-weensy bit nervous."

I glance over at her and try to hide my smile. She's totally rambling, but it's not annoying me, it's kind of endearing. We turn the corner and my shoulders slump as I look at the darkened windows of Betty's Fish Camp. It's only six-thirty. Betty's should be open and busy.

"Why is it dark and why aren't there any cars in the parking lot?" Lindsey folds her arms over her chest and looks around.

"I'm not sure, Thelma, maybe we should look around for some clues."

"Wait, why am I Thelma? It's because I'm short isn't it. I

want to be Daphne. I mean she would be with Fred anyway, right? Unless that makes you Shaggy." Lindsey giggles.

"Jesus, woman." I pull my phone out of my pocket. At least I have a signal. I type in Betty's Fish Camp. "I can't believe it."

"What?"

"Betty's closed last month. It's the most amazing place, how could it have closed?"

"Uh, maybe because it's in the middle of nowhere?"

"That's the charm of it..." I look around in disbelief. "Can you call Triple A? We'll hike back to the car in a bit."

Lindsey's stomach growls. She laughs nervously as she slaps a hand over it. "Ha sorry, I only had that banana today." She toes the gravel with her shoe. "Are we really going to hike back? We just got here and my legs are tired," she gripes as she fishes her phone out and pulls up the contact. She looks up at me when I don't answer. "You're really scary when you stare at me like that... Hi, yes, this is Lindsey Love, I need someone to come out to help with a flat tire. I'll need a new tire for a Fiat. Uh-huh. Hold on." Her eyes flicker to me. "What's our location?"

"Off of Route 55 heading north about ten minutes be-fore you get to Betty's."

She repeats the information to the operator. "Wait, are you serious? Not until seven a.m.? Ugh. Okay. Yes. Yes. Okay, thank you." She hangs up the phone.

"What's going on?"

"There's been a massive pileup south of here on 55. Can't send someone out until morning." She looks like she's about to have a nervous breakdown as she looks around the parking lot. "What are we going to do?" she cries out flopping her arms to the side as I assess the situation.

"Looks like we're stuck here for the night. We'll need to make a campfire, collect some wood because it's getting chilly." I eye her thin sweater she's wearing with jeans. "Luckily I brought a small tent. It's really only for one person, but you're small and—"

"I'm not sleeping in a one-person tent with you! I don't even *know* you. I'm going back to the car." She starts walking in the wrong direction muttering as she kicks gravel up with her shoe. "Who carries a tent around in their backpack anyway? That's so *creepy*. Like he was planning this all along." She gasps and turns around. "Oh my god, were you *planning* for this to happen?"

I try my best to look intimidating as hell because this woman is driving me batshit crazy. I fold my arms over my chest and glower at her. "Yes, Lindsey, I planned this just so I could get you in my tent. I *wanted* to take your shitty-ass clown car. I *wanted* to careen off the side of the road to miss a turtle. I *wanted* you to drive like a fucking maniac on bare rims shredding the tire. I'm so *fucking* glad Betty's closed down so that I could seduce you in a dark gravel parking lot with my *tent!*"

She stares at me a beat and huffs as she storms off giving me the middle finger.

"You're going the wrong fucking way!" I call out, my eyes narrowed on her cute little ass in her tight jeans.

"I'm going to look for firewood, *asshole!*"

Goddamn, Elliot, get your eyes off her ass and your head screwed on right. She drives you nuts!

I riffle through my backpack, thankful I grabbed it out of the truck right before we left. It's a survival pack in case anything goes wrong. Ever since *Naked in the Wild*, I'm obsessive about having one of these with me at all times. You never know when something can go wrong and Lindsey Love is like a beacon for bad shit.

I check around Betty's to see if there's anything we can use. Just some old wooden picnic tables. It's almost dark so I go in search of Lindsey because all I need is Simon down my throat for allowing her to get lost in Upstate New York.

Chapter 10

Lindsey

Snow White and the Snails

I STOMP OFF into the woods grumbling to myself. What a fucking asshole Nick Elliot is. I'm not going to lie, he's intimidating as hell when he folds his arms over his chest, his biceps bulging and he gives me that steely look. He makes me want to cry, kiss, and choke him all in one beat. I can't stand him.

My hair snags on a tree branch and I screech. I hate camping, I hate not having a bathroom and I fucking hate being lost. I want a soft bed, a shower, and Netflix. I collect a few sticks, staying on the outer edge of the woods because it's getting dark and let's be honest, boogiemen, ghosts, and Big Foot live in the woods. Oh, and It the clown. I shiver remembering those scary-ass pictures of people dressing like It and hiding in the woods. I pick up my pace because now I've scared myself shitless.

My stomach rumbles and I grind my teeth thinking about how a homecooked meal from Betty's sounded so good. You know where I should be right now? I should be in a posh New York City restaurant sipping champagne and eating filet mignon with Simon Blake, not trudging through scary-ass woods with spiders, collecting firewood with Nick Elliot. *Face it, Lindsey, this trip has been a nightmare.* I sit down on a log to take a break, feeling exhausted.

A cute little fuzzy gray squirrel scampers down a tree in front of me as he collects an acorn. I watch him as he nibbles the acorn in quick little bites. At least one of us is getting to eat. His little nose twitches and he's so stinking cute!

"Hi, little squirrel! Look at your cute little ears! I'm going to name you Ted, because you look like a teddy bear. Aw…"

A noise goes whizzing by my head and splinters the tree right above the squirrel. I scream and Ted jumps to safety. I whirl around and shriek again as Nick approaches me.

"Jesus Christ! Did you just really throw a dagger at me?"

"No, Colonel Mustard." He rolls his eyes. "It's a hunting knife, not a dagger, and I was aiming for the squirrel."

"I am *not* Colonel Mustard. Do I even remotely look like the guy from Kentucky Fried Chicken? Clearly, I'd be Miss Scarlett, thank you very much."

"I…" He scrubs his hand down his face.

"What if you missed? Huh? What about the poor squirrel? What about me?!"

He reaches over and pulls the knife out of the tree. "You moved at the last minute and I had to re-aim. Trust me, I never miss my mark."

I swallow. "Well, why the hell were you going to kill Ted?"

"Who the fuck is Ted?" He looks around the woods like some guy named Ted is going to pop out and wave a friendly hello.

"That adorable little squirrel."

"You mean dinner?" He actually has the audacity to smile.

I make a noise of disgust in the back of my throat as I pick up the firewood I dropped when the fucking squirrel murderer tried to kill me. "I would never eat Ted for dinner. That's disgusting. I'd rather eat snails than a cute little fuzzy woodland creature."

His hard gaze has me nearly peeing in my pants. He slides the knife back into a sheath and slips it into the back pocket of his jeans. He grabs a stick and hands it to me. "Alright, Snow White, if that's what you want." He turns to leave.

"I have enough firewood, thank you very much, but thanks for your one-stick contribution."

"It's not for firewood. It's to dig for your dinner."

"And what exactly am I digging for?"

He looks at me like he's trying to teach me two plus two. "You said you wanted snails for dinner, snails it is." He turns back around and leaves me standing there with my mouth hanging open.

"I was kidding!"

"I SAID PUT that pole together. You're doing it backwards," he growls in frustration.

I throw the two poles down on the ground. "Why the fuck are there poles anyway? Don't they have like a remote-control button you can just press and the tent pops up? This is like the caveman version of setting up a tent," I grumble in annoyance.

"Are you always such a pain in the ass? Just connect the two poles, it's not that hard."

"Maybe I don't want to play 'going camping'!" I shout back at him using obnoxious air quotes which makes his jaw tick. "I'm not even freaking going to sleep in it. I should be sleeping in a soft comfortable bed tonight."

"Well, sorry for our predicament, Snow White, but if you hadn't—"

"Gah! How many times are you going to remind me it's *my* fault?"

"Probably until my last breath," he mumbles. "You should sleep in the tent, it's going to be cold tonight." He snaps the pole into place and slides it into the canvas loop creating the arch of the tent.

"I'm not sleeping in a one-man tent with you, Elliot, so you can forget it."

"What do you think I'm going to do? Try and cop a feel?" His acid tone drips with disdain making my spine go rigid.

"Guys would *kill* to get me alone in a tent," I say indignantly.

"Yeah, just so they could suffocate you with their sleeping bag," he says under his breath.

"What was that? I can't understand you when you mumble."

"I said, I'm sure they would," he says clearly as he secures the sides.

It's really small, just enough room for him. If I did sleep in there, I'd have to curl up right next to his muscular side. I'd smell his woodsy scent and feel the heat from his body— nope, no. Not going to happen.

I stop arguing with him and sit down on the other side of the campfire and warm up my hands. It *is* getting chilly out. I watch him warily as he finishes the tent and then grabs his backpack and pulls out a small frying pan. It's like Mary Poppins frigging carpet bag. I wonder what else he can pull out of it...

"I'll be back." And with that he turns on his heel and leaves me alone to man the fire.

"You're leaving me alone out here?" I start to panic as I look around at the dark parking lot.

"You'll be fine."

"Where are you going?"

"To get dinner."

"Well, let me come with you!" I screech in desperation.

"No."

"But—"

He turns around clearly exasperated with me. "You can't leave the fire unattended. I'm going to go see if I can scrounge up dinner. Just stay put."

An owl hoots in the woods making me jump, my nerves frazzled. I pick up a baseball-sized rock that's near me and hold it in my lap. If anyone tries to kidnap me I can clobber them with it. Or maybe I'll just use it on Nick.

Chapter 11

Lindsey

No Turning Back Now

THE FIRE CRACKLES between us as the amazing smell of fish he's frying in a little pan makes my mouth water. "Where did you catch that again?"

"The pond out back. It's a fish camp, remember?"

"Oh, hmm…smells good."

"Want some?" He peers up at me and his sapphire-blue eyes glow in the campfire. If this were any other circumstance and he were any other man, I'd be all over him like white on rice. I look down at the pan-fried snails he graciously found for me and I want to vomit. "What's wrong with your snails?"

"I'm not French," I deadpan.

I swear I see his lips twitch before he bows his head and returns his attention to his fish. "That's a shame."

I set the snails on the ground and dig around in my bag hoping there's a mint or a Peanut M&M rolling around in there. I feel a cellophane wrapper and my stomach leaps for joy. Yes! It's an old granola bar. I have no idea how long it's been in there. The wrapper is torn, but I don't care. I'm so hungry I'll scarf it down. I bite into it and almost break all my teeth on impact. Nick is watching me and I swear I see his eyes glitter with glee.

"Is it good?"

I try to soften the bar with my saliva so that I can break it with my teeth, but that plan backfires as drool drips down my chin. Nick points to his own chin.

"You uh…have some—"

"Got it, thanks!" I quickly wipe my chin, mortified beyond belief.

"You sure you don't want some?" He holds his plate out to me. "It's pretty good."

"No, I'm good with this." I'd rather *die* from hunger than accept the bone he's throwing me. I bite down again and it's softer this time but it tastes like cardboard and makes me hate Nick Elliot all over again. I hope Ted pees on his tent in the middle of the night.

"Well, I'm sorry this was such a bust. If you still want me to film you for a practice run, I can."

"In the dark as I rave about my stale granola bar? Or my dirt-covered snails? No thanks," I say grumpily.

"Come on, it will be good for the show to get some practice in. I'll just do it with my phone."

"Fine," I growl as I pick up the pan of snails. God forbid he complains to the network that I was acting like an uncooperative diva. He gets a notebook out of his bag and holds his phone up, giving me a thumbs-up to let me know he's filming.

"Hey everyone, Lindsey Love here."

"Cut." Nick brings the phone down. "Do you always sound like someone just ran over your puppy?"

I roll my eyes and motion for him to go again as I try to drum up some spark of enthusiasm. "Hey, Lindsey Love—"

"Can you at least smile?"

"I am!"

"Wow, okay...*work on scary smile.*" He makes a note on his tablet.

"Ugh, do you want to do this or not?"

"Okay, go."

"Hi, it's Lindsey Love!" I sit up straight, my fake dazzling smile hurting my cheeks. "I'm sitting outside Betty's Fish Camp in a dark dank parking lot eating pan-fried snails. Why am I eating snails in a parking lot of a closed-down restaurant, you ask? Because my sadistic asshole producer dug them up for me to eat. They smell like dirt and ooh, look, one is still moving! What a treat!"

"Okay...I see we have some work to do. Let's do one with the granola bar."

Groaning, I put the snails down. I straighten back up and glare across the fire at Nick as I pick up the granola bar. "Hey guys, Lindsey Love is loving granola bars. This one is perfect for those who love to visit their dentist. It smells like..." I sniff the bar and scrunch my nose. "Well, it doesn't smell, and it has a distinct cardboard flavor to it. Definitely recommend this granola bar if it's the last edible thing in your purse. Unless you break a tooth, then you're shit out of luck."

"Take a bite of it." Nick smirks.

"I'd like to keep all my teeth, thank you very much." I throw the granola bar at him.

Nick stops filming as he catches the granola brick.

"Wow, that was an Emmy-worthy performance for sure."

"Yeah well, not really in the mood."

"You have a couple weeks to work on your smile and maybe not mention your asshole producer on camera."

"I'm exhausted. If we're done here, I think I'm going to just curl up on the picnic table. Thanks for the spare blanket." Of course, he had two blankets in his Mary Poppins backpack, but conveniently no food. I toss the snails into the fire.

"I'll leave the fire going if you need to come back over, but make sure to dump this water on it if you decide not to."

"Okay, whatever."

"Hey, Lindsey, I'm sorry I got mad earlier."

I shrug, bone-tired all of a sudden. "Forgiven. And I'm sorry I accused you of planning this and calling you an asshole."

"Forgiven. Night, Lindsey Love."

"Night, Nick Elliot."

I leave him by the fire and head over to the nearest picnic table. I wrap the thin blanket from his backpack around myself and lie down on the hard wood, using my lumpy purse for a pillow. The table smells like old ketchup and stale cigarettes. It's also a lot colder over here now that I'm away from the flames.

I try to close my eyes, but I can't get comfortable. The vinegar smell of ketchup and the hard table overwhelm my senses. *Just six hours and then you can get back to the car. You can do this.* I should have just walked back there and slept in it, but I was scared to walk back by myself and sleep on the side of a highway. Too many scary stories.

After a while, I hear Nick zip up his tent. I bet he's cozy-warm in there since it's close to the fire. And I bet it's softer than this table. And I bet it doesn't smell like stale beer, vinegar ketchup, and cigarette butts. Probably smells woodsy and campfire-smokey like Nick. I'd give anything to be cozy, even if it meant sleeping next to that jerk. I bet he puts off amazing body heat.

I bet if I asked him he would spoon me and make this shivering stop, because I can't stop it on my own. It's so fucking cold out here, I can feel it in my bones. I ball up into a tight fetal position but it doesn't do any good. *So cold.*

Maybe I'll just sleep by the fire. Yes, that's a good plan. People do that all the time, right? That's how cowboys sleep at night, it will be fun sleeping under the stars. I pass his tent and lie down by the fire. The ground is cold but the heat slowly thaws me. It's amazing…until it isn't.

The wind has shifted and now smoke is blowing right in my face. I cough a few times as the kindling crackles. I try to move but it just follows me. *Why can't this be fucking easy?* I get up and stand in front of Nick's tent, pissed that I have to acquiesce to the tent plan. "Hey, Nick?" I say softly, but there's no answer. "Nick?"

I remember to dump the water on the fire and watch as it sizzles out. No turning back now. I slowly unzip the tent. As far as I can see from the glow of the moonlight, he seems to be asleep. He even looks sexy asleep. How is that possible? And why isn't he wearing a t-shirt? It's freezing outside.

I zip the tent back up and lie down with my back to his as far away as I can get. I'm practically inhaling the canvas siding as I scooch away from him. I lay the blanket over myself and pull it up to my chin. I may hate Nick Elliot but I was right, his body heat is amazing. It takes me a few minutes to adjust sleeping next to him and then my eyes flutter closed and I drift off to sleep.

Chapter 12

Nick

You Devil

I CAN'T BREATHE. The snake wraps around my leg and squeezes. My heart jumps in my throat as I reach down to remove it. It slithers up my chest and wraps around my shoulder. I take my hand and run its length. It's warm and...soft? My eyes pop open. It's not a snake, it's an arm and a leg. And not just anyone's arm and leg, it's Lindsey's. She's spooning me, her leg pinning mine so I can't move.

She's like a giant koala wrapped around me. Her arm is tucked under mine, her hand on my shoulder. I don't think she could get closer to me if she tried. She murmurs something between my shoulder blades, but I can tell she's still asleep. How the hell did she end up in here and how did I not crush her in my sleep?

I must have been really tired not to have heard her come in the tent. I take a moment and breathe in her scent, feeling her warm body against mine. I want to turn around and pin her underneath me, dragging my tongue down her smooth creamy skin—*fuck*, why am I torturing myself like this? I glance at my watch remembering we are meeting Triple A at the car.

Shit, it's eight-thirty!

I grab her arm and shake it. "Lindsey, wake up."

"Mmm, I like it like that."

I choke on a laugh. "Lindsey, it's Nick. Seriously, wake up."

"Nick...mmm." She giggles. "You devil..."

Is she dreaming about me? I'd love to play along, but we don't have time for games right now. I roll over and face her. Her hair is a tangled nest, her mascara has left marks under her eyes, and she's sleeping with her mouth slightly parted, softly snoring. She's gorgeous.

I take my index finger and gently push her chin up, closing her mouth. She snorts, but doesn't wake up. I trace my finger down the side of her face as I blow on her. She groans and pulls the blanket up under her chin. She's so lovely when she isn't awake.

"Lindsey! Wake up!"

Her eyes pop open and she sits straight up. "Wuza happenin', omgodineedcoffeewherethehellamI." She rubs her bleary eyes and slowly looks over at me. "What time is it?" she whines as she starts to fall back down.

"Oh no you don't. We're late for Triple A. Didn't you say they would be there at seven?"

"Hmm, yeah." She curls into the blanket.

"It's eight-thirty."

She pops back up. "What?! Oh my god, we're going to miss them! Nick! Shit, why did you let us sleep in? Aren't you supposed to be a Marine or something like that? Why the hell aren't you wearing a *shirt*?!"

"Actually, a Navy SEAL." I look down at my bare chest wondering why she's freaking out about me being shirtless.

"Don't you wake up at four-thirty every morning? Shit, shit, shit!" She unzips the tent and scrambles out. "Ugh, I can't *believe* we slept in! I need to pee and oh my god, he needs to put his shirt back on. Where's my phone?" I hear her ranting outside as I scrub my face with my hands. She was so warm and *quiet* next to me and now I'm left here alone in the tent with a raging hard-on, feeling cold. "Nick Elliot, seriously let's not dawdle, get a move on! What is he *doing* in there anyway?"

I take a deep breath and gather the two blankets and fold them. So much for a peaceful morning. "Maybe you should see if they've called you while I break down this tent."

"Do *not* come outside!"

"What? Why? Weren't you just yelling at me to get out?"

She gives a flustered groan. "Because I have to go pee and you can't watch."

I stifle a laugh. "Okay. Let me know when you're ready."

"Um you wouldn't happen to have toilet paper in that magical bag of yours, would you?"

"No, Snow White, you're going to have to use a leaf or let it air dry." I smile knowing she's going to hate that answer.

"That's disgusting! Ugh, I fucking *hate* camping. Use a leaf...I'll tell you where to use a leaf."

"Are you done yet?"

"I'm blaming you if we've missed Triple A!"

"Sure, whatever. I wouldn't expect anything less," I mutter as I throw a shirt on, pack my backpack up with the blankets, and wait.

If this is how Europe is going to go, I'm in a shitload of trouble.

Chapter 13

Lindsey

Amalong

The next day

I'M EXHAUSTED AS I wheel my suitcase up the front walk. That was probably the worst trip I've had in the history of ever. Granted I signed on to the biggest deal of my career, but meeting Nick Elliot ruined everything. He's that kid in middle school that you can't stand because he always talks over you and thinks he knows everything. That was Donovan O'Brien for me. He used to pull my ponytail and call me ugly face. God, I hated that kid. Nick is my Donovan O'Brien all grown up.

I've already emailed Simon and put in a request for a new director. If I have to work with that douchebag for six weeks over in Europe I might implode.

I'm just about to put my key in the door when Mrs. Bixby's door opens a crack. I pretend not to see her beady little eyes as she peers at me above her security chain. She clucks her tongue.

I sigh. "I can hear you, Mrs. Bixby." This is seriously the last thing I need.

She unlocks the door and opens it wider. "In my day,

women wore dresses and heels when they would travel on an arrow-plane."

"I'm not a flight attendant, Mrs. Bixby." I sigh as I dig through my purse for my Mace in case she gets frisky.

"Where have you been? I hear that damn cat meowing all day interrupting my soap operas and *The Price is Right*."

"God forbid, Mrs. Bixby."

"You shouldn't use the Lord's name in vain. I'm telling Richie you need to get rid of that cat. He pees in my gardenias," she says sourly.

"Maybe I should tell Rich to just get rid of you."

She pretends to ignore me but her eyes narrow, so I know she heard me. "That company Amalong with the dreadfully ugly gray vans keeps dropping things off on my porch for you."

I look around but the porch is bare except for two rocking chairs and a couple potted plants. "You mean Amazon? Where are my packages?"

"They're in the dumpster. I was worried they might contain inappropriate things."

I grind my teeth. The last thing I want to do after my trip from hell is root around in the dumpster in the back alley for my shampoo and conditioner and the new dress I purchased. "Thanks a lot, Mrs. Bixby, really appreciate your consideration."

"You should have your packages delivered to your work," she says haughtily like she's got a knitting stick shoved up her ass. How many times have I told this old bat that I don't have an office?

"For the hundredth time, I work from home."

"Only prostitutes work from home. Explains the parade of men coming in and out of here." She slams her door shut before I can respond.

This woman is going to be the death of me. I shake my head in disgust as I shove my bag inside my door and then walk down the side alley. I feel no guilt now about leaving those retirement brochures on her doorstep last week.

I open the iron gate and walk out into our side alley and spy the large gray dumpster. I look for my boxes on the ground to see if she tossed them there, but no such luck. I open the lid and want to vomit from the rotten-cheese smell that wafts out. How the hell did Mrs. Bixby manage to throw the boxes in here? I look around and spot a plastic milk crate to step up on so that I can actually look into the dumpster. I have to stand on my tippy toes. I spot a brown Amazon box with spaghetti sauce splattered all over it. Lovely.

I gingerly grab a corner of it and slide it out from underneath the broken garbage bag. My butt is in the air as I hear a worker from the restaurant across the way whistle at me as he finishes his cigarette break. *A little help here, buddy, would be appreciated.* I manage to grab the box as I cling to the nasty dumpster with my other hand for dear life. I throw the box over my shoulder and look for the other package. I have to move some bags around, but I finally spot it. I have to dangle myself even more as I lean down to grab it. All I can see and smell is rotten garbage spilling out of bags.

I hate Mrs. Bixby even more than I hate Nick Elliot in this moment. I slide off the dumpster and glance down at my once-favorite white V-neck. It has spaghetti sauce and grime all over it. I grab the packages and march back to the front porch. I rip open the Amazon seal and take my things out, leaving the nasty boxes for Mrs. Bixby to deal with.

"You owe me a new t-shirt, Mrs. Bixby!" I yell at her door before I open mine, grab my bag, and huff up the stairs for a much-needed shower. My phone dings announcing an incoming email, so I take off my shoes and fall down on my bed after turning on the shower waiting for the water to warm up. Oh good, it's a text from Simon.

> Lindsey, I sincerely apologize that your meeting with Nick didn't go the way you were hoping. Unfortunately, at this time we are unable to process your request for a new director. You and Mr. Healy will be leaving for London in three weeks. I wish you much luck on your adventure. Sincerely, Simon Blake

On my adventure? What am I playing a game of Jumanji? What the hell? I throw my phone down in frustration. I'm stuck with Nick Elliot whether I like it or not. One thing is for sure, I'm not going to let him get under my skin.

Chapter 14

Lindsey

The Ducky Goose

Three weeks later

WHAT HAPPENS IN London stays in London. Yeah, that's actually a saying for Vegas and I hate that fucking saying, because it's not true. Shit always gets leaked by someone, and then you have to live with the memory of the time you got drunk, danced on a bar and acted like an ass, and all your friends were there to bask in the glow of it.

In this case, it wasn't all my friends, it was Nick Elliot.

Patrick and I just arrived this afternoon to start filming for the show. I haven't seen Nick yet, and I'm hoping I won't have to until tomorrow morning for our "strategy session". He's been here for a couple days and has been blowing up my phone with emails about locations and set up. I was supposed to be doing research on all the restaurants we want to visit in preparation these past few weeks, but every time I'd get on the internet I'd fall down some rabbit hole regarding celebrity gossip, or there would be a shoe sale and I'd get nothing accomplished. I did find a fresh open market in Germany I want to see, but no restaurants.

"What are we going to do first?" Patrick rubs his hands

together in excitement as he meets me down in the hotel lobby. Patrick and I have been friends since he dated my roommate Katie freshman year of college. He's tall and gangly with a swimmer's build. His curly brown hair and kind butterscotch brown eyes make you want to spill all your secrets at first meet. He's dorky and cool all rolled into one if that's even possible. He likes sci-fi and Harry Potter and is always peppering me with the most useless facts about these two topics.

He's going to be a dream husband to some Harry Potter sci-fi-loving junkie someday. Although he and Katie didn't work out, our friendship remained. We drunkenly kissed once, but then both wiped our mouths and said 'nope.' He's like the goofy annoying brother I didn't know I wanted, but always needed.

"I don't know, Trick, I was hoping for an early night. I'm exhausted from the plane ride."

Patrick gives me the stink eye as we step out into the chilly London evening. "You slept the whole time. Aren't you going to be cold in that skirt?"

"I was tired." I shrug, and tuck my arm in his as we turn right down the street. "Nah, I'll be fine. Isn't it cute? Got it on sale. I like the way it swishes when I walk. Where are we going?"

"Well I talked to a few locals at the hotel bar while I was waiting for you and got some great spots for us to film."

I squeal in excitement as I squeeze his arm. "You're the best, Trick! Now I won't have Nick biting my head off for not having a plan in place."

"Let's pop in here. This looks like a classic old-timey

London bar."

I look at the lead glass windows and the heavy red-painted door surrounded by black brick. "You don't want a cute little bistro? This looks…medieval." There's an ancient axe mounted above the door with cracked gold letters spelling The Ducky Goose. "Is it really called The Ducky Goose?"

"It's perfect!" Patrick pulls the heavy door open and my eyes have to adjust to the dark bar as he gently pushes me in. It's not empty like I was expecting, but it's not crowded or boisterous either. Patrick grabs a dingy little booth next to a window you can't even see out of because of the grime and lead glass. He excitedly looks around the bar. "This is so awesome, it's like Harry Potter-ish or something."

"Or something…" I wipe off my booth seat as I look around at the salty crowd. Pretty sure Ron Weasley wouldn't be caught dead in this place, but I don't want to pop Patrick's balloon.

"I already know what I'm getting. Look, Lindsey, they even have rugby on TV! This is so cool!"

"Fine, we'll have a beer—"

"And some fish and chips!"

"And some fish and chips. But I pick the next place."

"Deal." Patrick beams as a tired old waitress drops off two greasy plastic-coated menus.

"Welcome to The Ducky. My name is Judy," she says flatly. Patrick beams at Judy like she's the Queen of fucking England. He bounces in his seat like he's eight and we're at Disney World waiting for Mickey Mouse to come over to the table, sign his book and give him a hug.

Instead we get Pirate Judy, a haggard woman in her sixties dressed like a pirate wench. And I'm not talking the bright white and red satin costume either. This getup looks original.

This is definitely not the greatest place on earth and Judy looks like she'd rather throat-punch Patrick than give him a hug as she grunts out the specials.

We give her our orders, keeping it short and to the point, not daring to chitchat with Judy about where we should head to next. She grumbles that our order will be out shortly and then she disappears into the dark.

That's when I notice him. Nick Elliot is sitting at the bar drinking a beer as he watches the rugby game. Of all the fucking places in London, he has to be in *this* dive.

"Trick, don't look, but Nick is here."

Of course, Patrick immediately looks over his shoulder. "Where?"

"I said don't look!" I hiss as I slap his arm.

"Ow! Well shouldn't we invite him over? I haven't met him yet, and we *will* be working together."

"Are you *insane?* I told you about what happened in New York."

"Yeah, you guys went camping, big deal. I've got to meet him at some point, right?" Patrick starts to get up.

I grab his shirt. "You don't even know which one is him."

Patrick looks over at the three guys and two girls at the bar. "Pretty sure it's not the eighty-year-old man, and the other one just doesn't scream 'producer' like the good-looking guy." Patrick rips his shirt from my white-knuckled grip and moves toward Nick before I can throw myself down in his path.

I watch with bated breath as he introduces himself, gesturing toward our booth. *No, no, no, Patrick!* Nick looks over his shoulder and our eyes connect. I immediately pick up my beer and guzzle it down, averting my gaze. Minutes agonizingly tick by as they chat and laugh like long-lost sorority sisters. It's killing me not knowing what they're talking about, but my ears are burning, so I'm pretty sure it's about me. I covertly look over at them, deep in discussion.

Judy takes this moment to drop our fish-and-chip platters down on the table. She's blocking my view so I can't tell what's going on.

"May I have another beer please?"

Judy grabs my mug, grunting as she heads to the bar. Her ample bosom and hips were blocking my view a moment ago, but now I see Patrick and Nick laughing. *Great.* I pretend to ignore them as I unwrap the fish and shake some vinegar and salt over it. I dip a fry into the sauce on the side of the plate and angrily chomp down on it.

I just wanted a peaceful night before we started this hellish tour. I pull my phone out pretending like I don't have a care in the world as I sit by myself in the dim bar. Patrick's laugh floats across the pub causing me to bristle. Patrick is *my* friend. I pull up the article I was looking at earlier about the new Ice Bar opening up near our hotel. I thought it sounded awful. I hate the cold and everyone complained about how expensive the drinks are and how you have to wear coats they give you. No, thank you!

"Lindsey Love."

His voice pops my safe little reading bubble. It's deep, rough, and sexy like he just woke up from a long night of doing naughty things. The kind of voice that can make a woman's panties dissolve in her pants. But not this woman. Nope. I have underwear of steel when it comes to Nick Elliot.

"Nick Elliot." I angrily chomp down on another fry as he and Patrick slide into the booth. I haven't spoken to Nick since I left his house to head back into the city after our horrible camping trip. We didn't say a single word to each other after Triple A got us back on the road. I tried to engage him in conversation and he just turned the volume up on the radio. That was a fun road trip. When we had gotten back to his house, we discovered that Sasha had pulled my underwear out of my bag I had left in the room, chewed them up, and vomited them on his parents' pretty suede sectional.

Of course, Nick blamed *me* for leaving my door open.

Where the hell is pirate Judy with my beer? I quickly throw my phone into my purse.

"You hungry, man?" Patrick practically drools as he brings his plate closer in.

"Nah, I ate earlier. Not bad food here."

"Lindsey, stop!" Patrick shouts. I immediately freeze, my knife and fork poised to cut into the fish. "We should totally do our practice run, you know since all three of us are right here."

"Now?" My eyes cut to Nick who raises an eyebrow. "This isn't exactly the atmosphere I was planning on...it's kind of dark...and scary in here."

"Lindsey's right, Patrick. It's really dark in here, and I

don't think this is London's best-kept secret." He winks at me as he takes a sip of his beer. My mouth hangs open as I stare at him in disbelief. Not only did he just agree with me but he winked like we were in on some private joke together. *What the hell is going on?*

"Oh right, totally, totally. I wasn't thinking about that." Patrick babbles on about the weather forecast for the next couple days as Mr. Sexy Smirk and I hold a staring contest across the table. *Why is he even here right now?* I narrow my eyes and he arches an eyebrow in return. Damn his gorgeous runway-model good looks.

My eyes are starting to burn because I don't want to even blink and lose to whatever the fuck we're doing right now. He looks completely unfazed as he picks up his beer and takes another sip, not one fucking blink. They must teach this shit in the SEALs. Who the hell can keep their eyes open and not feel like they need a gallon of rewetting drops?

Judy chooses this moment to drop my beer down in front of me, liquid sloshing over the sides. I glance down breaking the connection and realize I made Interrogation 101 mistake *numero uno*. Nick sits back in the booth with a self-satisfied smile I'd like to wipe off his lips with Judy's greasy rag.

I tune back into what Patrick is saying when Nick looks at him and chuckles. I quietly chug my beer, needing all the liquid encouragement I can get to survive the next hour.

"So this guy in the lobby was telling me about this Ice Bar that just opened up."

Nick rubs the back of his neck. "I've heard it's a rip-off, super cliché."

"What a coincidence," I say, "I was just reading about it on my phone. Sounds great, Trick, I'm in!" I look over at Nick with a sugary smile on my face as I down my beer. The Ice Bar is the last place I want to go, but I'll freeze to death before letting that little nugget of info slip through my lips.

"You might want to slow down on those, tiger. They have a higher alcohol content than U.S. beers."

"Doing great, Nick, thanks for your concern!" I smile brightly.

Okay maybe I am starting to feel super lightheaded but he doesn't need to know that, especially after that jerky comment of fake concern. I'm in that perfect beer high where I feel giddy and good. Judy walks over and even she exerts enough energy to raise her eyebrow at my empty mug.

"I'll have another Nutbrown Judy, thank you so much." I discreetly burp into my hand as I shove three more French fries into my mouth. I'm not the most ladylike eater after a few beers.

"I'll have one as well, Judy. Patrick are you good?"

Patrick nods as he bites into his fish. Nick winks at pirate Judy and I swear to god I hear her murmur, *Of course, ye good sir.* Like Nick is some kind of knight in shining armor or shit. I roll my eyes and take a bite of fish so I don't have to make conversation.

I sneak quick glances at Nick while I eat because…how can you not? He's wearing a plaid button-down with the sleeves rolled up. His skin is tan even though it's almost October. His chocolate-brown hair is artfully mussed, but short on the sides. His dark blue eyes flash to mine as he laughs at something Patrick says. They quickly sober as he continues to stare at me, which means I've been staring at him too long like a psycho stalker.

Thankfully Judy arrives with our beers in record time. I'm pretty sure she curtsies as she backs away from the table, unable to take her eyes off Sir Nick. *I feel you, Pirate Judy, I feel you.*

"So Lindsey, have you picked out a restaurant for our first assignment? I'll need to check it out tomorrow and make sure they're okay with us filming inside."

"Um, what was the name again, Trick?"

Patrick takes a swig of his beer and wipes his mouth. "Oh, right, right. So someone was telling me about this place called Archipalios? Said it's off the beaten path and has really exotic stuff. It's a must-try."

Nick's gaze swings in my direction. He grimaces. "I've heard of it. I don't think it's your style, Lindsey."

I huff out a laugh. Like this guy even knows my style. "Actually Nick, it's *exactly* my style, and I can't wait to try it." I give him a warm smile, but my eyes say *screw you, Nick Elliot.*

He runs his hand across his jaw as he tries to hide his smirk. "Suit yourself. I'll check it out tomorrow."

"All right, you guys ready to blow this pop stand?" Patrick starts to pull out his wallet, but Nick stops him.

"I've got it. *Food and Travel* will be paying for all your expenses except for personal meals, but I'd like to treat on your first night here."

"That's awesome! Thanks, man." Patrick beams at me. "Isn't that nice of him Lovie?"

"Mmm," is all I can manage while trying to figure out

his end game. Patrick kicks me under the table. "I mean, yes, thank you."

"Let's go get a cab. I can't wait to ride in one of those!" Patrick bounces out of the booth. I smile goofily back because I'm feeling pretty damn good at this point, and his excitement over London is infectious.

Nick pays Pirate Judy and we head out into the cold night to go to the Ice Bar, because we're smart like that.

Chapter 15

Nick

I See London, I See France. I See...

I KNOW LINDSEY is freezing her ass off right now as she shimmies on the dancefloor with Patrick in her short skirt and open-toe booties. The jacket they make you wear when you enter the bar engulfs her, but she doesn't seem to mind. In fact, she doesn't have a care in the world about anything right now as she downs another drink. I lean against the bar and do a quick reconnaissance of the room. It's a small place, but seems to be filled to max capacity. Because of the temperature they only let you stay for a maximum of forty-five minutes. I'm hoping we'll only be here for fifteen. Lindsey and Patrick move over to where I'm standing.

"Let's do another shot!" Lindsey pumps her hand in the air.

I try to maintain a mask of indifference, and pretend like I don't care what happens to her, but I don't really want to watch this train derail. She's my responsibility, so I need to keep her safe and hopefully not piss her off.

"Look, I don't care if you drink shots until you puke, but remember we're filming tomorrow and you don't want to look haggard and hungover."

"As if." Lindsey smirks as she knocks on the iced bar with her glass to signal another round, completely dismissing me. This woman loves to worm her way under my skin and make me twitch. "Oh my god, I love this song! Woo hoo!"

Before I can stop her, she's hoisted herself up on the bar made out of ice and starts dancing as if she were auditioning for a job at the bar *Coyote Ugly*. One thing she's nailed…it's ugly. The bartender is trying to get her to get back down, but she's lost in the song, her eyes closed as she moves her hips.

I'm willing to admit, as every guy in the bar turns to watch her, even though she may be sozzled, she's absolutely mesmerizing. I want to grab her off the bar, hoist her over my shoulder, spank her until she begs me to take her back to my hotel room…but instead I stand back and watch. Her carefree smile is infectious. Patrick, my new best friend, stands beside me.

"Is she always like this?" I lean into him.

"Only when she does shots." He grins. "Shake it, Lindsey Love!"

Okay, maybe Patrick isn't my new best friend. "Dude, don't encourage her. She's going to hurt herself."

"Nah, she's fine."

"So what's your story with her anyway?"

Patrick looks over at me with a sly smile. "She was roommates with my girlfriend in college. We both ended up in Charleston after school and she asked me to start helping her with her blog." He chuckles and gives me the side-eye. "Dude, don't worry. I'm not really into feisty short brunettes. I like the shy curvy bookish girls. Lindsey and I are just friends. She's like a sister to me."

I shake the ice in my glass ignoring Patrick's knowing smile. "I'm not interested in her. I was just curious."

Patrick shakes his head. "Whatever you say, man."

Everyone in the bar has now noticed her doing the electric slide as patrons start to whistle and clap. Encouraged by the attention and the alcohol Lindsey tries to up her dancing game, but she's either forgotten she's on ice, or she doesn't see the rubber mats placed haphazardly on the bar, because she trips and skids, losing her balance. She crashes down onto the bar, her short frilly skirt flying up as she flashes everyone her pink unicorn panties. Everyone cheers as several camera phones go off.

I growl like a tiger as I advance upon her, wanting to rip every single camera and smash it to smithereens. I grab Lindsey as she dizzily sits up, rubbing her backside looking like she just woke up from a dream. More like a nightmare. I wrap my arm around her and carry her out of the bar against my side.

"I'm calling it a night, you've had enough," I bark, pissed at myself that I stood by and watched her make an ass out of herself. "You're a pain in my ass, Lindsey Love."

"Sir, ma'am! We need our jackets back!" the hostess calls after me right before I burst from the lobby. I set Lindsey down, who strangely enough hasn't said a peep, rip my jacket off, then hers, and hand them to the young woman. Patrick is right behind us looking flustered.

"Shit, Lindsey, are you okay?"

"My butt hurts. I need to go night-nights," she says drunkenly, as she stumbles toward the door. I quickly pick her up. She looks into my eyes and smiles. "Whoa there. So strong, Sir SEAL." She pats my cheek like my grandmother does. "Aw, I love my boys. I'm so happy to be happy."

I grunt as I look into her glazed eyes. "Sir SEAL?"

"Sir SEAL, so sexy. Simon sexy too." She hiccups. "That's a lot of s's. I need chocolate cake…"

And then she passes out in my arms.

Chapter 16

Nick

Peri and Poppy

THE NEXT MORNING the sky is blue and the air is crisp, so I grab a coffee and a newspaper and head over to the park next to our hotel to sit and relax for a bit before I set things up for tonight. I wonder how Lindsey is doing. After I got her back to her hotel room last night in one piece, I made sure she was breathing normally before I tucked her into bed. I told Patrick to call if he needed me.

It took all my self-control not to lie down next to her and make sure she was going to be okay through the night, but I knew she wouldn't want that. She wants Simon Blake. It's a bitter pill to swallow that she thinks so highly of that sleaze, and so little of me. I sit down and unfold the newspaper. I glance over at a yoga class going on in the park. I nearly spit my coffee out as I do a double take.

No way. That *can't* be her. There's no way she's functioning at...I look down at my phone, eight a.m. I get up from my park bench and move inconspicuously closer to another that gives me a better view of the brunette doing downward dog in hunter-green Lycra. I sip my coffee and stare at her ass while I wait for her to stand back up. A woman pushing a pram walks by and gapes as she notices my laser focus on the group of women. I look down at my newspaper and pretend to read, feeling like a complete perv as she hurries by.

Damn, Lindsey Love, if that's you, I'm going to wring your neck for making me toss and turn all night worrying if you were okay.

The woman in green stands up and reaches to the sky, then turns to the side and reaches down. Oh, it's her alright. How the fuck did she pass out in my arms at midnight and is up doing yoga in a foreign country at eight a.m.? Most people have a difficult time adjusting to the time difference, let alone doing *namaste* the next morning. I watch as she bends down and points her arm to the sky. She looks fucking good in Lycra.

I wait for the group to finish and then practically run over to Lindsey as she wipes her face off with a hand towel.

"Lindsey!" I bark out, a little more harshly than I intended. She looks up sharply, her eyes wide like I caught her doing something wrong. *Oh, you did something wrong alright. You kept me up half the night worrying about you.* The whole group turns to look at me and I shrink back a little.

"Well, aren't you fit?" One woman from the class sidles up next to me and squeezes my arm, not letting go.

"Back off, Peri, I saw him first. He's totally lush." Another woman grabs onto my other arm.

"Uh, actually I'm here for—"

"Look at that smolder, Poppy. Don't be a cheeky one." Peri giggles as she blows into my ear. "I'm not wearing any knickers." She squeezes my bicep for good measure. Lindsey looks over at me as she gulps water from her bottle and smirks as the women grope me. She's enjoying this.

"Yeah, *don't be cheeky*, Elliot." Lindsey laughs as she walks by me on her way back to the hotel, swinging her towel over her shoulder.

"Oh Elliot, you *are* tidy. Are you up for it?" The other one pulls me out of Peri's viselike grip. I'm not sure what she's up for but I don't want to hang around to find out.

"Uh, excuse me ladies, but I'm here for someone else." I disengage from them as Peri and her friend Poppy start arguing.

"We were going to boff!" Peri screams causing all the other ladies to look in our direction. I don't think twice as I run from the group to catch up with Lindsey.

"Were you really going to leave me back there to be clawed apart?"

"You were handling yourself just fine." She smirks as she types something on her phone. "Besides, they were just going to boff you…whatever that means…sounds harmless."

I growl in frustration. "Boff means they wanted to have sex with me."

"Huh, really? At eight a.m.? Didn't see that one coming. Who knew Poppy was a dirty-talking whore?"

"Lindsey, stop." I gently grab her bicep. Her eyebrow arches as she looks down at my hand engulfing her arm. I immediately drop my hold.

"What do you want, Nick? Why are you even here? You're like poison ivy, you keep showing up in random places uninvited."

"I came out to the park to have coffee." I hold up my

cup and paper waving it in front of her face feeling insulted. It annoys me she just referred to me as a bad itchy rash. "What are *you* doing here? How did you even know they have a yoga group in the park?"

She rolls her eyes at me. "I asked the hotel clerk yesterday if there was a yoga studio nearby and she said they hold a class on Saturday mornings in the park if the weather is decent, which it is." She shrugs and takes another sip of her water. Her eye twitches in annoyance.

"Aren't you hungover?"

She looks at me indignantly. "No, do I *look* hungover?"

My eyes travel from her head to her toes. She doesn't look the least bit hungover which baffles me after her performance on the bar last night. Her glossy brown hair is up in a cute high ponytail. Her creamy complexion has a rosy glow after her workout. Her mossy green eyes are bright and shiny. It pisses me off that she caused me so much worry all night and here she is like a spring daffodil smiling cheekily at me. I glower at her as I cross my arms over my chest, refusing to respond.

"I'm going to check out the restaurant in a bit, I think you should join me. I don't think this place is your cup of tea." After spending time with her in New York and watching her previous YouTube videos, I know without a doubt in my heart she's going to hate this place.

She shrugs off my invitation like I'm an annoying gnat. "I'm good, but thank you for going to arrange it. If Patrick likes it then I'm onboard. We're actually going to do a little sightseeing. See if we can make a palace guard crack a smile, you know the usual touristy stuff. I trust you to make the proper arrangements." She looks longingly toward the hotel across the way and asks weakly, "Do you want to join us?" Her invitation is pitiful at best.

I want to go with them. Not to see the sights, I've been there and done that; I want to watch her laugh and be carefree. The pull is so strong in me it makes me angry. *She doesn't even like you, Elliot, get it through your thick head.* She likes Simon the snake.

"I'm good," I say gruffly.

"Suit yourself."

"I will."

"Okay then."

"Fine!" I grit out wanting to stomp off because she's making me feel like I'm twelve years old fighting with Missy Thompson on the playground when she refused to be my girlfriend.

"Fine!" Her long ponytail swings around as she turns on her heel and stomps off toward the hotel.

I sigh and hang my head, then chuck my now-cold coffee and newspaper in the trash bin as I turn in the opposite direction and go for a run to burn off the infuriating energy this woman has ignited in my veins.

Chapter 17

Lindsey

He Started It

HUNGOVER DOESN'T EVEN describe what I'm feeling right now. My pounding head is silently screaming at me to shut my eyes and crawl in a dark hole, but I can't, because I'm sightseeing with Patrick and I don't want to ruin this Harry Potter moment for him. We walk to King's Cross station where platform 9 ¾ resides. I insist on stopping in a coffee shop on the way so I can kickstart my brain. I can't seem to escape the image of Nick's pissed off face from this morning as Patrick prattles on about fun-filled Harry Potter facts.

I have no idea why I got out of bed at the ass crack of dawn, but when my alarm went off I panicked. I couldn't remember who I was with, where I was, until the memories of the night before flash-flooded my brain. I rarely forget anything, and unfortunately this was one of the times I wished I could have. I'm so embarrassed that I got up on the bar and shimmied my way from a dance move to my ass, showing everyone my pink unicorn underwear. I mean, it's not like I'm going to wear my sexy-time underwear out with Patrick, that's just a waste. If I had known how the end of the night would turn out, I would have splurged. My butt now sports a nice purple bruise.

I thought a little yoga time would make me feel better. Sweat out the toxins and all that good stuff. I was wrong. When Nick barked out my name at the end of class I was sure I was hallucinating. He's the last person I expected to see at yoga. Watching a muscular tall sexy god storm up to you while you're in child's pose makes funny things happen to your stomach. Or maybe it was just the alcohol making a comeback.

Either way, I've never popped up out of a position that fast before. And when Poppy and Peri started manhandling him, my gurgling upset stomach turned into a volcanic explosion. It was all I could do to keep from throwing up all over Nick's running shoes. He kept peppering me with questions which annoyed me even more because I just wanted a hot shower, a gallon of coffee, and for the ringing in my ears to stop.

"Earth to Lindsey…"

"Oh, sorry Patrick, yeah that's totally fascinating. Lovely, actually." I nod my head vigorously which makes it feel like someone put it in a salad spinner at top speed.

"You think so, huh? Did you just use a British accent?" He smirks as he hands me my coffee.

"Yup, I did."

"Have you been listening to anything I've said?"

"What? Yes!" I wasn't listening at all. I have no clue what we're talking about.

"So you think it's totally fascinating and *lovely* that Snape dies at the hands of Voldemort and that the real-life actor Alan Rickman died of cancer?"

Oh shit. "Wait, Alan Rickman died? Of cancer? Well, that just made me super sad. I loved him in *Love Actually*, and really no one can replace him as Severus Snape. When did this happen?"

Patrick sighs as he pushes the door open. "A while ago, where have you been? Ugh, just drink your coffee so you can be human again." We walk in silence for a bit.

"I'm sorry, Trick, I'm a terrible friend. I'm a little bit hungover if you can't tell."

"Oh, I can tell."

"Hey!" I bump into him as we walk down the sidewalk. "So on a scale of one to ten, how bad was I last night?"

"Probably an eight."

"Okay, that's not good, but not terrible either."

"I mean your unicorn panties might be a meme by now." He shrugs and quirks a smile.

"Uh, that would make it a ten if my undies have their own meme."

"Okay, then last night was a ten." I elbow him in the ribs causing him to grunt. "Your new producer boyfriend didn't seem too happy about it. Especially after you mentioned some guy named Simon."

I groan out loud. "He's *not* my boyfriend." Weird, I don't remember saying anything about Simon. "I mentioned Simon? In what capacity?"

"Sexy Simon?" He arches an eyebrow up at me as I suddenly feel like I'm walking in molasses.

"Great. That's the executive producer for the show."

"I thought his name sounded familiar."

"Yup."

Patrick flings an arm around my shoulders. "Well, Lovie, today is a new day. Maybe you can wow Nick with your charm over dinner tonight."

"Why do I need to *wow* Nick?"

"Because you like him."

"I most certainly do not," I scoff. "He's pigheaded and stubborn. He always wants his way and he throws a tantrum if he doesn't get it. And might I remind you, he made me eat snails in New York."

"He didn't *make* you."

"He tried to kill me! With a knife!"

"I mean sometimes, I'd like to kill you…"

"Patrick, that's not nice!" I sulk as I try to keep up with his long legs.

"I'm just kidding…kind of." He's silent for a moment, lost in thought. "Actually Lindsey, I'm pretty sure you just described *you*. I've only known Nick a few hours but he seems honest, straightforward, and responsible."

"Whose side are you on anyway?"

Patrick chuckles. "I'm not on anyone's side, Lovie. Just give the poor guy a chance." At the long line of visitors waiting for a picture with the trolley sticking out of the wall, Patrick excitedly gets out his camera. "After this I want a picture on the Millennium Bridge!"

I crossly fold my arms as we stand in line with the rest of the chatty tourists, but all I can think about is what Patrick just said. Give him a chance. First my sister and now Patrick.

As if.

I APPLY A layer of gloss and check my appearance in the bathroom mirror. I'm finally feeling put back together after lunch and a long nap. I check my phone and notice a new text from Nick requesting our presence downstairs in five minutes. I roll my eyes. He's so demanding. He might as well have just said: Lobby, 1800 hours. I throw my compact, phone, keycard, and my small brush into my purse before leaving my room.

I hold my stomach and take a deep breath as the elevator trundles down. I'm not sure why I feel nervous. It's not like this is the first time I've critiqued a restaurant. Maybe it's because it's in a different country and it's not just Patrick and me goofing around on my YouTube channel. This is television—the big leagues. I'll also have to look at Nick's judging eyes the whole evening as I eat and comment on the meal. I'm not sure why his opinion matters to me, but it does.

I step off the elevator. The people milling about in the lobby fall away as Nick turns around. He's so good-looking it hurts. I take in a lungful of fresh O$_2$ as his gaze quickly and discreetly rakes over my body. He looks handsome in tailored navy dress pants and a white button-down that fits his body like a glove. If we were two strangers who happened to bump into each other on the street, and he never opened his mouth except to ask me if I wanted to have wild crazy monkey sex, I would say yes in a heartbeat.

His brown wing tips move toward me as I stand stock-still in front of the elevators. I shift nervously as he approaches. So much for trying to look cool and uncaring. His gelled hair is artfully mussed, his dark blue eyes giving nothing away. He looks like he's on a Navy SEAL mission to take out his next victim; a lion hunting his prey.

If you haven't pieced it together yet, I'm the prey.

He stops and stands in front of me. He cocks an eyebrow and folds his muscular arms over his chest. If he's trying to intimidate me, he's doing a damn fine job. He smells as good as he looks—cedar, woodsy, expensive. I want to bury my nose right in the column of his throat.

"Lindsey Love."

My imagination wanders as my name leaves his lips. *Me walking toward him on an empty street. He reaches out and pulls me to his hard chest. His hand gets tangled in my hair as he looks down into my lust-filled eyes. 'Hot monkey sex?' he asks.* "Yes!"

He arches an eyebrow at me. "What are you saying yes to?"

My daydream pops like a bubble. So much for the hot monkey sex invitation. I clear my throat. "Yes, Lindsey Love is my name." I laugh lightly like I'm not totally certifiable. His expression begs to differ. We stare intensely at each other. "Please don't let this be another staring contest, my eyeballs are still exhausted from the last one."

"What are you talking about?"

"Ha, oh gosh, nothing. What's up?" My eyes dart around the lobby looking for the quickest exit.

"We have a few rules to go over this evening."

"Oh, we do, do we? And what might those be?" I smile sweetly which causes a muscle in his jaw to tick.

"Tonight is about business. I want you to have fun like you normally do for your show, but we can't have a repeat of last night."

I bristle. *Oh...this guy.* "Uh-huh. And what if I happen to make an ass out of myself? What are you going to do about it?"

He blows a breath out through his nose. "Why are you always so difficult?"

"Why do you make things so difficult?" I put my hands on my hips ready for a faceoff.

"Okay, okay, wow, let's take a few steps back." Patrick nervously looks around as he steps in between Nick and me, his camera equipment bumping into me making me take a step back.

"He's being rude, telling me not to get drunk again." I step back and fold my arms over my chest.

"And dance on bars and show everyone your underwear," Nick bites back.

I blanche, because it's true. I did make an ass out of myself. I was totally unprofessional when I'm here to do an assignment.

"Jesus, can you two just take a breather?" Patrick gives me a hard stare. "The cab is here, let's go."

I trail behind the two men, feeling completely deflated when Nick holds the door open for me and whispers, "I'm sorry, I was out of line. You look beautiful tonight. Forget what I said earlier. You're going to be great."

I'm so stunned, I let him guide me to the cab with his

hand pressed to the small of my back. "Thank you," I murmur as he helps me inside the cab and then slides in and closes the door.

As we drive to the restaurant, Nick and Patrick discuss direction and where Patrick should sit at the table to get my best angle. I usually start my spiel outside the restaurant and then cut to me sitting at the table. Nick wants to change it up a little, do a few shots of the signage and then have me walking into the restaurant to greet the owner.

I look out the window at the passing buildings and traffic as the guys talk, not really wanting to open my mouth again and sound like an immature ass. I'm tired of arguing with Nick and just want to get this night over with.

"You okay, Lovie?" Patrick asks.

"Yeah. I think the time difference is finally catching up to me." I shrug. "I can't wait to eat. I'm starving."

Nick shifts in his seat as he types something out on his phone. He puts it away and asks what we did today which launches Patrick into the gazillion Harry Potter sights we saw. I tune him out the next few minutes until we get to the restaurant.

Chapter 18

Lindsey

Soup du Jour

PATRICK TAKES SOME shots of the outside of the restaurant and signage, then he and Nick go inside while I wait for Nick's cue on my cell phone to come through the door. I nervously wipe my hands on my dress while I give myself a quick pep talk telling myself this is going to be great. My phone buzzes making me jump. That's my signal.

I enter and paste a big smile on my face as a tall thin man dressed in a tuxedo greets me at the front desk. He looks like an old English butler with graying hair and bifocals. "Ah, Miss Love, welcome to Archipalios. We are so excited to have you dining with us this evening. My name is Nigel and I will be taking care of you and your guests." He slightly bows toward me and I swear I'm about to curtsy when I look up and see Nick frown, slightly shaking his head no. I stand there awkwardly and smile as Nigel guides me over to the dining area.

"Don't look so stiff," Nick whispers in my ear before we get to the table.

"I'm sorry, I'm really nervous and his formal British accent is throwing me for a loop."

I look in awe around the restaurant. It's dark with black polished wood floors, red-papered walls and black tables with red candles. Diners speak in hushed tones and look over at us as we follow Nigel into a private area.

"We thought it might be better to have you away from the crowd so that we can give you the ultimate Archipalios experience," he says with a flourish as he scoots my chair out.

"Thank you, Nigel, this is beautiful." I look around the table as he picks up my napkin and gently puts it in my lap. "Do we have menus or…"

"The executive chef has taken it upon himself to prepare his favorites just for you. Do you have any food allergies or restrictions, Miss Love?"

"None, thank you." I smile back at him feeling excited. Nigel departs after Nick orders a bottle of wine from the Sommelier. I waggle my eyebrows in excitement. "This is awesome!"

Nick looks at me blandly, clearly not sharing my level of enthusiasm as he turns to Patrick. "So Patrick, I'd like you to film her receiving the food and her reactions to each bite. That initial reaction tells everything in my opinion. We'll cut and splice stuff together later and do voiceovers if we have to."

"Sure, sure, got it." Patrick quickly sets up a light box on the other side of the table to help illuminate the dishes when they come out.

"It's kind of strange not being able to choose something from the menu."

"In restaurants like this, executive chefs like to offer what they are best known for, not necessarily crowd-pleasers or the regular menu fare."

"Well I know, but you would think they would want to advertise their regular fare. The restaurants I feature back in the States want people to come in for the food on their menu."

Nick gives me a withering stare which does nothing to help my nerves.

Patrick sets his camera on the table tripod, pointing his microphone in my direction signaling that he's rolling as he adjusts the sounds on his belt bag. A waiter brings over the first dish. Nigel accompanies him and explains the dish as he places it in front of me.

"Miss Love, this is off our à la carte menu and is called Moroccan Nights."

I arch my eyebrow at Nick. Point one to me. "Ooh, that sounds exotic and beautiful," I say dreamily as I take a bite of the dish that looks like tabbouleh. I mull over the spices that hit my tongue and then bite into something crunchy. Hmm, interesting. The waiters leave a small plate for Nick and Patrick.

"The spices blend together so nicely especially with the dried fruit, but I'm not quite sure what the crunchy ingredient is…"

"Ahh, yes. Moroccan Nights is our signature dish of pan-fried chermoula crickets, quinoa, spinach and dried fruit. *Bon appétit.*"

Nigel bows before he backs away from our table and it's all I can do not to spit the mixture out on his polished black shoes. I look up at the camera. "Wow, wasn't expecting that." I gulp down an unhealthy amount of water.

Patrick grins as he presses something on the camera and dives into his dish. "This is awesome. It's like Fear Factor meets fine dining."

"Uh, yeah." I switch from water to wine and take a swig. "Mmm, at least this is good."

Nick's jaw ticks as he looks at me, taking a bite of the cricket dish. He doesn't say a word, but he doesn't have to, I know what he's thinking. *Don't get drunk.* I mimic his facial expression except mine is telling him to politely fuck off. He chokes on his food.

"Did you get a cricket down your windpipe?" I ask innocently.

"Something like that." He grimaces as he pushes the plate to the side.

Patrick stands again as he adjusts his camera and sound. I flash a smile at both of them.

"Do I have anything in my teeth?"

Patrick gives me a thumbs-up.

The waiter places an oval bowl in front of me. It looks like pea soup garnished with fresh flaky croutons and parmesan cheese. He then sets down a zebra-patterned plate with skewers on it for all of us to share.

"Mmm, this smells so incredible." I pick up my spoon and am about to dip into it when Nigel clears his throat and starts to speak. Dammit, I'm so hungry. I quickly place my spoon back down and focus all my attention on him.

"This is from our à la carte menu. The chef has prepared our signature flash-fried zebra skewers. This is zebra meat dipped in cornmeal, flash fried and served on a bed of crisp curry leaves and tzatziki. For our second delicacy, the chef is excited and pleased to serve you one of his specialties tonight, his soup du jour—turtle soup."

Nigel continues to describe the cream sauce and spices blended lovingly with the turtle meat that was freshly prepared just for us.

I can't breathe. I can't do anything but stare down at my bowl of soup in horror. How could anyone want to eat a sweet innocent turtle? I nearly killed myself to save one a few weeks ago and here I am across the pond and he's being served up right in front of me. I want to vomit. Sweat starts to trickle down my spine. Nigel bows and leaves as I look up at Patrick, my mouth in the shape of an O.

"I can't." I shake my head. "Nope, not going to do this. This poor turtle and zebra. What the fuck did they do to anyone? I can't even look at that fucking black and white zebra-patterned plate. That is some sick shit, serving zebra meat on a zebra-patterned plate. They might as well have the pelt as the tablecloth."

I'm starting to shake. Nick grimly sits as the waiter brings two more bowls over. I take a deep breath.

"I can't, y'all. Tucker deserved to live. He was probably just moseying along and this sadistic asshole chef from *The Little Mermaid* picked him up and shoved him into a bag and then kept him barely alive in a cage until his untimely death. Oh my god, I'm so sorry, Tucker!" I cry out as I shove the bowl away from me.

"Hey Lindsey, it's okay." Patrick lowers the camera while Nick coughs into his hand, looking away. "The turtle was probably raised just for this kind of thing anyway, like at a turtle farm. I doubt they got it from the wild. And I doubt his name is Tucker. It's probably like Turtle A1-12."

"They have fucking turtle farms for this?" I whisper in horror.

"You're not *helping*, Patrick." Nick leans forward in his seat.

My eyes return to Nick as thoughts start making me doubt his character. "Did you plan this? Did you see this on the menu and tell them they *had* to serve this just so you could get a reaction out of me? Because that's some—"

"Lindsey, no," he says sharply. His jaw ticks as he looks at the soup bowl. "I tried to tell you this wasn't the right fit for *Lindsey Love Loves*...but you wouldn't listen. This restaurant serves unusual exotic food."

"Well a fucking heads-up would have been nice!"

Nick shakes his head in exasperation, his lip curling into a snarl. "Look—"

Patrick clears his throat as he turns the camera back on and starts recording. I grind my teeth and take another gulp of wine as another waiter appears moving the soup to the side and sets a plate down in front of me. Nigel appears faithfully at my side and I really want the pompous ass to just go away, but he's here on assignment and he's going to get the job done. I take a page out of Nigel's book and take a deep breath as I smile up at him. I can do this. I can be professional and get through this awful meal.

"We will have three main courses this evening for your dining pleasure. The first will be a Durban 'bunny chow' with moong bean and lentil Indian curry and green mango atcha."

I look up at the camera and mouth *bunny chow?* Before I

can stop myself, I interrupt Nigel as I hold up my hand. "Excuse me, Nigel, but is this actual rabbit? Were Peter Rabbit and friends harmed in making this dish?"

Nick snorts into his closed fist as I glare at him.

"Uh, no Miss Love, Durban bunny chow is actually a South African dish of hollowed white bread bowl filled with curry."

My cheeks flame as I quickly nod. "Ah, of course. Thank you for clarifying."

"Of course, madam." The waiters bring over a second platter that smells mouthwatering.

"The second dish is one of our most popular, Zhug-marinated kangaroo skewers, candied beets with a goat cheese and balsamic reduction. And our third dish is Python-seared rare wrapped in grape leaves with a pine nut and honey glaze. Enjoy."

My mouth hangs open before I can remember my manners as I look at the steaming plates of kangaroo and python. I quickly snap it shut. "Thank you, Nigel, wow, this looks...um...honestly rev—"

"Thank you, Nigel," Nick smoothly cuts me off. "You've rendered her speechless, for once." His angry laser eyes zero in on mine and tell me to shut the fuck up before I say something I'll regret. "This looks amazing."

Nigel bows like a dutiful servant and backs away from the table.

"Cut, Patrick," I say sourly as I look at the table laden with exotic dishes. "Nick, I...I don't know what you want me to do."

He looks at me and smiles. "I want you to be the professional I know you are and try each dish."

"You want me to actually *eat* this?"

"Yes, it's in your contract."

I look at Patrick who gives me a shrug. "I'll try the python."

"No, Lindsey has to eat it," Nick says firmly. Our eyes lock. "Maybe next time she'll do a little more research on the restaurant she's critiquing."

I have never despised someone as much as I do him in this moment. I narrow my eyes at him in pure hatred. "Fine," I grit out, "but I'm not touching the soup. I have a sudden severe allergy to turtle."

"Fine," he says calmly. "The soup can be the one you don't eat."

Damn, that was too easy. I should have bargained for more. "Which do you want me to try first?"

"Whatever your heart desires."

My heart desires for him to get severe food poisoning is what it desires.

Patrick turns the camera back on and starts to film. I take the smallest bite of meat off the zebra skewer with my front teeth. "It's tough and chewy like jerky." *Disgusting.* I shiver as I set the skewer back down. "If you like gamey meat, you'll like the zebra."

"Uh, try that one again." Nick looks down at his phone like this whole production is completely boring him. "You need a little more *oomph*. You sound like a robot."

I growl as I pick the skewer back up. I want to stab him in the eye with it. This time I slide the meet off the skewer and cut a small bite. I pretend to savor the meat in my mouth. "The zebra is crisp. It's not as tender as I like my meat to be, but it definitely carries an exotic flair." I smile at the camera.

"Better," he grunts. "Next."

After eight more takes I manage to swallow down two bites of python—which I almost gag on—three bites of kangaroo—which I make sure is heavily doused in goat cheese—and one bite of bunny chow which I actually enjoy. Patrick enjoys it all. I look over at enemy number one. "Are we done here?"

"Maybe next time you'll listen to your producer." He grins at me across the table making me want to punch out all of his perfectly white teeth.

Before I can come back with a snappy reply Nigel sweeps over with his two waiters who start clearing the plates. "How was the soup, Ms. Love?"

"Marvelous, Nigel, thank you. I must say the bunny chow was my favorite, it had such great flavor."

Nigel's smile slips a bit as he surveys our dishes. He looks down his long patrician nose at me, his voice turning nasally. "Ah, yes, the South African fast-food dish. A popular dish for sure, but not unique."

Clearly, I've disappointed him by picking the *McDonalds* hamburger over the filet, but I couldn't admit it was the only dish I didn't gag on. His expression tells me my culinary taste buds are not up to snuff for his restaurant. He clears his throat and straightens his shoulders.

"For dessert, our chef has created one of our favorites especially for you."

Oh for fuck's sake, can't this nightmare just be over? I smile grimly at Nigel. "Can't wait."

I swear Nick's eyes light up with mirth as he leans back and takes a sip of his wine. I hope he gets a running rash on his balls.

A waiter brings over three small dessert bowls for each of us. I look down at my red porcelain bowl and want to cry with joy. Vanilla ice cream with chocolate sauce. Many thanks to the chef for not being a complete sadistic asshole.

"For dessert we offer you French vanilla bean iced crème with dark chocolate sauce drizzled over a charred jalapeño-infused scorpion. Enjoy."

"Are you fucking kidding me?" I say under my breath. Nick is shaking in his seat, he's laughing so hard. I want to dump my charred scorpion right on top of his head.

"This is awesome, I've always wanted to try something like this!" Patrick enthusiastically digs into his ice cream as I just stare down at my bowl. I hate my life right now. I look up and almost vomit when Patrick holds up the scorpion tail he just found in his bowl like the toy at the bottom of a cereal box.

"This is so wicked!" Patrick joyfully takes a selfie of himself eating the scorpion. I roll my shoulders back and snap my big-girl bra into place because there are starving children in the world, and I am not going to let Nick Elliot win this round. And if Patrick can enjoy it, then so can I.

"Patrick, start filming," I say resolutely.

I take a bite of the smooth velvety ice cream. The sweet flavor hits my tongue and I sigh because it really is so good. The crunch of the charred jalapeño scorpion is gritty and ruins the whole experience for me, but I power through it like the champion I am. I smile as I swallow it down.

I eat the whole goddamn bowl, grimacing every time my teeth crunch down on scorpion, and rave about how good it is. Nigel is positively delighted when he sees my empty bowl.

Fuck you, Nick Elliot. Fuck you.

Chapter 19

Lindsey

John from Florida

"LINDSEY WILL YOU just sit in your seat and relax?" Patrick complains.

"Well, I don't understand why he gets first class and we're stuck back here in coach," I gripe as I grab my e-reader out of my purse. "Shouldn't we all travel the same? Why is he so special he gets first class?"

Patrick sighs, clearly annoyed with my tirade. "I dunno, maybe because he's the producer?"

"And maybe because my legs are so long, and I have broad shoulders I have a hard time fitting in a coach seat." His hard voice chafes my nerves like sand stuck in the crevices of a swimsuit.

I look up at him as he leans over our seats. His blue eyes pierce through me. He raises an eyebrow challenging me, but I don't take the bait. I open up my reader and pretend like he's not looming over me smelling fucking incredible. I can practically hear him grind his teeth as I chance a glance up at him from under my eyelashes. His sharp jaw ticks in annoyance as he gazes down the aisle.

"See you when we land in Germany." He thumps Patrick's chair once with his fist.

"*Klingt gut*," Patrick replies.

"You know German?" I hiss. "What did you just say?"

"Yeah, I took it in high school. I said, 'Sounds good'."
He shrugs like it's no big deal.

"Great, so now you and Nick can both converse in German and I'll have no idea what you're saying."

"Nah, I promise I won't do that to you."

"I'm nervous, Trick." I sigh heavily.

Patrick looks over at me. "Why are you nervous?"

"So far this whole experience has been a total disaster. I mean, I've gotten drunk and flashed a whole bar wearing unicorn underwear, I've had the worst eating experience of my career, and that man has turned me into a total craze ball...I'm a loser."

"No, you are not. Remember that time we checked out that taco stand near Folly's Island?"

I groan. "Hard to forget places that give you food poisoning."

"You threw up all over that dorky wannabe surfer lifeguard."

I laugh and cover my face with my hands. "Oh God, that was so embarrassing. He was cute until I puked on him."

He grabs my hand and squeezes it. "My point is, it may seem bad in the moment but we'll look back on this whole trip in a year and laugh about it. Everyone has gotten drunk and made a fool of themselves. Who cares what anyone else thinks?"

"I don't."

But I *do* care. And it rubs me raw with irritation that I

care what Nick Elliot thinks of me. I know our first filming disappointed him. I should have listened to him when he said I wouldn't like the place. He is my director and producer after all and he reports directly to Simon.

Oh God, Simon. He has the ability to pull the plug on this whole project if I can't deliver. He's going to be so disappointed in last night. I heave another sigh as I flop my head against the headrest.

"Don't worry, Lovie, I promise I won't let you do anything stupid from here on out."

I huff out a laugh. "Not even you can make promises like that, Trick." I smile wryly at him. "I'm glad you're here."

"I've got your back."

GUESS WHO DOESN'T have my back? My ex-best friend Patrick, that's who. As soon as we land in Germany, he meets a girl in the lobby of our hotel as we wait to check in. We have the night to do whatever and instead of sticking to our original plans of dinner, just the three of us, he is now going to dinner with Gabby from Australia. I tried to cajole them into joining, but Patrick shooed me away like an annoying fly and said he wanted to check out a place that I would probably hate.

I hope he chokes on a cricket or whatever nasty Fear Factor thing he's found.

So now it's just going to be Nick and me.

I take a sip of my martini as I pull out my phone, calling my sister as I wait at the hotel bar for Nick to come down from his room.

"Well, it's about time! Jesus, I was over here having a heart attack thinking you had been kidnapped and sold on the black market."

So dramatic. "Okay, take a breath, Liam Neeson. I'm sorry I haven't called since I landed in London—"

"Texted. You *texted* me."

"Same thing. I've been busy. How's Mac? How are Dan and the kids?"

"They're all fine. Mrs. Bixby called the police on Dan the other day for breaking and entering when he went to go feed Mac, even though she knows who he is."

"What? Oh Shannon, no! I am so sorry. Ugh, I hate that old bag."

"It's fine. We got it all straightened out. So, tell me what's been going on?"

I turn my attention to the bank of elevators as I wait for Nick to step off of one. "I only have a couple minutes. London..." I blow out my breath, "...was a total disaster."

"Oh no! Why? What happened?"

"Well, the first night Nick our producer—"

"The hot serial killer with the cabin in the woods?"

"Yeah, that one. Anyway, he—"

"Did you ever have sex with him and relieve all that sexual tension?"

"What? No! I told you everything that happened in New York. Stop interrupting me. Besides, there's no sexual tension between us."

"Didn't you say he was a hot Navy SEAL?"

"That was before he opened his mouth."

"Uh-huh. There's sexual tension."

"*Anyway*, he joined us for drinks our first night and it annoyed me so much that I ended up drinking my weight in beer because Pirate Judy kept bringing them. Then we went to this Ice Bar where everything is made out of ice. It was so cold so I danced and kept drinking to keep warm. I might have gotten up on the bar and fell on my ass flashing the whole bar."

"Wait, slow down. Who is Pirate Judy?"

I sigh dramatically. "Really not the significant part of my story and yet that's all you pick up on. Did you hear about me flashing the whole bar?"

"Oh no."

"Yes."

"No, I mean, oh no, there's a gif of it."

"Wait, what?" I hiss. *I thought Patrick was kidding!*

"Uh yeah, it's titled Lindsey Love Loves…Unicorns."

"Fuck me. Who the hell would be there that knows me?" I groan as I sink back into the bar stool. "As if it doesn't get worse, the next night we go to some weird exotic place—"

"Like naked women?"

"Exotic as in weird food. Shannon, they served turtle soup with actual turtle meat, kangaroo kabobs, zebra satay, and boa constrictor."

"That's disgusting."

"I know! And serial-killer Nick made me eat it. *And* he had the nerve to fly first class while we flew coach."

"That bastard."

"Yes! Thank you for finally agreeing with me."

"Oh, sorry, no I was talking about the asshole who just took my parking spot."

"Oh." I slide an olive off my toothpick.

"Ugh, now I have to circle around again. Look, Lindsey, I'm sure he's not as bad as you're making him sound. The unicorn panties gif is unfortunate, but that will blow over in a couple years."

"A couple *years?*" I screech causing several people to look in my direction. "You are not helping, Shanny."

"Sorry, what are you doing now?"

"Patrick ditched me for some girl he met in the lobby so now it's just Nick and me going to dinner."

"Ooh, *tres romantico.* Remember to use protection."

"No, *tres tragico*—condoms not needed. We can't stand each other and we have nothing to talk about."

"So then just talk about sex. Men love talking about sex."

"No, they don't."

"Lindsey, it's on their minds constantly. Men are simple creatures. Look at Dan. He always has sex on the brain. Trust me, I'm an OB/GYN, I've got babies popping out the wazoo. Ooh, found a spot. Look, I gotta run. Call me tomorrow and let me know how tonight goes. Just be yourself, you'll be fine! Love you, bye!"

"Love you, bye."

I check my phone and see that Nick is five minutes past our appointed meeting time. He's never late. Maybe he got stuck in his hotel room or got hit by a car. *That would be a shame.*

I sip my martini. I'm still pissed at him for making me

eat all those weird meats last night. His eyes said what his mouth wouldn't—I was acting juvenile. His penetrating stare spoke volumes causing me to feel ashamed that I couldn't pull my shit together, be professional and eat Tucker the turtle. I felt like I wasn't good enough to do my job or that I didn't deserve this show. I know he thinks I'm a spoiled little princess, and that irks me the most because I'm not. I've worked my ass off to get here.

"Is this seat taken?" I shake my head as the good-looking man sits down next to me. I check him out discreetly as he orders a scotch and a can of Sprite. "Hello."

I smile over at him. "Hello."

"American?"

"Yes," I say, taking another sip of martini.

"Me too. I'm John from Florida."

"Hi, John from Florida. I'm Lindsey from South Carolina."

"You're too pretty to be sitting here all alone. Are you waiting for someone?"

He has a nice smile and even though he doesn't initially sweep me off my feet, he's a decent-looking guy. I ignore his question because even though he's nice, he doesn't need to know if I'm alone or not.

I slide my last martini olive off the stick and pop it into my mouth. "What are you doing in Berlin, John from Florida?"

"Uh, business."

"Hmm, me too."

The elevator doors open, a group steps off, but there's no sign of Nick. I check the time again. Ten minutes late. I can't believe he's standing me up. He doesn't even have the balls to come up with some half-ass excuse. Well screw him, I'll just go eat by myself. I signal the bartender to close out my tab.

"I hope I haven't scared you off."

"Oh no, not at all. I was supposed to meet a friend, but he's been held up."

"Well, I'm here…" He has a point. Better to hang with John than go off into a strange city by myself.

I smile and send John a flirty wink. When I peer over his shoulder I see Nick stalking toward me, a dangerous look in his eyes, with a tall blonde on his heels.

"Lindsey, I've been looking everywhere for you."

"Well here I am. What's up?"

The woman stops next to Nick and smiles at me. Clearly, he has a dinner date.

"Dinner reservations?" He cocks an eyebrow like I'm completely dense. The blonde says something in German and Nick responds with a tight smile. "*Nein.* Lindsey, this is my friend Claudine. She lives here in Berlin. She'll be joining us for dinner tonight."

"Oh, okay! It's very nice to meet you." I muster a fake smile. The last thing I want is to be a third wheel. Especially *Nick's* third wheel. "This is John from Florida. John, this is Nick and Claudine. John is *my* dinner date."

Nick appraises John quickly, his mouth set in a grim line. "Great. Let's go."

"Oh, uh…" John looks around the bar. "I'm not—"

"Yes, John, I insist. Dinner. As. My. Date." The words come out stilted as I stare Nick down.

"Shall we?" Claudine says in heavily accented English. She's tall and thin like a model. She reminds me of Charlize Theron, and it makes me feel short and frumpy. She immediately grabs onto Nick's arm, holding him tight as they walk across the lobby. Her body moves fluidly like water as she walks, like the whole world is hers and she knows it.

I grab John and pull him off his barstool. "Put his drink on my tab," I shout to the bartender.

"Uh, thanks? Listen, I'm—"

"Look, just roll with it, John from Florida. I need you as my wingman right now."

My short legs try to keep up with Nick and Claudine as I drag John behind me, but my heels prevent me from running a sprint, so I give up. They're conversing in German, so I can't understand them anyway.

"Mark! What the fuck are you doing?" John halts pulling me to a stop. We whirl around to see a frizzy brunette with a toddler in one arm and a five-year-old being dragged behind her.

"Shit," John mumbles next to me as he unlatches my hand from his.

"Um, do you know this woman?" I ask behind the smile that's permafrozen on my face as she comes charging up to us.

"*Who the hell is this?* What are you *doing?*" the woman shouts causing everyone in the lobby to stop and stare. I feel Nick come up to stand next to me.

"Rita, I swear, it's not what it looks like. She grabbed my hand. I couldn't get away!"

Rita's eyes want to stab me to death and I can't say I blame her. I chew my bottom lip as I slowly back away. "So…I'm guessing you're not John from Florida."

"No, he's Mark Shapiro from New Jersey!" Rita seethes. "What the hell, Mark? Were you going to go have a quickie with this floozy in the hotel bathroom? I thought you were getting a Sprite for Anna! Is she a German prostitute you picked up at the bar?"

Oh boy.

"Um, I'm not a prost—"

"I think there has been a misunderstanding here." Nick steps in, cutting me off. "Lindsey is with me. She mistakenly thought Mark was a part of our group. I'm so sorry if there was any…mix-up." Nick pulls me to his side. I actually want to turn into him and bury my nose into his hard chest. Jesus, I'm so embarrassed.

Rita eyes me with pure hatred as Nick's words seep into her brain. She nods her head once. "Come on Mark, our room is ready." She pulls him from the group with her older child in tow staring back at us with wide eyes. "You are in *so* much trouble!" she yells at him.

I just want to hide where no one can see or speak to me again. Nick shifts away from me which makes me realize I did indeed bury my head into his side. God, I hope I didn't leave a drool stain on his starched button-down.

His lips are set in a frown, but his eyes hold something akin to sympathy. That's the last thing I want to see from him. And I can't even look at Claudine.

I push out a laugh that falls flat. "Well, that was…hilarious."

Jesus, *hilarious*? Is that the only word I can come up with to describe the most humiliating moment of my life? That just made my unicorn panties gif look like fun times.

"Why don't you two go on to dinner, I'm suddenly feeling really tired." My traitorous stomach decides that now is the perfect moment to make the loudest growl ever.

"Your stomach says otherwise," Nick smartly points out. My stomach is a hateful bitch is what she is as she rumbles again. "Come on, let's go." Nick winks at Claudine as I pathetically trail behind them like a stray puppy.

Nick hails a cream-colored Mercedes with a taxi sign on top. "Aren't we going to take the U-Bahn?" I ask them as I rifle through my purse making sure I have my phone.

Claudine snorts. "If you want to ride the underground system, be my guest, but it's not the quickest way to the restaurant and your feet will be begging for relief after."

"Ah, I see," I say, feeling small once again. We head to The Sky Lounge which Claudine boasts has the most amazing views of the city. "So how do you two know each other?" I ask, trying to get the last thirty minutes permanently erased from their brains. I wish I had that cool little pen like Tommy Lee Jones carried around in *Men in Black* that erased memory.

"Ah, I've known Nicky for a long time." She laughs and looks at him lovingly. My teeth click together in irritation. *Nicky?*

"I spent the summer of my junior year of high school abroad over here and Claudine was in the same program. She's actually Russian but now lives in Berlin."

"Oh, that's nice," I lamely reply as I look out the window

feeling like Skipper on a date with Ken and Russian Barbie.

Claudine says something in German or Russian, who the hell knows, and they both smile lovingly at each other. *Vomit.* She continues to speak in her foreign tongue leaving me out. Nick answers her in English, but it doesn't matter because she's doing most of the talking and I can't follow. I may just be plain old American Skipper, but that doesn't mean you have to be rude.

Ugh, what does it matter anyway, I don't even *like* Nick. He's gorgeous, yes. And he smells so freaking good tonight like cedar, cut grass, and manly I-want-to-have-sex-with-you pheromones, but he's...infuriating! His eyes graze over me causing me to squirm in my seat, but I pretend not to notice as I watch the city race by. He probably thinks I'm the biggest idiot for picking up that guy at the bar.

We get to The Sky Lounge and it does not disappoint. It's in a high-rise encased in floor-to-ceiling glass walls. The Berlin skyline sits under a painted sky of oranges and blues as the sun sets.

"Wow, this is breathtaking," I say in awe as the hostess guides us to a tabletop underneath a large glass lantern. The furniture is modern and simple, but that's all you need with views like this. "Claudine, this is amazing."

She smiles at me. "It's beautiful, no? It's impossible to get a table here on short notice." And yet, here we are. It's a tiny dig letting me know she's someone important.

I turn to Nick who is intently looking at me, but not in a creepy way. His gaze flits down to his menu. I grab his hand in excitement. "We should film here tomorrow night!"

His eyes land on my hand and he looks back up at me.

There's something peculiar in his expression, but before I can analyze it, his eyes shutter as he pulls his hand back. "This restaurant has been featured so many times I've lost count. Isn't your whole schtick to do something unique and off the grid?"

Claudine laughs. "This is definitely not off the grid. Nicky's right, this has been featured a lot." She says something in German and Nick nods his head in agreement. She could be saying I'm an orangutan ass for all I know. I certainly feel like one.

I smile wide as I peruse the menu, my voice a touch off-key as I swallow my pride. "So Claudine, what do you recommend?"

"The lobster tail is to die for."

"Lindsey doesn't like eating any kind of animal."

"Ah, you're...what's the word...vegetarian? Vegan?"

I glare at Nick as I look over the menu. "I'm not either actually. I love lobster tail, so that's what I'll have. There are just certain animals I refuse to eat."

I look down at the English prices and almost have a heart attack. Holy shit, one hundred and twenty dollars for lobster tail? Is it fucking gold-plated? I know the show is paying for our meals, but it doesn't include non-work-related dinners. I start to sweat having already committed to the lobster and not quite certain if I paid my credit card bill on time. I try to tamp down the anxiety rising up like bile in my throat as Nick orders wine for all of us. Great, add that to my bill. I can only imagine what that will cost.

"So Claudine, what do you do?"

"I work in luxury."

I look at Nick. What the hell does that even mean? I'm tired of feeling like an ass so I just nod enthusiastically. "Ah, that sounds amazing." I notice a large solitaire diamond necklace around her neck and wonder what kind of luxury she's talking about.

Claudine says something to Nick in German and they both chuckle. She continues to converse with him and I might as well not be at the table. *Oh haha, yes, that was funny. Lindsey Love is a complete idiot. Yes, she's a total pain in my ass. This is fun, let's keep talking about her in German.*

The waiter fills my glass with red wine and I pick it up and gulp it. Screw trying to be polite or savvy. I just need to eat my lobster and say adieu…to you and you and you. Okay, maybe I shouldn't drain my glass of red wine on an empty stomach since I'm now singing the farewell song from *The Sound of Music* in my head. Nick looks at me strangely.

"What?"

"You just bid us adieu. Are you okay?"

Crap. "Peachy." I smile breezily. *Make conversation, Lindsey. Be a Barbie not a Skipper!* "So Nick, is it true guys only think about sex?"

Nick chokes on his water as Claudine looks at me quizzically. Damn you Shannon for putting that in my head!

"Never mind, forget I asked that." My cheeks are on fire as I look out over the skyline. I don't think I've ever been this strange or awkward around a guy before. This makes throwing up on the lifeguard look like common first-date mishaps.

We order our food, and of course I'm the only one that goes for the lobster. Claudine and Nick order the fish special which in all honesty sounds a lot better, but there's no way I could renege after I insisted I had to have it.

"So Lindsey, you are a food critique? How charming is that." Claudine takes a sip of her wine. I sense that she thinks it's about as charming as a toothache.

"Yes, actually, it's a lot of fun, but it can get tiring too."

"Mmm? How so?"

"Well, every meal becomes about tasting food. I automatically break apart every aspect—the taste, the texture, the smell. Even if it's something as simple as scrambled eggs. Sometimes I wish I could get my brain to shut off and enjoy the meal."

"That makes two of us," Nick mutters.

"Oh, I don't like eggs. I'd be big as a cow if I ate everything shoved in front of me." She smirks. "How do you maintain your cute figure?"

"Ha, you're being kind. I've actually gotten into the habit of just trying small amounts of food, so I never eat the whole plate. That helps."

"Lindsey likes yoga too."

Claudine's eyes flit from mine to Nick and back. "Ah, me too. I'll have to take you to my favorite yoga studio tomorrow. You two seem to know each other pretty well, no?"

"No," we both say in unison. My eyes lock onto Nick's sapphire-blues. Claudine's prickly laugh and the approaching waiter interrupt the weird energy pinging back and forth between us.

The waiter sets the fish plates down and they look amazing. My plate is set down and I do a double take. Why does my lobster look like it went through the dryer and shrunk down five sizes? It's about the size of a pickle spear and it's on an eighth-cup of saffron rice with a solitary rosemary sprig for garnish.

For a hundred and twenty dollars I was expecting a lobster the size of a Mack truck.

"Is something wrong with your lobster, Lindsey?" Claudine asks.

Nick is trying to wipe the smile off his face with his napkin and I want to pinch him with my mini crustacean claw. I smile tightly at Claudine. "It's perfect, thank you."

The waiter comes by with a pepper grinder. "Um, excuse me, is this the appetizer by chance?"

"No, Fraulein, that's the entrée. Pfeffer?" He shoves the grinder over my plate. What does he expect to pepper? The claw is as big as my pinkie.

"No, thank you."

I swallow past the colossal ball of anxiety building as I take a bite, summarizing the events of tonight in my head. I just blew one hundred and twenty dollars on a lobster the size of a crawfish, I tried to coerce a stranger—a married man—into being my date and was publicly called out on it by his wife, and now I'm third-wheeling it with Ms. Russia who is giving Nicky googly eyes at a swanky restaurant. I just want to drown in a bottle of red in my hotel bed, have a good cry, and call it a night. But no such luck.

"Is your dinner okay? You can have some of mine if you want." Nick leans toward me. Why is he being so nice? Clearly, I'm encroaching on his date feeling like Skipper all over again.

"I'm good, thanks."

The waiter comes by to ask if we would like dessert but the other two are stuffed. My two bites of lobster did nothing to appease my appetite, but I'm not about to tell them that. He sets the bill down and I dig my wallet out and quickly throw my card down.

"Lindsey, I've got this." Nick places his card on the black leather and hands mine back. I refuse to take it.

"I can't let you pay for my meal."

"It's ok—" The waiter swoops down and gathers the two cards and leaves before we can argue further.

"So Lindsey, I'm a little confused about your date earlier. Was he *married*?" Claudine smiles at me, but it digs.

Nick says something sharply to her in German and she looks hurt. "Sorry, Nicky says I'm being rude."

My gaze quickly darts around the room. "Oh, it's okay. He was someone I met at the bar. I didn't realize he was married." *Could this get any worse?* I laugh lightly. "So...yeah."

"Fraulein Love, uh, your card has been declined." The waiter materializes out of thin air. Yes...yes this can get so much worse.

"Oh crap," I mutter as I dig around for my ATM card. Guess I didn't make the payment on that card before I left.

Nick says something quietly to the waiter in German and he quickly leaves. "Oh, wait I've got—"

"Lindsey, I've got it," Nick says, leaving no room for argument.

I fold my napkin next to my plate in resignation. What do you do when you've had the worst night ever? You run to the bathroom and hide.

Chapter 20

Nick

Watch Your Back

I WATCH LINDSEY quickly excuse herself and head to the bathroom. I frown wondering if I should check to make sure she's okay, but this provides me with the time I need to discuss serious matters with Claudine.

"She's funny, Nick...I like her. Not your usual type, no?" She looks at me over her wineglass.

"Look, we don't have much time. Do you have any information you can give me?"

"No...not at the moment."

An uneasy feeling washes over me. "I'm running out of time, Claudine."

She waves her hand casually. "I'd be more worried about the man your friend picked up at the bar. Do you think he was working for someone?"

"No."

"Be careful. We're being watched. Or I should say, *you're* being watched."

I keep my head looking at her as I smile, but my eyes dart around the restaurant memorizing every face sitting at the other tables. Nothing seems out of place, but that doesn't mean anything.

"Hurry up, my time here is running out."

"Don't tell me to hurry. He's very paranoid…he set this meeting up so that he could photograph us together. He's setting you up, so you better watch your back."

"Does that include you?"

She smiles wickedly at me. "We were good together once, no?"

"That was a long time ago."

"Too bad you have a thing for the little brunette. We could rekindle that flame."

"Let's go. Next time we meet, I expect more."

She angrily scoots back from the table. "Next time we meet, we'll both be dead."

I grind my teeth as I pick up my credit card and head toward the elevators to wait for Lindsey.

Chapter 21

Lindsey

The Bathroom

I QUICKLY EXCUSE myself and dart to the restroom where I try not to cry because my eyes will get all red and puffy. I send a quick text to Shannon.

> **Me:** *Charlize Theron as Nick's date, I picked up a married man...wife, kids...German prostitute...oh god...sounds so bad when I text it. I just ate a thousand-dollar lobster the size of a quarter and my card got declined. I'm hiding in the bathroom. Say something so I won't burst into tears.*
>
> **Shannon:** *Wow.*
>
> **Shannon:** •••
>
> **Shannon:**
>
> **Me:** *What the hell! You can't three dot me after that and then drop whatever you were going to say!*
>
> **Shannon:** *Use a condom.*
>
> **Me:** *What??? That's all you have to say? WTF kind of sisterly advice is this? I'm in crisis mode!*
>
> **Shannon:** *and wear a smile.*
>
> **Me:** *Are you drunk? Weren't you just at the grocery store two hours ago?*

Shannon: *Yup. Dan's mom has the kids so we're letting loose.*

I roll my eyes even though she can't see me. This is perfect. When I need her most, her drunk advice is to bang Nick with a smile and a condom.

Shannon: *Gotta run, Dan is doing a striptease!*

Me: *It's like four pm there. What the hell is wrong with you guys?*

Shannon: *You'll understand when you have kids one of these days.*

I shove my phone back in my purse, wash my hands, and slink out of the restroom. Nick and Claudine are arguing in German so I can't tell what's going on. I paste on a big smile.

"Everything okay?"

"*Nein!*" Claudine spats as she turns on her heel out of the restaurant, leaving Nick and I alone.

"I hope that wasn't because of me," I whisper.

"No, it was because of John from Florida."

I look up at him confused. "John from Florida?"

"Come on, let's call it a night. I need to call in a favor for tomorrow and I need a good night's sleep."

"Okay." Relieved, I lean into him and wrap my arm around his waist feeling a little loose from the wine and lack of food. "I'm sorry you had to pay for my uber-expensive lobster. I'll pay you back."

"I don't want your money."

"And I'm sorry if I ruined your date."

"It wasn't a date," he growls.

"I guess this means no yoga tomorrow."

"Not with Claudine."

He hails a cab and we sit in silence as we head back to the hotel.

Chapter 22

Nick

The What-Ifs

I LIE IN bed the next morning and contemplate texting Lindsey. I did not get a good night's sleep like I intended, Claudine's words making me toss and turn. I need to make sure Lindsey stays safe. She's all I can think about.

God that woman makes me so furious. One minute I want to strangle her and the next I'm so fucking drawn to her that I want to drop everything and kiss her. I've never had this kind of turmoil over a woman before and it's interfering with what I came here to do.

I text her before I lose my nerve.

Me: *Want to take a walk and get some coffee?*

Three little dots appear and then disappear. Then they reappear and disappear again. Clearly, she's struggling this morning with wanting to hang out with me. I quickly type out a text to save face.

Me: *Oh sorry, I meant to text Patrick*
Pain in My Ass: *Sure*
Pain in My Ass: *Oh, oh okay…no problem!*

"Fuuuuck," I groan as I lay back in bed. I pick up my phone.

Me: *You and me. Downstairs in 15.*

Pain in My Ass: *Are you talking to me or Patrick?…*

Pain in My Ass: *Besides, I don't take orders from grumpy a-holes.*

I grunt in amusement. God, she drives me bananas.

Me: *You. 15.*

Pain in My Ass: *So demanding. Maybe I don't want to. Maybe I need 20.*

Me: *15. Please, with a cherry on top.*

Pain in My Ass: *Fine.*

I quickly brush my teeth, wash my face, and grab a bottle of water after changing into running shorts, a t-shirt and a fleece. I'm downstairs waiting when she appears in hot-pink running tights with sexy cutouts along her leg and thigh causing me to swallow my tongue. Her long ponytail swishes as she walks up to me.

"Are you taking me to yoga?" She smiles and it makes me want to pull her to me and breathe in her sweet scent.

"Where's the other half of your shirt?"

"What do you mean?" She laughs as she looks down. "It's a crop top."

I grunt because it's sexy as hell and I'd like to rip it completely off of her with my teeth. "No yoga."

"One of these days I'll get you to relax and say *namaste*."

I side-eye her as we step out of the hotel. "I doubt it.

We're heading over to Tiergarten."

She shrugs. "As long as I can get some coffee, I'll be good."

I hail a cab and we stop at a café near the gardens and grab some pastries and coffee. I really want to go for a run to burn off this weird energy, but I'll drink a coffee with her first. We walk into the beautiful gardens. It's still early so the tourists haven't descended on them yet.

"Wow, this is like Central Park in Germany."

"Hmm, kind of."

"Let's go this way." She leads us down a gravel path next to the Spree river. We sip our coffees and walk in companionable silence.

"Want to talk about last night?" I offer up.

"Did I ruin things between you and Claudine?"

"No. We're fine."

"Is she…is she your girlfriend?"

I catch a glimpse of her as we walk. Her cheeks bloom pink as she quickly catches my eye. Is she jealous? Damn she's so cute. "No, we're just friends. That's all we've ever been."

"Can I be blunt?"

"Are you ever not?"

"Touché." She's silent a moment as I wait. "I thought it was rude of you guys to talk in German when you know I can't understand what you're saying."

"Yes, it was." I drink my coffee as we continue silently down the path.

"Wait, that's it?"

"What do you want to know?"

She gives me a dubious look. "What were you talking about?"

"Stuff that would bore you."

"You're driving me crazy right now."

"Welcome to the club." I sigh as I take a sip, taunting her just a little more. "We talked about the weather, about her job, about you."

"About me? I knew it."

"Mostly about you."

"What about me? That I'm an orangutan ass?"

I nearly spit out my coffee as I quickly glance at her profile. "What?"

"Never mind."

We talked about how crazy you make me. I clear my throat. "We talked about this project."

"Aah, the project, yes." She twists her cup in her hand. "Do you have a girlfriend?" She trips and I quickly reach out to make sure she doesn't faceplant. "Thanks. I mean I'm just curious, but you don't have to answer. I'm just trying to get to know you, that's all."

"Do you have a boyfriend?" I quirk an eyebrow up at her.

"Aah, I see what you did there. Deflecting the question. I do not have a boyfriend. It's been a while."

"The crazy keeps them at bay?"

"Ha ha ha," she deadpans and takes a sip of her coffee. "Having to go out to dinner several times a week for work isn't as great as it sounds. When your boyfriend wants to take you to dinner or go to a party and all you want to do is stay in and chill…well, you become the boring one. So then he starts going out without you. The next thing you know your girlfriend is texting you pics of him hooking up with random girls at the Oyster Bar while you're at home on the couch waiting for him to call, watching Bobby Flint in your pjs with your cranky old cat."

"Wow, that's...detailed."

"Yeah. Your turn."

"I had a girlfriend for a while. It was getting serious, but we wanted different things."

"You wanted to go out and party every night and she wanted to stay at home, have your babies and live the life of leisure?"

"Hmm, not exactly." Smiling, I rub my hand over my head wondering how much I want to share with her. For the first time I don't want to kill her or push her away. I actually *want* to get to know her and vice versa. "We wanted different things. Namely, she wanted the fame, the money, and the party lifestyle. I didn't."

"Why don't you want the fame and money?"

"Because that's not what drives me. I want to do shows for National Geographic, not reality television. I don't need the money."

"Mmm, so y'all ended it?"

"Kind of. A third party got involved."

"Oh no. I'm sorry."

"I'm not."

She looks up at me and smiles. "So how do you know Simon and why does he call you Scar?"

I bristle at the mention of Simon. I don't want to talk about him or my past.

"Hey, it's okay, I'm sorry I asked." She places a hand on my bicep. Her touch makes me shiver.

"It's complicated."

"It's okay, we don't have to."

But I need to. I want to share myself with Lindsey, and that worries me more than reliving my past. I tell myself I can share some parts of me with her. "When I was in the SEALs, my team was on a classified mission that I still can't talk about to this day, even though it's been ten years."

I look over at her and she nods in understanding. I take a sip of coffee and look at the scenery as we walk, but I'm not seeing the trees and river, I'm back in Afghanistan in a bullet-ridden hellhole. "My best friend Mike was like my brother. We came up through BUD/S together. I'd do anything for him and he for me. I got my nickname Scar when we were out on a mission." I shake my head. "A room was cleared, but Mike and I stayed behind to secure it. We were ambushed. I saved his life that night by throwing myself in front of him. I was stabbed several times before the assailant was taken out."

"The scars on your side…"

"Yeah, the whole unit nicknamed me Scar to tease me, but truthfully we were all pretty shaken up by it. It was pretty touch and go for me. Mike carried me for three miles back to the helicopter where we were all transported back to base." I breathe in deeply through my nose. "They were out on another covert mission while I was on medical leave. I wasn't there to save him this time. Simon, a rookie on our unit, wasn't watching Mike's back like he should have and Mike was killed. At least, that's the story I've heard."

"Oh my God, Nick. I'm so sorry." She places her hand in mine guiding us over to a bench. I didn't even realize I was shaking. "Okay, that's enough."

I shake the memories away. "I'm okay."

"Hey, it's not your fault. You know that, right?"

I nod. "Years of therapy have gotten me through it, but I still can't fight the ghost calling to me that if I had been there. The what-ifs. Fuck, Mike was like a cat with nine lives. He always jumped right into danger and asked the questions after. He was a fucking cowboy." I smile remembering his craziness. "Sasha was Mike's dog. He loved her like she was his kid. Found her in an alleyway one night in Bagram and took her back to base and trained her even though he wasn't supposed to have her. I couldn't leave her behind. It would have been like leaving Mike behind so I petitioned to have her brought back to the States. My parents took her for me."

She squeezes my hand as we sit in silence for a few moments. I hadn't even realized my fingers were threaded with hers. "Do you blame Simon?"

"It's hard not to, but the truth of the matter is I wasn't there. I don't really know what happened that night. I mostly blame myself. Simon contacted me, knowing I was doing film producing. He asked if we could collaborate on *Naked in the Wild* and being former SEALs together I automatically said yes."

I look over at Lindsey's innocent face. She doesn't need to know the sordid details. I pull my hand away from hers and run my fingers through my hair.

"Anyway, that's my past and how I know Simon and

how I got my nickname."

"What's the skeleton frog tattoo on your side signify?"

"The Navy SEALs are called the Frogs. When you retire, it's tradition to get a tattoo. Mike and I had ours picked out as soon as we passed through buds."

She gives me a soft smile. "Hey, Nick Elliot?" She looks at me from under her eyelashes as she chews her bottom lip. I want to kiss her lips so badly.

"Yes, Lindsey Love?"

"Can I have a do-over?"

I snort and shake my head. "I've never had someone ask me for more do-overs than you."

We sit in silence as we finish our coffees. Mike would have fucking loved Lindsey. He would have loved her sassy, goofy personality. I shake my head and laugh to myself.

"So what now?" she asks, looking around at the scenery.

"Want to go for a run? There's a cool little restaurant up the way where we can sit and watch boaters."

"Uh, I'm not much of a runner. I don't sweat very well."

"Really? Do you overheat easily?"

"I get red, but that's about it." She looks down at her shoes.

"Let's just see how it goes. I need to burn off some of this energy."

"Ugh, fine. I'll try it, but in return you'll have to try yoga with me at some point."

I ignore her yoga comment as I look down at her Nikes. "Are those brand new? Have you even broken those in?"

She shrugs. "I'll be fine, start running. But remember my legs are half the length of yours."

"I'll go slow."

Chapter 23

Lindsey

A Quarter and Cargo Shorts

"YOU OKAY?" NICK looks over at me as I trudge along next to him.

"Yeah, why?"

"You're looking kind of splotchy and you're breathing heavy."

"I'm fine. I'm not breathing heavy, I'm panting. There's a difference." I barely get the words out.

He looks at his watch. "We're only a mile in and you're tomato red. I'm scared you're going to stroke out."

"Who me?" I wheeze as my muscles feel like they're about to seize up. "No sweat, remember?" I motion around my face with my hand which takes an extreme amount of my energy reserves. Not even sweat can save me now. I'm fucking dying. Death by running torture. "How much farther?"

"Seriously, stop." He pulls me, slowing me down, and I have to lean over with my hands on my legs as I gulp in a lungful of oxygen. I peer up at him and of course he's perfect. Not a hair out of place, not a bead of sweat. He's not even breathing heavy and his face is a normal color. Meanwhile my once-bouncy ponytail hangs limp, and my face matches my hot-pink leggings. I look at his athletic physique, his leg muscles cut to perfection.

"You're too perfect." I wave my hand up and down his body.

"What does that mean?" He grins cockily.

"I mean, I could never date a guy like you. *Clearly.* Look at me, I can't even run beside you without looking like a hamster on a wheel."

A look of irritation sweeps over his face, but then he quickly replaces it with a mask of indifference. "More like a sloth."

"That paints a pretty picture. Nothing screams sexy like being called a sloth."

"Are you trying to be sexy?"

I look over at him, because he's the epitome of sexy. If you looked the word up in a dictionary the definition would read, Nick Elliot. "Ugh, now you're just annoying me."

"Nothing wrong with a sloth. They're cute and slow." He slings an arm around my shoulder, causing my body to freeze up, his close proximity making my heart pound faster. "Come on, champ. Let's go check out the boats."

WE SIT AND people watch, lounging in the sun. So much has happened between Nick and I this morning that I need to process, but it's hard to do with him sitting two feet away from me looking like a hunky cover model for broody runners. I'm annoyed with him that he changed our dynamics once again. I want to hate him, but after our talk this morning, I got to see a deeper side to him. The chamber of my heart reserved for icing out Nick Elliot thawed out just a little bit more. "So, what kind of documentaries do you want to film?" I take a drink from my bottled water as I watch a couple take a rowboat out. If Nick were my boyfriend, I'd insist on taking him out in one...*but he's not*, I quickly remind myself. We're just friends. Well, maybe not friends. We're platonic work companions who are spending the morning together. Yes, that sounds good.

I watch his perfect kissable lips move as he talks. I bet he's a good kisser. I'm pretty sure he's good at everything he does. *Pay attention to what he's saying and stop looking at his mouth!*

"I have a friend who is a wildlife veterinarian. He's brought to my attention the dwindling numbers of black rhinos and elephants out in the wild due to poaching. I want to spend some time with him over in Africa and make a documentary about it, bring it to the forefront."

"What does he do, just observe them?"

"No, he and a team locate them and grind down their tusks so that they won't be killed for them. It's a pretty cool process and it doesn't hurt the rhino. They actually don't need the tusks to survive."

"Sad that we have to take those measures." I shake my head. "That makes me mad. People can be really selfish, can't they?"

"Unbelievably so, especially when it comes to the near

extinction of an animal. But there are good people out there too, people that want to help."

"People like you." *Dammit, he's making me like him even more.* I drum my nails on the table between us. "Do you see now why I didn't want to eat exotic animals at Nigel's house of horrors?"

Nick snorts. "I get it, Lindsey, but for the record I did try and talk you out of that place."

My thumb glides under the plastic label of my water bottle. I hate admitting when I'm wrong. "I know you did," I say quietly as I pick at the label.

"Holy shit."

"What?" My head snaps up as I look around at the crowd.

"You just admitted you were wrong."

"Hardee-har-har." I roll my eyes. "I can be the bigger person and admit when I'm wrong."

"Really?" He looks at me dubiously. "Bigger than five-two?"

I huff, "I'm five-three and a quarter, thank you very much."

"Don't want to forget that quarter." He winks at me.

"Quarters are important. You can phone a friend with a quarter."

He rubs his hand across his jaw, smothering his laugh. "Pretty sure it's fifty cents to phone a friend." He looks at me and smiles, his dimples making a rare appearance. It's devastatingly attractive and completely transforms his face. "Hypothetically speaking, if you could make a call with just a quarter who would you call?"

"You," I blurt out and then clamp my lips shut. *Shit.* I did not intend for that to come out.

"Me?" He smirks in delight. "Not Patrick?"

I wave a hand in front of my face. "Don't get so cocky. I chose you because you're like ninja Navy SEAL warrior and all that shit. If anyone's going to get me out of a jam, it would be you. Trust me, Patrick is not going to broker a deal with the bad guy out of a James Bond movie with his useless Harry Potter trivia."

Nick laughs and I want to make him do it again. "Fair enough."

He drinks his water and I watch it slide down his throat. Who knew an Adam's apple could be so sexy? I shift uncomfortably in my seat. What I really want to do is walk over to his side of the table, straddle him, and lick his throat. *Focus Lindsey, you're in the middle of a conversation.*

"What about you? Who would you use your one quarter on? I mean if you had to choose between me or Patrick. Who would you choose?"

He thinks about it for a moment. "Patrick."

"What? Why?" I pathetically whine in protest.

"Because Patrick would pepper the James Bond villain with such useless info that he'd shoot him first out of annoyance and buy me time to get the ropes untied and tackle him. Or if we had to stop a bomb, I feel like Patrick would actually *listen* to my instructions and have the steadier hand to cut the correct wire."

I look at him indignantly. "I can cut the right wire."

"Please," he huffs. "When have you ever followed directions from me? You'd go all rogue on me and cut the pretty pink one and blow us all to smithereens."

"That's sexist."

"It's true."

"I could totally take out the bad guy."

He eyes me over his bottle. "You're right, I can absolutely see you outrunning him."

"Low blow." I sit back, folding my arms over my chest, and pout. "Pink wire…that's insulting. You owe me a Coke if I ever manage to help you out of a sticky situation."

He side-eyes me. "I think my eight-year-old nephew says crap like that."

"Patrick and I say it all the time. He usually ends up owing me the Cokes."

"Figures." He smirks and I want to kiss it right off. Yikes, dangerous thoughts there, Lindsey. Don't look into his hypnotic blue eyes. Think chocolate cake…rich buttery choco-late cake.

I look over at a guy walking by in cargo shorts with about a hundred useless pockets. "Why are guys so obsessed with cargo shorts? I don't get it. What happened to a good ol' pair of chinos with two pockets?"

His eyes flicker from me to the guy in question. "Because they have pockets to carry stuff. They're useful."

"Like what? What does he need a hundred pockets for? He probably has a tube of Chapstick and a piece of bubblegum."

"Guys don't chew bubblegum."

"So sorry. Big League Chew." I roll my eyes and he arches an eyebrow. "And why is it an unspoken rule that guys can't blow bubbles?"

Nick shakes his head. "Your rambling has seriously gotten out of control."

I strum my fingers on the table impatiently waiting.

He chuckles. "Would you really find it attractive if a handsome guy, such as myself, sat here chewing a wad of Big League gum, blowing bubbles?"

"So modest." I smile as I picture him doing exactly that. This guy can make eating a pink confetti cake pop look sexy. "You're right. You'd look like a moron."

"So…no cargo shorts, no blowing bubbles—"

"Or cake pops."

"I didn't even know that was in the equation, but okay, no cake pops…what else drives Lindsey Love bonkers?"

"For the record, blowing bubbles was on your list. I blow bubbles and smack them loud."

"I have no doubt." He chuckles.

I shrug as I cap my water bottle. "I just think when a guy wears cargo shorts or athletic shorts he just looks sloppy. It's like he's not even trying. He might as well be wearing a sign over his head shouting, "Look at me, I've got Chapstick and a hammer and some useless doodads."

"Don't forget Big League Chew."

"I wish I could."

"I'm wearing athletic shorts." He arches an eyebrow in challenge.

I look at the shorts in question showing off his tan muscular legs with a dusting of dark hair, just the right amount. He could wear athletic shorts to his own wedding and no one would bat an eye because his legs are that fine. "Uh, well you're the exception. We were running."

"Uh-huh. I'll make sure never to wear cargo shorts in your presence, athletic shorts only for a run, chew bubblegum or eat cake pops. Any other rules?"

"There's a lot more, but you're a quick study, Elliot. I like that about you." I wink.

Smiling, he holds my gaze for a moment putting me under his spell. And in the blink of an eye he clears his throat while looking down at his watch. "Should we head back? See how Patrick made out on his date last night?"

"Sure, I guess." But I'm scared to pop this magical bubble of truce we've created. I don't want this morning to ever end because for once in the short period of time I've known Nick, I'm truly enjoying his company.

"Aw, don't look so sad, *meine schöne*. I got us dinner reservations at the best schnitzel place in Berlin tonight."

"Schnitzel, huh?" I'm going to pretend he didn't just make my heart flutter. *Meine schöne*. I'll have to remember that and look it up later. He could have just called me *my sugar* or *my shit*. It's hard to tell with Nick these days.

"Yes, don't worry, Germans use pork instead of veal. Trust me, this little hole-in-the-wall is the best."

And for some reason, I do trust him. He's my twenty-five-cent call, after all.

Chapter 24

Nick

Heartburn

MY EYES GRAZE over her full pouty lips as she laughs at something Patrick says. She looks up at me and winks and my heart stutters in my chest. I rub the spot unconsciously as I try to wrap my brain around what's happening.

"Do you have heartburn?" She looks up at me with concern.

"Something like that." I clear my throat. "Let's do the intro one more time."

"Sure, okay." She smiles at me and it has my defenses up.

"You're not going to argue with me?"

She looks over at Patrick with a smirk. "Why would I argue? You're the boss. If you want me to do it again, I'll do it again."

Did I enter another space dimension? What the hell is going on? "K, go," I grunt as drink her in.

I'm pissed at myself that I'm trying to sabotage the night, because up until this point the three of us have been laughing and having a good time at the little hole-in-the-wall my friend owns. The only reason I'm acting like a prick is so that Lindsey and I can stay on even ground.

Patrick points his index finger at her indicating he's rolling. "Hey guys! It's Lindsey Love here! I'm so excited to be in Berlin, Germany and share the best-kept schnitzel secret in the city!"

"Cut. Do it again." Lindsey looks at me and I can see her eye twitch. "Was there something wrong with that?"

"A little stiff." She was perfect. She blinks and turns toward Patrick.

Patrick indicates for her to go again. "Hey guys! It's Lindsey Love here and you're probably wondering what I'm loving this week. It's schnitzel! We're in Berlin, Germany to hunt down the best schnitzel in town."

"Again."

"Oh for fuck's sake. What was wrong with that?"

There's the Lindsey I know that drives me insane. But we don't have a chance to do a third take because my friend Lukas approaches the table.

"*Willkommen*, Nick! Ah Lindsey Love, so nice to meet you!"

"*Danke, dass du uns Freund hast.*" I get up to give him a hug. Lukas and I have a long history together.

"What did he just say?" Lindsey whispers to Patrick.

"Uh, thanks for having us, I think."

Lukas claps his hands. "Good to see you again, friend. Shall we go back and see how we make the schnitzel? The secret is in the air bubbles."

"Lead the way!" Lindsey enthusiastically smiles. Her face falls as soon as Lukas turns his back. She pulls my arm stopping me as Patrick and Lukas chitchat about the restaurant. Her vanilla scent wafts over me weakening my knees.

"Nick," she whispers. "Is he going to make me cook?"

I chuckle wanting to kiss the worry right off her face. "No *fraulein*, you're just going to watch him make it."

"Oh, thank god, okay." She visibly relaxes. "Hey, are we okay?"

I clench my jaw. "Yeah, why wouldn't we be?"

She smiles and pats my chest. "I just wanted to make sure."

I watch her butt in her jeans as she walks into the back kitchen. My chest starts to ache again. I don't want to get involved with her. I don't want to like her, but I can't help myself. She's gorgeous, feisty, and adorable. She makes me want to kiss the smirk right off her lips and bury myself so deep inside of her that I can't find my way back.

It will never work. The first problem is, I'm not her type. She's told me that twice now. The second problem is that I don't want to be in a relationship. I have too much going on in my life right now. I have the unfinished business with Claudine, and I want to go off to Africa after this and film wildlife conservatory documentaries. Having an unpredictable bossy food critic tied around my ankle would just drag me down.

But if you were falling for that bossy little unpredictable food critic would it really matter? No. I can't let my head go there. *What the fuck is wrong with me?*

I take a deep breath and rub the spot on my chest as I follow her to the back kitchen. I'm just going to have to hide my feelings and bury them deep for the next two weeks. If I can survive being a Navy SEAL, I can survive Lindsey Love.

Chapter 25

Lindsey

Schnitzel Sticks

"SEE THE TRICK is to add a little lemon juice to your egg mixture. It has to be lightly coated with breadcrumbs so you can get little air pockets, making the coating light and crispy."

"Lukas, you know what would be fun? If Lindsey tried her hand at cooking schnitzel," Nick says with a straight face.

"What?!" I shoot daggers at him. "No, that's a bad idea." *Didn't we just have this conversation in the hallway? What the fuck is he thinking?*

"Ah, Ms. Love, it would mean so much to my great-grandmother Helga VonWeber if you would make our family schnitzel recipe."

"Uh…" I gurgle as I look from Nick to Lukas. "Yes, of course, thank you so much. It would be an honor." I pass by Nick to wash my hands. "I hate you," I whisper harshly.

"Good," he breathes out.

It leaves me feeling confused. Weren't we just laughing together a few minutes ago? I go stand next to Lukas at the counter where the ingredients are laid out. Patrick maneuvers around to the other side to get a better view as Nick stands off to the side texting someone on his phone. This annoys me thinking he might be texting Claudine even though he said they're just friends.

"Hello, Mr. Director? Don't you think you should be paying attention?"

He gives me a lazy stare. "It's not rocket science, Julia Child, just listen to Lukas."

I grind my teeth because I want to leap across the counter and strangle him. What the hell happened to the Nick from thirty minutes ago sitting across from me giving me emoji heart-eye vibes? We were laughing and flirting and having such a good time as we teased Patrick about his date. Now all of a sudden, his evil twin *Nick the Dick* has taken over. The one who sadistically likes to push all my buttons.

"Okay Lindsey, you're going to pound the meat flat with this hammer." Lukas hands me the meat mallet and I pretend the pork is Nick's face as I pound down on it hard. "Whoa, there. We don't want to kill it, it's already dead." Lukas laughs at his own joke as I lighten my pounding by a fraction. "You'd eh make a good zimmermann...eh carpenter."

"Ha, yes, when I picture something in my head I go after it with gusto." My eyes narrow as I stare at Nick. He returns my icy glare.

"Okay, next we will season it and dip it into the flour."

I season the four pieces and then dip it into the flour, then into the egg and lemon mixture, and finally transfer it into the breadcrumbs.

"We don't want to coat the meat too heavily. Ah, yes, perfect." He turns around to the stove. "Now we pour some vegetable oil into a pan and get it hot so that the meat sizzles. I've already had it heating up, so be my guest. Just two pieces at a time. You don't want to do too many pieces or it will get overcrowded."

I slide the pork into the oil and it immediately sizzles. I'm so proud of myself that I'm doing this and not fucking it up.

"We wait three to four minutes and then we'll flip and brown the other side. The trick is to swirl the pan which helps create air pockets, giving you a lighter schnitzel."

"Cut. We need to do that part over."

"Ah, sure, sure." Lukas gallantly takes the pan and moves it to the side. He immediately heats up a fresh pan of oil. I bite my tongue intentionally not meeting Nick's gaze. I can't let him know how much this annoys me as I pick up the meat mallet and paste on a smile that tells the audience I'm having the time of my life. I repeat all the steps and then slide the pork into the hot oil.

"Do it again," Nick idly says from across the counter as he looks down at his phone. What the hell was wrong with that? *Was he even paying attention?*

I whirl around with the tongs in my hand. "What? Why? You're acting like Martin Scorsese over there. It's just a freaking thirty second bit about making schnitzel."

"Uh, Ms. Love?"

"Hold on, Lukas." I put my hand up immediately shutting him up. I point the tongs at Nick. "I don't know what's crawled up your butt tonight, but I'm tired of it—"

"Ms. Love—"

"I didn't want to cook in the first place, and now here I

am because *you* insisted. It shouldn't take three takes to watch me prepare the schnitzel."

"And yet, here we are, needing to do three takes." Nick looks up from his phone giving me a flat stare.

"Ms. Love, *entschuldigen sie*, excuse me...your schnitzel has burned."

I turn back around and see red. "And now you've made me burn my schnitzel! Ugh, I hate you!" I throw the tongs down and storm out of the kitchen.

I lean against the hallway wall and try to fight back the sting of tears. Damn that man is infuriating! I let him into my heart just a little bit and what does he do? He digs a knife in and twists it. The door swings open and I'm expecting Patrick, maybe even Lukas, but instead it's Nick the Dick. I quickly wipe away a tear that has managed to escape. The last thing I want for him to see is me crying. I don't want him to know he has that kind of effect on me. His jewel-toned eyes rake over me. I'm embarrassed I just exploded in front of Lukas, but this man standing in front of me has a way of bringing out the absolute worst in me.

"Lindsey..."

"Nick, I'm sorry I lost it. I just...need a minute, okay?" I hold my hand up as I try to keep it together.

But he doesn't give me a minute. He grabs my hand bringing it down to my side, pushing me up against the wall, his body bracketing mine. He doesn't even give me a chance to breathe before his lips swoop down and capture mine in a dizzying kiss causing me to jolt in surprise. His large hand cups the back of my head, angling it just the way he wants. Weeks of pent-up frustration pour out of us as his demanding lips coax mine apart.

I sigh in defeat as he deepens the kiss, my hands curling up into his hair. His hands cup my ass as he easily lifts me up. Without thinking, I wrap my legs around his waist as he pins me against the wall. I can hear waiters pass by us on their way to the kitchen, but I don't care if they're staring because all I can smell and taste is Nick. Who the fuck wants chocolate cake over this?

Damn he's an amazing kisser. I moan as he pushes into me and I can feel how hard he is for me. Jesus yes, take me against this wall. Right here, right now!

He breaks the kiss, our chests rising and falling as we fill our lungs with much-needed oxygen. His eyes are hooded, his lips parted, as I trace my thumb over them. A thousand unanswered questions flicker between us when Patrick clears his throat.

My legs slide down as Nick steps back giving me room. The sudden loss has me shaking because seconds ago I was ready to throw down the gauntlet and let the waiters have the show of the year right in the hallway. It would have been the most amazing sex of my life, because I know with a hundred-percent certainty that Nick Elliot wouldn't just be a subpar lover.

Hell no, he would make my body hum like a harmonica. He would have me strung so tight, not even Slash would be able to play that shit. And the orgasm…oh my god, the orgasm would be epic. I shiver just thinking about it.

"Are you guys done yet? I'm hungry. I'm ready for some schnitzel," Patrick whines like a famished five-year-old as he pushes back through the kitchen door.

I look up into Nick's bottomless blues. "Are we done yet?"

"Not even close." His nostrils flare as he turns and leaves me slowly sliding down the wall as he heads back into the kitchen.

Well, schnitzel sticks, I'm screwed.

Chapter 26

Nick

Kermit and Miss Piggy

WE LANDED IN Paris a few hours ago and checked into our hotel. Things are a little weird between Lindsey and I after I kissed her in the hallway. We sat and ate our incredible schnitzel dinner that Lukas prepared for us in awkward silence. Every time I looked away from her I could feel her curious gaze slide over me, but when I'd try to engage, she'd quickly avert her eyes. Patrick went out with Gabby again, while Lindsey and I retired to our hotel rooms. I wanted to ask her back to my room for a nightcap, maybe explore that kiss a little more, but she looked exhausted and I didn't want to push her. Besides, I had some work to do.

My brain may have decided I didn't want Lindsey Love, but my heart had other ideas. When I saw her crying in the hallway, I felt like such a jerk. I didn't think, I just went with my gut instinct, picked her up and kissed the hell out of her. Her sweet taste and vanilla scent invaded my senses and made my need for her kick into overdrive. And she reciprocated which surprised me. I half expected a slap after I let her go, but when I looked into her glazed confused eyes, they mirrored my own.

So here I am waiting in the lobby for her and Patrick so that we can go to a quaint little French bistro that serves "authentic" French cuisine. I'm already doubting this place, but the three of us agreed to try it. If we like it, we'll come back tomorrow night to film.

The elevator opens up and Patrick walks off with Lindsey, both of them laughing. Damn she's so beautiful. It hits me like a ton of bricks that I want to make her laugh and smile like that all the time. I don't want her to hate me or be irritated with me. I'm tired of pushing her buttons, I just want us to be friends.

She smiles at me and it takes my breath away. Scratch that. I want to be more than friends.

I stand up to greet them. "What are you guys laughing about?"

Lindsey winks at me. "Patrick's date didn't end so well last night with Gabby."

"Oh no, the Aussie?"

"More like saucy." Lindsey chuckles earning a light shove from Patrick. "Romeo here tried to spoon-feed her a meatball over candlelit dinner but he couldn't quite reach her."

"I might have dropped the meatball down her cleavage." Patrick turns a tomato sauce shade of red.

"Oh man." I shake my head and grin.

"It gets better." Lindsey beams as she flicks Patrick's ear to continue.

Patrick groans. "So, there was sauce on the spoon and apparently it was hot. When the meatball fell off, I accidentally tipped the spoon and sauce went with it. Meatball, sauce, boobs…it wasn't pretty. She had a hard time fishing it out…there was a lot of cleavage."

Lindsey snorts as Patrick makes a motion with his hands indicating her large breasts.

"So anyway, she's shrieking and crying, red sauce smeared all over her chest. It looked like I stabbed her. She left me to go to the bathroom and never came back," he says sadly.

"I mean, seriously Trick, who serves a meatball on a spoon?"

"I was trying to be romantic like *Lady and the Tramp!*"

"Wasn't that spaghetti?" I quirk an eyebrow. "Didn't they meet in the middle with a noodle?"

"Yeah, I tried that before the meatball." Patrick sends Lindsey a dirty look when she starts to giggle again. "It didn't exactly work. The spaghetti broke in half and there I was sitting across from her with a string of spaghetti hanging from my front tooth."

"Ah, better luck next time champ." I cover my laugh with a cough. "Sorry she pulled the old bathroom trick."

"Yeah. I hope she doesn't have second-degree burns," Patrick says glumly as he shuffles between Lindsey and me.

"Nothing a little aloe vera can't help." I hail a cab as we stand waiting in front of the hotel.

"She was a Berlin fling, Trick. Maybe tonight you'll meet a French goddess." She winks at me.

"Yes, definitely a lot of pretty girls in Paris." I smile back at Lindsey but her lips downturn into a frown. *What?* I mouth. She rolls her eyes at me as we climb into a taxi. I'm still trying to figure out what I said wrong when we get out at our destination.

We walk into the restaurant and Lindsey and Patrick immediately start chatting about the dark wood-trimmed booths with red, cream, and gold striped cushions and how good that would look on camera. The waiter leads us to a table for four near the windows because Lindsey asked for a view. It's crowded in the small restaurant but thankfully not too loud. Waiters gracefully buzz from table to table, wearing long white aprons over black shirts and pants. The French language rolling off their tongue effortlessly—soothing and romantic.

Lindsey pops open the heavy menus. "I love this place already! What are you all going to have...oh, oh no... no, no...yuck."

I smile knowing exactly what she's reading. "What's wrong, Snow White?"

She gives me a flat stare. "Nothing."

"Are you going to have the snails tonight?"

"Totally!" Patrick interrupts completely excited by the idea. Lindsey grimaces, her eyes scanning the menu. "Omg, I think I've found something even worse. *Foie Gras*. Is that frog legs? Are they seriously serving Kermit up?"

I cough trying to swallow my laugh. "It's not Kermit. It's duck liver."

"Ugh, no thanks. Oh my God! Pig's head? Miss Piggy too? What fresh hell is this place? Are they really serving a pig's head?" Lindsey desperately looks around at the other diners and sure enough someone has a deep-fried pigs head at their table. "I think I'm going to vomit."

"Look, they have pig trotters too."

"I can only guess what that is. No, thank you."

"Ooh, wait! Pig trotters and snails in a crisp pastry. Two for one." I wink at Lindsey as she scowls back at me. "Oh shucks, they do serve Kermie here. It's under appetizers."

"So much to try...it all sounds amazing." Patrick's eyes are as big as saucers as he peruses the menu. Lindsey frowns at him.

"Patrick?" I waggle my eyebrows at him. "Snails and trotters or Kermie's legs and Miss Piggy's head?"

"You're having way too much fun over there." Lindsey scowls.

"I might try the frog legs but Lindsey might kick my ass if I get the pig head."

"There's no *might* about it. Where the heck is Coq a Vin and Salad Niçoise? It's all pork products. Even the freaking salad has grilled pig ears, snails, and pork belly. I think I'm going to be sick."

"So, it's safe to say this place is not where we will be filming tomorrow night?"

"I think it's awesome!" Patrick enthusiastically takes a sip of water. Lindsey glares at him and he immediately back tracks. "I mean if you like pork...which I don't. Yeah, this place sucks."

I snap my menu closed. "Perhaps we should blow this popsicle stand and go somewhere a little less—"

"Cringy? It's like they're trying to murder the Muppets in here."

"Uh, I was going to say pork-product based, but sure..."

"Aw man, think I can get mine to go?"

Lindsey rolls her eyes. "Fine, we'll wait for you outside."

"You're sharing your pig ears with me!" I shout over to Patrick who gives me an enthusiastic thumbs-up in return.

"Ugh, y'all are disgusting. I can't even."

"Can't even what?" I grin over at her as we walk outside into the cool autumn Paris evening. I want to scoop her up and repeat that kiss from Germany, effectively wiping that perma-scowl off her face. "Let's wait here for him and order a drink."

We sit down at a little bistro table under a red and black stripe awning next to the restaurant. I text Patrick our location and order a bottle of red from our waiter.

"Cheers."

"What are we celebrating?"

"Being in Paris. We only have Italy and Spain after this and then we're done."

She looks sad as she looks over at me. "Are you happy to be done?"

"I'm excited to start editing our footage, we've got some great stuff, but no I'm not excited to leave you…guys."

Patrick spots us and sits down at the tiny table. "This food smells amazing. I can't wait to try it."

"Hmm…we'll have to figure out a place for tomorrow night."

"I'll ask someone at the hotel." Patrick sniffs his food in the bag.

"Because that worked out so well for us in London." Lindsey smirks.

"Would you guys like to go up in the Eiffel Tower?"

"Oh…um, sure."

I sense her disappointment. "Do you not want to go?"

"No, I do, I was just thinking maybe it would be better during the day…"

"If we leave now, we'll just catch the sunset. It's beautiful, and Paris is called the city of lights for a reason. Besides, during the day the lines are ridiculously long and when you get up to the top it's so crowded and claustrophobic. We can stop at a creperie after for dinner."

She laughs. "Okay, sold." She finishes her glass of wine. "Trick, you in?"

"Nah, I think I'm going to head back to the hotel and eat this food that's oinking my name."

"You are seriously disturbed."

"Have fun, kids! Don't do anything I wouldn't do!"

Chapter 27

Lindsey

The City of Lights

NICK IS RIGHT. Paris at sunset from the Eiffel Tower is breathtaking, but it's cold in the crisp autumn evening, so we pop in to the little bar at the top where they sell overpriced champagne in flutes that light up. I don't know which I'm more excited about, watching the sunset over this exquisite city with the most handsome man at my side, or my light-changing champagne flute.

The waiter comes back with the champagne. "I've never opened a bottle of champagne before. Can you believe that?"

Nick whispers something to the waiter and he hands over the unopened bottle with our glasses. "Here's another first for you."

"I'm scared I'm going to shoot it in someone's eye. I don't have the best of luck. Have you seen those videos where the woman popped a cork into her boyfriend's nuts?"

He chuckles. "No, thank goodness. I'm not sure why she would be aiming in that direction in the first place. If you take it nice and easy, you should be fine. Take the foil off, or I can do it if you don't want to ruin your nails."

I hold up my unpainted short nails. "No problem there."

"Okay, so slowly untwist the wire. You want to carefully edge the cork up for a nice pop." He covers his fingers over mine in case I do hit someone and my stomach flutters with the contact.

"Can you imagine blinding someone with a champagne cork while they're at the top of the Eiffel Tower? I'd never live that down. There would be gifs for years."

He smirks at me as I slowly edge the cork out and it gives a nice pop sound. "Oh my god, I did it and I didn't send anyone to the hospital!" I giddily clap as Nick takes the bottle.

"Pour it into a champagne glass like you do a beer, and here you go." He hands me the glass, his gaze eliciting goosebumps on my arm. My blood sparkles and pops like the champagne bubbling in the glass. Our eyes hold each other as we both take a sip. The liquid chills my tongue, the tangy grapefruit flavor fizzing down my throat. He licks his lips.

"This is pretty good." He takes another swallow and I watch his throat move. I want to lean across the small table and plant a soft kiss right under his jawline. I want to run my tongue along his five o' clock shadow. I want to climb into his lap and...

"Okay! You ready to head back?" I drain the rest of the champagne from my glass.

Nick laughs. "We just got here." He refills my glass. "Would you like me to take a picture of you with the city in the background before the sky darkens?"

I shrug. *What I really want is for you to take my clothes off in your hotel room, but sure let's take a picture.* "Sure."

He lifts his phone as we exit the bar on to the little walkway that wraps around the tower.

"Wait!" I laugh. "I'm not ready."

"Just filming a little for the show."

I look out at the incredible city glittering below us. The wind whips my hair back as I smile at Nick. I sip my champagne and watch the blueberry colored clouds scuttle across the sky as the sun sinks down into the city. I turn to him and he takes a picture. A couple passes by him and offers to take a picture of us.

"Oh, it's okay, he's not—"

"Sure," Nick says easily as he slips in next to me and wraps an arm around my waist. His body is warm and I want to snuggle into him. The couple takes our picture and hands Nick his phone back. We look out over the city of lights as we sip our champagne.

"It's beautiful, Nick. Thank you for dragging me up here."

"You're welcome."

Everything looks so small below us. It makes me feel small. Like something big is about to happen and I'm nervous, excited, and scared. As much as Nick Elliot drives me crazy, he also makes me want more. He makes me want to be better. He makes me want him. I'm terrified that after this is all over I won't be able to walk away from him.

The wind ruffles his dark hair making me want to run my fingers through it. His smile is carefree and relaxed as he looks down at Paris and it makes me smile. Goddamn you, Nick Elliot, you're making me fall for you.

"Ready to head back to the hotel?" He arches an eyebrow.

"Yeah, you going to feed me first?" I smile up at him as I loop my arm in his, leaning into him.

"Ah, how could I forget to feed my little Gremlin?"

"Gremlin? Please...I'm the cuddly, soft, gentle thing. What's it called before it turns into a Gremlin?"

"A Mogwai?"

"Of course, he knows the answer," I grumble as he grabs our flutes and pulls me into a hug. His eyes are alight with humor. "You are so far from a Mogwai it's not even funny."

I smile teasingly at him. "What are the rules? Don't feed after midnight..."

"Don't expose them to bright light." He dips and kisses my nose causing me to lose my breath.

"And don't get them wet." My voice sounds sultry and breathy. He arches an eyebrow and I literally want to melt down into the ground from embarrassment. "Ha...that sounded really bad."

"I don't know what you're talking about. It's one of the rules," he says with a devilish smile. "Ohhh...do I make you wet, Ms. Love?" he asks silkily.

"No!" *Goddamn* these wire cages covering the side of the Eiffel Tower because what I really want to do is throw myself off right about now.

"Your cheeks are quite rosy." He runs a finger down the cheek in question causing my skin to ignite with just his touch. He looks at me like he wants to devour me. "Let's go before you pass out. I know a great little creperie near here."

He flings an arm around me as we head to the elevator. I swear this man is intentionally trying to drive me crazy with either lust, embarrassment, or hate. I just haven't figured out which yet.

Chapter 28

Nick

Diaper Pants

SO, LINDSEY LOVE has finally shown her true colors. She's got it bad for me. She can deny it until the cows come home, but I saw the truth in her eyes tonight. They're like an open book. A book about sex and longing and need. She needs and wants me and that makes my chest puff with caveman pride. I look down at her, grabbing her hand as we walk home from the creperie stand. She's stuffing her face with a butter and brown sugar crepe, groaning with every bite. And with every bite, my dick gets harder.

"This is so good. Like I could get run over by these crazy ass taxi drivers and I'd be a happy woman kind of good. You sure you don't want a bite?"

"I'm glad." I squeeze her hand. "Thanks, but I'm full from the mushroom spinach one."

"Mmm...so so good."

And my dick pulses again.

The problem is, I need and want her too. I find myself drawn to her. I love her quirky sense of humor, her goofiness, and the way she doesn't let me get away with shit. We only have a few weeks left together and then we'll go our separate ways. At the beginning of this whole thing I would have said hallefuckinglujah, but now…now the game has changed. I've fucking fallen for her and I don't want to get up. I want to pull her down with me and drown in her.

"Oh my god, did you see that?" She laughs about something we passed, but I'm lost in my own head. "Why do guys think it's okay to wear that?"

"We're not going to get into another cargo shorts discussion, are we?" I ask wearily. "Because for a food critic, you're very opinionated on men's fashion."

She quirks up her lip. "No, but can I just say, unless you're a skinny man, please don't wear skinny jeans. Especially the ones where the butt sags in the back. Let me tell you, Nick Elliot, women like butts. It's not just a guy thing. If a woman sees a fine ass she is going to want to squeeze it. If you're wearing fucking diaper jeans—"

"Diaper jeans?" I chuckle.

"Yes! The jeans that have the saggy ass, looks like a diaper."

"I feel like we *are* having another cargo shorts discussion, just in different form."

"No, we are on a whole nother topic at hand."

"Is nother even a word?"

"Yes! It is, don't steer me off in a different direction."

"Speaking of direction." I pull her hand as we get to a crosswalk. "The hotel is this way."

"No it's not, it's this way." She pulls in the opposite direction.

I groan in annoyance. "Can't you just trust me for once? I swear if I say go, you immediately stop."

"Can't you trust me? I have a very keen sense of direction."

"Fine, lead the way, Christopher Columbus."

"Don't think I didn't catch that little insult. He was an egotistical tyrant that got lost on several occasions."

"Hmm…"

She rolls her eyes as she throws her wax paper from her crepe in the trash. "I can't believe you think I'm a tyrant." She sulks as we turn a corner.

"I never said that."

"Yeah, but you didn't disagree. You just hmm'd."

"You have your moments…"

"Good or bad moments?"

"Sure." I smile down at her as she scowls. We walk in silence for a bit as she leads the way. She pauses as she looks down a side street.

"Are we lost?"

"No! Just…I swear I saw that street sign earlier. They all sound the same. Rue de something. Come on, this way."

We walk down another street, turn a corner and walk to the same crosswalk where we started. I cough in my hand trying to smother a laugh. She growls in frustration as she spins in place. "Ugh, fine, we'll do it *your* way."

"I thought you'd never ask, Pain in the Ass."

"I didn't ask," she huffs. "Did you really just call me a pain in the ass?"

I pull her in the direction I originally wanted to go. We turn down another street. "Oh good, we're back at the hotel."

"Lucky is what you are," she mumbles as we walk into

the hotel lobby. "I had fun tonight," she whispers as we ride up in the elevator. I'm still holding her hand, unable to let it go.

"Me too." I turn to her. It's now or never. I could shut this shit down once and for all, say goodnight and pretend like this crazy chemistry between us doesn't exist, but I don't want to. I have so much going on in my head right now, but the one thing that is clear as day is that I want Lindsey. I tug her to me causing her to gasp. "Come back to my room with me."

Before she can answer, I dip by head and capture her lips in a soft kiss, coaxing them apart. I release her when the elevator stops at our floor.

I arch an eyebrow as she touches her lips. "Well?"

"Yes," she whispers. "Screw chocolate cake."

Chapter 29

Lindsey

The Choke Hold

HIS SAPPHIRE-BLUE EYES glaze over with need as he leans down and softly kisses my lips. I'm momentarily dazed because I can't believe this is really happening, but it quickly evaporates as his tongue tangles with mine. I didn't realize how much I wanted him until this moment. We peel each other's coats off and dump them on the floor as we stumble into the room. I twine my fingers up into his hair and tug him closer. I can feel him smile against my lips as I groan.

He angles my head as he pulls slow tender kisses from me. But I'm not in the mood for sweet. I want to feel alive. I don't want the prince who gallops in on the white horse to save me. I want the tattooed beast who rides up on his chopper and takes me to hell, because that's where I'm going if I continue this make out session with Nick.

He grunts in surprise as I hop up and wrap my legs around his waist and kiss him with fervor. He matches my pace, and holy hell can this man kiss. He's like the Bruce Lee of kissing, taking no prisoners. He walks me over to the bed and gently lays me down as he does that incredibly sexy move where he reaches back and pulls his t-shirt off in one swift move. Like he can't be bothered with things such as shirts because he's got a breathless goddess looking up at him with *come fuck me* eyes. She's waiting with bated breath for him to shed his pants as well.

That goddess would be me by the way.

He doesn't disappoint as he unsnaps his jeans and I quickly tug my shirt over my head, but unfortunately not as smoothly as he made it look. My sweater tag snags my hair because I forgot to cut out the little fancy plastic piece from the price tag. I have to rip it from my head with a quick yank which make my eyes smart. The cuff gets stuck on my wrist and I'm violently trying to shake it free. I look more like a convulsing octopus than a sexy siren trying to seduce her man. I finally get the damn thing free as I quickly fix my hair and scoot back on the bed with my best come hither smile, inviting him to join me.

Damn this man is fine, cut like a freaking stone statue. He hasn't taken his pants off, but that's okay, I can work around them. My eyes linger on the trail of hair from his belly button down to his…heaven have mercy, I don't think he's wearing any underwear. Unless it's made of dental floss, I'm not seeing it. I bite my lip as he leans over me, his tan muscular arms bulging as he holds his weight.

I'm not going to lie…the size of his body is a little intimidating at six-foot-something compared to my five-foot-three-and-a-quarter. I'd bet on Mrs. Bixby's prized gardenias that little Nicky isn't so little. Let's be honest, I haven't had sex in ages, so if he wants to go all caveman on me and try and fit his big club in my tiny cave, then I'm going to let him. And if he wants to smother me to death with his muscular body while burying himself in me, then I would die a happy woman.

He kisses my neck and I sigh; his smell is so intoxicating. "Smother me, Nick."

"What?" He quirks one side of his lip up in a grin. "I was going to ask if this is okay, but you want me to *smother* you? Didn't peg you as a kink, Miss Love."

"Uh…" *Did I say that out loud? Backpedal!* "I said *don't* smother me. Please don't put me in a choke hold." I lean up and pull his mouth to mine sufficiently ending the topic that will hopefully never come up between us again. *Ever.*

"Are you okay with this?" He looks over my flushed skin with concern and it's so adorable I want to lick him like a lollipop.

"I'm good, more than good. Your body is sinfully sexy and the kissing's not too shabby either."

Now I do wish Nick would snuff me out. Who the hell says *not too shabby* in the throes of passion? That old crochety Southern detective Matlock, that's who. I bet Mrs. Bixby watches Matlock. Gah! Why am I thinking about Mrs. Bixby at this very moment? *Concentrate, Lindsey, for fuck's sake, get your head back in the game!* I bet Claudine wouldn't use the word shabby. She'd say something incredibly sexy with her Russian accent like, "Nick, fuck my brains out."

Nick looks down at me and his face splits in a wide grin. "You want me to fuck your brains out?"

Fuck, fuck, fuckity-fuck. Just stop talking and for the love of god *thinking* out loud, you moron! My cheeks feel like they are on fire as I look up at him, his eyes dancing with mirth. In the sweetest Southern drawl I can muster, I channel my inner Scarlett O'Hara, although I'm ninety-nine-point-nine-percent sure Scarlett would *never* ever say this to Rhett.

"Why I never, Mr. Elliot. What I meant to say is *please* fuck my brains out."

He laughs and dips his nose under my chin as he kisses me. "You're so weird, but I love it. I'm glad my kisses aren't too shabby." He pauses and I swear to god I see him blushing. He clears his throat as he leans down and kisses my collarbone. "I'm sorry, Lindsey, but I'm going to have to say no to the choke hold. Not my thing."

Jesus Christ. Why can't Nick be a stranger that I'll never ever *ever* see again. *Ever.*

"I swear on grandma's diamond ring I'm not into that either. It came out wrong."

He smiles as he kisses his way down to my satin bra and peels the silky material down, capturing my tight bud in his mouth. All embarrassing thoughts quickly melt away as his wicked tongue flicks my nipple. He kisses his way down my hip and slowly slides my panties with him.

"I've been wanting to do this to you from the moment I met you."

I grip his hair as he runs his nose along my seam. I can't argue, I can't think, I can't send him any kind of witty retort because for once in my life I am completely speechless. Damn he is good at this. He licks and sucks on me like I'm his favorite dessert. Like I'm the creamiest, richest, silkiest chocolate mousse he's ever tasted. He licks that spoon until it's completely clean and then he dives back in for more. Forget about an S.O.S. because this ship is going down, taking me under with Nick at the helm, and I'm going to drown a happy woman. My orgasm hits me so hard that I'm left panting, completely spent. He looks up at me with a devilish grin.

"You're uh…you're really good at that," I say breathlessly as he stands and takes his pants off. Thank god, because I don't think I have the energy to push them down. I watch his muscles bunch as he rolls a condom over his impressive length. Thank you, Jesus, for not making Little Nicky small like a gherkin pickle.

He holds himself over me, his eyes asking permission that he doesn't need to ask. Yes, Nick, a thousand times yes. I grab ahold of him and guide him into me. He sinks in slowly, but I don't want it slow. I tilt my hips up and take him until he's fully seated.

"Slow down, Linds, I'm not going to last long," he pants which fucking amps me up even more. The fact that I can bring Nick Elliot, the man that never loses his cool, to his knees is empowering. We move in tandem as he grabs my hip, his thrusts hitting me right in the sweet spot. He takes his thumb and rubs my clit, the room tilting as I buck against him. Goddamn, this man knows what he's doing. I crest the waves, my fall hitting me so fast it's blinding.

"Shit, I'm going to come," he shouts as he pounds into me hard. I feel his cock pulse inside of me as he lowers himself down on to one arm so that he doesn't collapse on top of me. I wipe the sheen of sweat from his brow and smile up at him. He makes my heart feel like it's going to explode with happiness as he grins back at me.

"So worth it," I murmur as I trace his jaw with my fingertips.

"We finally agree on something." He laughs, making my heart sing. He kisses my lips and gets up and heads to the bathroom. I snuggle in his sheets wondering if I should stay or hightail it back to my room. I mean let's face it, this isn't a love story. We're more like star-crossed lovers doomed from the start.

The bed dips as he gets in and pulls me to his side. He's a cuddler, and that just makes it worse because I love to snuggle. My head falls right into the dip of his shoulder and chest as I breathe in his masculine scent. I vow to remember his smell right up until the day I die. Even if I fall in love and get married to another man, Nick's scent will forever be tied to the night I had the best sex of my life.

Damn him.

"Your popularity is going to explode after this," he murmurs as he draws lazy circles on my arm.

"After having sex with you?"

His chest vibrates from his chuckle. "I do have a reputation."

I snuggle closer to his side knowing what he really meant. "I'm scared."

"What are you scared of?"

"That it's going to flop and ruin what I've worked so hard for."

His fingers still on my arm and then start up again. "Nah. People are going to love your honesty. Your expressions and commentary are gold. They will be flocking to the restaurants you go to just to see what all the fuss is about and if they have the same reaction. They'll be going with their friends to try the boa constrictor because you gagged on it. They'll wait an hour in line to get a table at Lukas' restaurant because you practically orgasmed when you ate his schnitzel."

"I did not." I smile against his chest.

"You did. I just saw your big O face." I try to pinch his side, but pinching a wall of muscle isn't easy. He grabs my hand and pins it over his heart. It beats steadily against my palm, causing my own heart to slow down, syncing with his rhythm. "So, no, Lindsey Love, you will not fail. I won't let that happen. This will catapult you into the spotlight."

"What if I don't want the spotlight? What if I want the simple Lindsey Love from before?"

He releases my hand. "I'm afraid that's not possible." He turns on his side so he's facing me. He runs a finger from my temple down my cheek. "Face it, Lindsey Love, everyone is going to want a piece of you."

I swallow felling incredibly vulnerable as I whisper, "And what about you, Nick Elliot? Will you want a piece of me too?"

His mercurial blue eyes search mine looking for an answer that I'm screaming right back at him. He leans in and slides his nose along my neck. The simplest touch from him makes my body hum. He kisses his way up my neck until he reaches my lips. I arch into him needing more. Part of me is frustrated he won't answer me, but the other part protecting my heart doesn't want to hear his truth.

I trace his scar with my tongue and kiss the tattoo he has on his side. I kiss every inch of his body because I can't get enough of this man, and even though he doesn't give me an answer, his eyes, his lips, his fingers, and his tongue do the talking for him.

We make love slowly, leisurely getting to know one another's bodies. And I'm pretty certain all my hate for Nick Elliot before was actually just foreplay to kickstart my heart.

The truth is, I never really hated Nick, we just needed a do-over.

Chapter 30

Nick

A Little Bistro in St. Germain

I STRETCH AS the morning sun filters through the drapes that I forgot to close last night. I'm alone in bed, but I'm not surprised. I knew Lindsey would freak out, over think this new turn of events between us, and run. I sigh as I reach for my phone. There's a text from her which surprises me.

> **Pain in My Ass:** *Patrick and I headed out to get coffee. Didn't want to wake you, you looked so peaceful. I'll bring you back a cup. L*

She's right, I did need the sleep after I stayed up half the night ravishing her body. My appetite for sex is insatiable when it comes to her, and when I did finally succumb, I slept like a baby. That hasn't happened in a long time.

I sigh as I set my phone down. Perhaps it's best if Lindsey did run from me. I'm committed to other things I can't share with her and this project in Africa after the new year. I wasn't lying when I said this show would catapult her career. She'll have obligations she'll have to fulfill for *Food and Travel*. Heck, we don't even live in the same state. We might as well be on different planets.

I take a shower and check in with a local French restaurant that has classic French dishes to see if we can film there tonight. The only table they have available is at nine p.m., so I take it. I head down into the lobby and bump into Patrick and Lindsey with their coffees.

"Hey, sorry it took so long. Patrick had to eat like three baguettes."

"They were right out of the oven. Oh my god, they were so good...what? I couldn't help myself."

Lindsey rolls her eyes. "Sorry Nick, your coffee might be a little cold now."

"It's okay." I smile warmly at her. I wonder if she's confided in Patrick about last night. "I made a reservation at a small little bistro not too far from here around nine tonight. They have very traditional food. But I will warn you, they will have snails, raw meat, and duck liver on the menu."

"Hey, I'm okay with it as long as I don't have to have Miss Piggy staring at me."

"Noted." I smile. Damn, I want to lean down and kiss her.

"Don't knock it 'til you try it." Patrick smiles as Lindsey jabs him in the side.

"So, we were thinking of going over to the Louvre. Would you like to join us?"

My how things have changed since London. I smile to myself. "Can I make a suggestion?"

"Of course."

"The Louvre is a zoo. The Musée d'Orsay has some beautiful art in it, and not nearly as crowded. Unless of course you're dying to see the Mona Lisa, which by the way is quite small. We can always do a bike ride by the Louvre to see the pyramids."

Patrick shrugs. "Eh, I don't really care. I just want to see some art."

"They have Monet, Van Gogh, Renoir, Degas…"

"Oh, I love Edgar Degas and Monet. Yes! Let's do it. I wish we had more time to see Monet's gardens."

"Hmm, maybe we can stay one more day here and fit that in."

"Really?"

I shrug. "I'll call Simon and see."

"Thank you!" Lindsey squeezes me into a tight hug.

"You guys are acting weird. It's making me uneasy," Patrick gripes as he turns toward the elevators. "Meet you down here in an hour."

I smile down at Lindsey as I hold her in my arms. "I take it you didn't tell Patrick about us."

"Nah, I like making him uncomfortable."

"Are you okay?"

"Completely." She smiles, her eyes bright and shining. "So according to Patrick we have an hour." She waggles her eyebrows at me suggestively.

"I can chug my coffee on the way up."

She grabs my hand and we make a run for the elevators causing nearby Parisians to look at us with disdain, but I don't care as long as I have Lindsey.

"GUESS WHAT I'M loving tonight? Paris. We are here tonight at Brindilles, a cute little French bistro tucked off of a quaint little cobblestone side street in The St. Germain district. I am so excited to try some French cuisine tonight!"

"Good, that works." I pick up the menu and ponder what I feel like tonight.

"You guys seriously...what the hell is going on between you?" Patrick looks between us as he lowers the camera. "All day the two of you have been laughing and making jokes. I even saw you holding hands."

It's true. Lindsey and I couldn't keep our hands off each other all morning and I loved every minute of it. Gone are the loathing stares. We shared secret smiles and laughter over the most mundane things. It's like my whole world has suddenly gone from black and white to a kaleidoscope of colors. Lindsey bulldozed her way past my defenses and unearthed the real me. The me before Mikey died. As infuriating as she can be, she's made me laugh again. She's made me *desire* again; she's made me feel.

"Aw Patrick, are you feeling left out?" Lindsey pats his arm sympathetically.

"No! But in a normal universe he would have made you redo that opener six times!"

"Maybe she's getting better." I smile to myself.

"Bullshit, she was fine all the other times."

"Should we tell him?" I wink at Lindsey.

"And ruin the surprise?"

"Ugh, mom, dad! Just tell me!"

"We slept together," Lindsey says matter-of-factly, causing me to cough as I take a sip of water.

"I was going to say we were friends…" I laugh.

She smiles at me and blows me an air-kiss. "I think I'm going to get the French onion soup and coq a vin."

"Well, it's about fucking time."

"No need to get snippy…I couldn't decide." She shrugs.

"I'm talking about you and Nick, not the food."

"So was I." She smiles coquettishly.

I laugh as I gaze at Lindsey, but something out on the street catches my eye beneath the string of lights hanging between the buildings. A man dressed head to toe in black quickly approaches the restaurant's front entrance. He places a box on top of a car and pulls out a key fob.

"Get down!" I shove the table over as a bomb explodes and total chaos ensues. Smoke fills the dining room and all I can hear is screaming and people running. "Get under the table!" I shout but I can't find Lindsey or Patrick anywhere.

Another bomb goes off.

Everything else falls away except for the man in black.

Chapter 31

Lindsey

I've Got You

SMOKE BILLOWS UP blurring my vision as I gasp for fresh air. Bullets ricochet off the table above me and I scream Nick's name, shooting my hand out as I try to grasp his shirt, but I just grab air. Patrons are screaming as I curl into myself blocking out the sounds and the carnage around me. I can't breathe. Please God, I don't want to die alone under a café table. I hear Nick shout but there's just too much smoke.

Another loud bomb goes off as more people scream. I wrap my arms tightly around my knees and bury my head into them. I know I'm crying but I can't feel anything except for a fiery heat in my ankle as I rock back and forth.

"Nick, please help me. Nick! Nick Elliot, please be alive. Please help me," I chant as I cry.

I can't see anything because of the smoke, but I'll never forget the sound of people shouting, glass breaking, bullets lodging themselves into the café walls around me as sirens roar in the distance. I pray that Nick and Patrick are alive. I don't want to survive this if they aren't.

I feel like hours have gone by, but in reality, it's only been minutes. A woman at a table next to me starts wailing.

Please God, make it stop. I need Nick. I need him to hold me and tell me it's going to be all right. I need him to make it all stop. Tears blur my vision as I rock. Suddenly a hand grabs my arm and I shriek. "Please don't kill me!"

"Shh, Lindsey, it's me. I've got you. Come on, we have to get out of here. Quick," Nick whispers in my ear as he pulls me into his hard chest. I sob in relief against him. "Shh, I've got you. You're safe. Come on, I need you to move your feet."

"I can't," I cry back. "It hurts. I think I've sprained my ankle."

Strong arms quickly lift me as I bury myself into his chest, gripping his t-shirt.

"Whatever you do, keep your head down and your eyes closed." His breath tickles my ear as we start to move.

I disobey him and look up and see the lifeless body of a man in body armor I can't ever unsee. "Oh my God, oh my God…" I mumble hysterically. "Where's Patrick?"

"Goddammit woman, do you ever listen to me? Close your eyes! He's safe."

I immediately close my eyes and say a prayer thanking God that both my men are safe. Nick stops jogging as someone speaks to him harshly in French. He answers back, his tone just as severe, and then he continues to jog. If I weren't freaking the fuck out I would have commented on how flawlessly the French language rolled off his tongue. But I can't think about that. I don't want to think about anything. I whimper and Nick's arms tighten around me.

"I've got you Lindsey, you're safe now. I've got you."

"Nick, don't leave me." I hiccup on a sob as I grip his

shirt. "Don't leave me alone."

"I've got you." He kisses my forehead as he jogs toward a waiting car. "I'll always have you." The car door opens and Nick shouts to the driver, "We need to get her to a hospital. Can you take her while I—"

"No!" I shriek. "No you can't leave me! No hospitals." Fear bubbles over into hysteria. "Please, I can't be alone. I just want to go back to the hotel."

Nick lowers himself into the car and speaks to the driver in French. He keeps me cuddled on his lap, safe in his strong arms.

"Oh my God, is she okay?" Patrick leans over as he inspects me. "Oh thank God, Lovie, I tried to find you but I couldn't see anything. I'm so sorry." His voice breaks causing my heart to lurch.

"It's okay, Trick. Are you okay?" I reach out and squeeze his hand.

"I'm fine, just shaken up."

I bury my face into Nick's strong warm chest. The beat of his heart and his familiar masculine smell is like a soothing balm to my soul.

Nick begins speaking French into his cell. I pull away from his chest wondering who he's talking to. He looks down at me with concern as he ends the call. "How does your ankle feel?"

"It hurts but not as bad as before."

He nods. "You might have just twisted it. I have a doctor coming to the hotel. Are you sure nothing else hurts?"

"Thank you. No, the table protected me from everything," I mumble into his chest. He squeezes me and kisses the top of my head. My whole body trembles as the taxi races to our hotel.

THE FRENCH DOCTOR sent over by *Food and Travel* exits my hotel room.

"I'm glad it's not broken or sprained, Lovie." Patrick pats my leg as I lie in bed. "Do you want me to stay?" He tries to stifle a yawn.

"No, I'll be okay. Go get some sleep. I'll see you in the morning, yeah?" I give him a reassuring smile as he leans down and hugs me. He stops and says something to Nick before he quietly closes the door to our suite. I pull the duvet up to my chin. I can't stop shivering for some reason. Nick heads over to the minibar fridge. He pulls out a small bottle and pours it into a glass.

"Here, drink this."

"What is it?"

"It's whiskey. Drink it, it will help warm you up." He stands next to the bed, his muscular arms crossed over his chest. He's doing his intimidating stance tactic, and it's working.

I eye him warily as I take a tentative sip. It burns like fire going down my throat and I cough. The liquid heat spreads like wildfire in my belly. He's not wrong though, it does ease the shivering.

I take a bigger sip, prepared for the gut-punch reaction.

"Thank you for coming back for me."

He raises one eyebrow. "What do you mean?"

"You know, after the bomber was…" I can't even finish the sentence so I take another gulp of whiskey. "Who was he anyway? Where did he come from?"

"You really think I would leave you there?" he says irritably.

"I mean, I wouldn't have blamed you."

"Lindsey, Jesus I…" He sighs, frustrated, then rakes his fingers through his hair as he starts to pace. "Look, it's my job to protect you. I'm so pissed at myself for letting this happen!"

I snort. "Letting what happen? The bomber? You couldn't have known he was going to show up tonight. I mean there was no warning. One minute we're talking about…shit, I can't even remember… Is that normal?"

He stops and looks at me, concern written across his features. "Yes, it will all come back eventually. You're just in shock."

"I appreciate you trying to protect me, but don't think for one second this is your fault."

He turns his back to me, and I watch his shoulders rise and fall. I slowly get out of bed and hobble over to him. The doctor said I have a grade-one sprain, so no surgery or casts needed, just rest. I slip my arms around his waist, startling him.

"Thank you for coming back for me and carrying me out of there. You could have left me for the authorities to find." I place a kiss between his shoulder blades which causes his lungs to expand. "Just accept my gratitude."

Nick whirls and tilts my chin up so our eyes connect. "I'd never leave you behind."

A tear slips down my cheek. His calloused thumb sweeps across my skin making me shiver. I look into his midnight-blue gaze. It reminds me of a clear crisp night when you look up into the inky sky and try to find Orion and the Little Dipper. It's comforting and grounds me.

He picks me up and carries me back to the bed where he gently lays me down and brings the covers up over me. I grab his hand before he can turn away from me. "Please don't leave me. Stay."

He nods, and slips off his boots. He climbs into the bed and spoons me. "The doctor left you a sedative. Do you want to take it? It will help you sleep."

"Not right now." I turn over and slip my arms under his. "I just want to lay here with you. Was anyone killed tonight? Where did that guy even come from? Was he a terrorist?"

Nick puts a finger on my lips. "Shh…we'll talk about it in the morning, okay? Right now just try to rest. I don't know the details yet." He gathers me closer and gently kisses my forehead, then lazily strokes my back.

"I've never been so scared in my life," I mumble into his chest as my fingers trail up under his t-shirt tracing his smooth skin. His heartbeat kicks up a notch. My limbs move like liquid and I'm exhausted, but I need to feel him. I need him closer.

"I know. You're safe now, *Meine Schöne*, I've got you. You're a pain in my ass, Lindsey Love, but I'd never leave you behind. I was so scared you'd been hurt tonight…" He kisses my temple.

I look into his twilight eyes. *"Meine Schöne...*you called me that in Germany. What does it mean?"

"My beautiful." He traces my lips with his index finger.

"Will you make love to me, Nick? I...I need you. I need this."

"Lindsey..." He sighs and runs his fingers through my hair. "What about your ankle?"

"My ankle will be fine, but I might just break apart into a million pieces if you don't touch me. I need to feel, Nick. Something other than this terror that is clawing up my chest. *Please*," I whisper, tenderly skimming my fingers across his lips.

He searches for something in my eyes, but he must only see my desperation because he nods once and slowly lifts my t-shirt. He flicks his tongue across my nipple and I arch off the bed. He kisses every inch of my skin slowly and tenderly, careful not to touch my ankle, worshiping my body as if it were a priceless statue he doesn't want to break.

Tonight, we are two different people than the ones who woke up this morning. Forever altered by the turn of events. We make love slowly and deliberately, whispering words of promises not meant to be broken.

Chapter 32

Lindsey

It's Over

PINK SUNLIGHT DAPPLES the curtains as I rub my eyes. I reach for Nick but the bed is empty. He probably went to get coffee. I pick up my phone on the nightstand and look at the time. It's early, seven a.m. I scrub my face trying not to think about last night as I head to the bathroom.

After I brush my teeth, I take a hot shower trying to scrub away the memories from last night, but I can't. Everything plays out in my brain like a movie trailer. I had just told Patrick we had gotten together when Nick's eye's lasered in on something and his face went blank.

We were near the open front windows of the restaurant because I remember the cool breeze. I remember shouting and Nick roughly pushing me down where I then crawled under the table he flipped. My ankle is better but still tender from where I must have twisted it when it got wedged between the table and a chair.

I'm crying again so I wash my face with a washcloth. I'm lucky to be alive and I owe it all to Nick. I quickly towel off and get dressed, anxious to see him and Patrick this morning. I also need to call my sister and Margot in case this incident makes the news back in the states.

I walk out into our living room that Patrick and I share and stop dead in my tracks. "Simon? What are you doing here?"

Simon turns around and hangs up on his call. "Good morning, Lindsey. How are you doing this morning? It's been a crazy twenty-four hours."

"It has." I glide my finger along the back of the chair. "What are you doing here?" I rudely repeat. He clears his throat looking uncomfortable. "I mean, not that I'm not happy you're here, I'm just surprised. I didn't know you were coming." I sit down on the couch.

Simon sits in the chair across from me, crosses his leg, and stares at me. "Well, Nick called me as soon he got you and Patrick to safety. Obviously, *Food and Travel* doesn't want to put you in harm's way and we care about you."

Patrick walks out of his room looking like he just rolled out of bed and pauses when he sees me talking to Simon. I get up and cross to him and give him a tight squeeze.

"Is your ankle better? I heard voices. Who's this guy?" he whispers.

"Yes, still sore, but it will be fine."

"You must be Patrick Healy. Hi, I'm Simon Blake. It's nice to finally meet you. I wish it were under different circumstances."

"Nice to meet you, Simon." The two men shake hands.

"I'm glad you are both here. Please have a seat."

Patrick eyes me warily as we sit down on the couch. Simon chooses to stand.

"To be honest, Simon, I'm surprised you're here. How

did you get to Paris so fast?"

"I was in London when Nick called me last night. Look, Lindsey, I'm going to cut right to it...we've decided to pull the plug on the show."

My heart plummets as Patrick grabs my hand. "Wait, what? After all we've been through, after being bombed last night you're just going to say forget it? That's bullshit!"

"Lindsey..." Patrick quietly admonishes.

"I understand your frustration, I really do, but we can't have that kind of liability on our hands. You had Paris, Italy, and Spain to film, which isn't going to happen. I can try to see if we can do a two-show episode, but I doubt the network will go for that."

"So, what now? You're just sending us home?" I get up and pace despite my injured ankle.

"Lindsey, I don't have a choice."

"There's always a choice." I throw my arms out to my side in exasperation.

"Not this time."

"Where is Nick? Shouldn't he have a say in this?" I sit back down beside Patrick.

Simon looks down at his clasped hands. "Nick is gone."

"What do you mean Nick is gone? Gone where?"

"I was wondering the same thing, actually..." He sighs and looks at me, the silence making me uncomfortable. "How much do you two know about Nick?"

I bite my lip as unease washes over me. "I know he's an ex-Navy SEAL and a producer for this show...was a producer."

"Anything else?" he hedges.

"He was hired to protect us. He speaks a crazy amount of languages…" Patrick shifts forward in his seat as he speaks up.

"Did you happen to see him take out the assailant last night?" I look over at Patrick dumbfounded. "Ah, by the expression on both of your faces, clearly you didn't."

"What do you mean *take out*?" I swallow thickly.

"Nick Elliot is all the things you listed, but he's a dangerous man. I'm obligated…well, never mind, I shouldn't have gotten you two involved with him. He's a producer and a director, yes, but he also gathers intelligence for a private group on the side. He was doing that while in Europe unbeknownst to me."

"He's CIA?" I hiss.

Simon chuckles. "Not exactly."

"Oh my god, he's an assassin? A killer for hire?" My eyes widen as I bite my knuckle. "I knew it. I knew he could fucking take me out with a twitch of his thumb," I mutter.

I had the most unbelievable sex of my life with…

"He's Jason Bourne?" I squeak out. "No wait, wait…he's the guy played by Mark Wahlberg in *Shooter*."

"Uh…" Simon looks helplessly over at Patrick.

"Just ignore her. Please, continue."

Simon nods. "Look, I've said too much already, but it's probably best if your relationship ends here. He's not a good guy."

"He's not a good guy? What do you mean he's not coming back?" I sputter.

"It's best if you just let it go." Simon stands and Patrick and I follow suit. He places his hands on my arms giving me a charming smile. "Why don't you go and pack your things. You and Patrick have a flight out tonight."

"You can't just dump all this vague information in our laps and not expect me to go crazy. I have questions, lots of them!"

"Questions I can't answer at the moment. Look, I promise, I'll do everything I can to see if we can get this aired." He pulls me into a hug and it feels awkward and uncomfortable. I once thought Simon was appealing and handsome, but that was before I fell for my asshole, multilingual sexy-talking assassin, Nick Elliot. I quickly shrug out of his embrace and step back.

"What if Patrick and I shot the last three episodes?" I look over at Patrick for approval and he nods his head.

"It's too dangerous, Lindsey."

"Well, it's not like we were exactly safe last night. Please, Simon. Think about it before we have to leave. I know we can do this. We've invested so much into this...*Food and Travel* has invested so much. Give me a chance to show you I can be a true professional and get this job done."

He sighs and looks down at his phone. "I'll talk to the higher ups and see."

"Please. I need this."

"No promises, Lindsey, but they did love the footage Nick sent...I promise to see what I can do. And please don't mention our conversation about Nick to anyone. It could be a matter of life and death for him...and possibly for you too."

Well, that's fucking ominous.

Patrick nods. "Of course, of course. I'm going to go pack

up."

I swallow feeling suddenly ill at ease. "Okay, I promise. I'm going to go call Margot and my sister and let them know I'm okay. As soon as you hear from *Food and Travel*, please let us know. We are willing to see this project through, with or without Nick Elliot."

"You don't take any prisoners do you, Ms. Love? I like that about you." He winks at me.

Three months ago that comment coming from Simon would have turned me into a hormonal glob of goo, but this morning it just makes me want to punch him. Everything Patrick and I have worked so hard for is about to go up in flames and he's over here winking at me and being inappropriately flirty.

I quickly walk back into my bedroom, my brain spinning with all the new information. I sit down on the bed as I wipe away the tears that start to fall. I tried to keep up a brave front in front of Simon, but the truth is I'm heartbroken and angry. Not only did Nick lie to me about why he's really here, but he just up and left without saying goodbye. No explanations. Simon says he's a bad guy and to stay away from him, but that doesn't add up to the man I got to know.

He held me in his arms last night, promises whispered between us. He wouldn't say and do those things and just vanish without a note or anything, would he? I don't know anymore. I have so many questions and no one can give me the answers. Everything I thought I knew about Nick Elliot was a lie.

I pick my phone up off the bedside table and that's when I see it. I swear on my life that wasn't there when I woke up this morning. I would have definitely noticed it.

"Nick, are you in here?" I ask foolishly to a silent room. I pick up the shiny silver quarter and hold it in my palm. I trace the edge of it as more tears leak from my swollen eyes.

Where the hell are you when I need you most, Nick Elliot?

Chapter 33

Nick

End of Story

"YOU TRIED TO have me fucking killed!"

"Not me per se..." Simon gives me a smarmy smile. "Look, Scar, you knew the danger. The Russians are a very tetchy group." He sits across from me at my desk, twirling a pencil.

"I told you back in Cartagena that I was done. Yet here we are again barely escaping another botched mission you've created. I can't believe you fucking put Lindsey and Patrick in that situation."

"Well, it's not like I knew the informant you talked to in Berlin was a double agent. You're lucky she didn't kill you that night. They must have been following you."

"Jesus." I scrub my hands down my face as I think back to dinner with Lindsey and Claudine. If anything had happened to Lindsey that night, I never would have forgiven myself. I trusted Claudine wouldn't hurt us, but I wasn't so sure about the rest of the Russian gang she was involved with.

"I told Lindsey and Patrick."

Murderous rage makes my blood boil. "You did what?!"

"She wanted to continue the show. I had to convince her it was a bad idea. That you were dangerous."

"So giving up my fucking identity warranted that? You're putting *all* of us in jeopardy."

"Well, it didn't work. She's a ballbuster that one. I caved and told her she could continue. After all, *Food and Travel* thinks they're getting five episodes and you told me yourself the execs loved what you sent them."

All I can see is red. "I told you to tell them we were pulling the plug on the fucking show! What if someone is still following her?"

Simon casually waves. "I sent one of my guys with them. Besides, it's you they wanted, not her. My guy is good, don't worry. I told her it was the only way she would be allowed to go."

I shake my head. "I can't believe this. I'm done, Simon. I'm out. Just let me live my life in peace from here on out. I don't want to be a part of the Syndicate anymore."

"Scar, you don't mean it. What about Mikey?"

"Don't fucking bring up Mike to me and stop fucking calling me Scar. I need you out of my face before I launch across this desk and strangle you."

"No wonder Whitney left you for me. You're so fucking uptight and moody." He eyes me over his perched hands. "Now, Lindsey, she's a firecracker. I bet I could bring the tiger out of her in the bedroom."

I go blind with rage as I strike Simon with lightning speed. He crumples to the floor as he holds his bleeding nose. He didn't even have time to register that I got up from my desk.

"Shit, I think you broke my nose, you fucking son of a bitch!"

"I want to do more than just punch you in the nose, motherfucker. Don't even think about getting near Lindsey, you fucking cockroach. Get out."

"There's one more mission the senator needs from you." He stuffs some Kleenex under his nose, staunching the blood as he sits down in the chair across from me.

"Fuck you," I grunt, using all my self-control not to murder the bastard.

"I just need you to meet with a guy in Morocco. It's important, Nick. Senator's orders."

My jaw clenches. "I told you, I'm done."

Simon sits back and smiles. "It would be a shame if something happened to Miss Love in Italy or Spain, now wouldn't it?" He knows exactly what he's doing as he taunts me. He exposed my underbelly and now he has me by the balls.

"I'd rip your heart out while it was still beating and shove it down your throat."

"Exactly. One last favor, and you and I will never have to see each other again."

"End of story."

"End of story."

"Your word means shit to me."

"Go fucking take your videos of gazelles and turtles and live out your pathetic life. But just remember, you're no longer under the Syndicate's protection."

"I'd happily trade death than to be tethered to you."

"I can make all your dreams come true." Simon Blake

winks at me as he gets up. "You'll be leaving for Morocco tomorrow. Here are the details; burn it when you're done." He throws a manila envelope on the table and casually walks out.

Chapter 34

Lindsey

Herman Munster

Eight days later

I STARE ACROSS the table at Rico, the security guy Simon sent with us to Italy and Spain. Let me tell you, he's no Nick Elliot. He looks more like Herman Munster from the old classic television series, *The Munsters.* His head is long and square. His black hair is matted to his forehead with fringed bangs, his face sallow. It would not surprise me in the least that if we looked closely enough, we would see bolts coming out of his neck. The most disturbing part is that he doesn't talk, he just grunts. I don't even know if he speaks English.

Italy was beautiful but sad for me. As angry and confused as I am with Nick, I also miss him like crazy. What's making me even crazier is the fact that I still haven't heard from him. Not even a text letting me know he's okay. I blew up his phone with questions that have gone unanswered. And I know he's seen them because he was *always* looking at his damn phone. Every street I walked down, every corner I turned, I looked up hoping I'd catch a glimpse of him.

We also had Herman Munster joined to us at the hip. Nothing spells incognito with a six-foot-five lumbering

Frankenstein following you around. Patrick and I tried to ditch him on several occasions but somehow, he always found us. Patrick thinks Simon put tracking chips on us. Nothing would surprise me anymore.

It's hard for me to concentrate while Patrick is filming because Rico is next to me chewing what sounds like nuts and bolts. My eyes widen as he picks up his water glass and makes a whistling noise with his teeth while he drinks through the straw. *What the fuck?* I mouth to Patrick who is trying not to laugh.

"Uh, Herman, I mean Rico, are you almost done there? We're trying to film." Patrick looks over at Rico who just grunts in response.

I'm seriously doubting Rico's talents as a security guard. There's no way this guy could take down a badass like Nick Elliot. I just don't see him jumping up and doing a scissor kick or a karate chop to someone's throat. It's hard to determine Rico's age since I'm pretty sure he dyes his hair with shoe polish, but I'm guessing he's in his sixties. And it's a hard six-oh.

I look over at the man in question as the whistling noise starts up again. He's sitting with his back to the door. Everyone knows that's a Mafia 101 rookie mistake. You never sit with your back to the door or else someone can sneak up behind you and...fuhgeddaboudit.

Patrick and I have discussed the merits of Rico's body mass at length. He's bulky. We both agree that if someone comes at us with guns blazing or bombs dropping, we would just use Rico as a human shield.

What? It's his *job*, people.

Rico chews on an ice cube and it makes my eye twitch. It sounds like he's chomping on a brick. "Okay!" I clap my hands together which causes his heavy head to lift up and look around the restaurant. *Way to be alert there, Herman.* "Let's do one more take and then I think we can go. Sound good?" I smile cheerfully at Patrick and Rico. Only one smiles back. You can guess who.

"Uh, Rico, if we can hold off on the ice-chewing, bud, that would be terrific." Patrick gives him a wink and holds up his fist for him to bump. I snort as Rico indifferently stares back at Patrick who quickly drops his hand. He may seem useless in the kung-fu, guns-blazing department, but he still scares the shit out of us.

Rico pauses so Patrick and I jump into action. "Go, Lovie."

"What makes you think of dreamy sunsets, acoustic guitars—"

"Blehhhhurp…ehh."

My jaw hangs open as I look over at Patrick in disbelief. Did Rico seriously just fucking belch during our filming? Patrick looks nervously between Rico and me. He motions for me to continue as Rico's eyelids slowly droop down.

"What makes you think of dreamy sunsets, acoustic guitars, and flamenco dancers? Spain, of course," I whisper.

"Cut! Why are you whispering?" Patrick hisses.

"Why are you whispering?"

"Because you are!"

"I don't know! I don't want to wake up Rico."

"Fuck Herman, just get this done!"

I nod as I take a sip of water. I paste on a bright smile.

"What makes—"

Loud snores erupt from Rico, causing me to jump.

"Jesus Christ, he sounds like a trucker using his jake brake," Patrick mutters. "Wake him up."

"Why me?" I whine.

"Because he likes you better than me!"

I reach a finger out and poke Rico but he doesn't stir. His snores have increased in volume causing other diners to look over at us. This is so embarrassing. "Hand me that churro."

"What are you going to do with it?" Patrick looks at me uneasily as he hands the plate over. I pick one up and run it under Rico's nose, but it doesn't do anything. I bang it on his head and it breaks in half.

I sigh in frustration as I grab another one. "Worst security guy in the history of ever." I stick the churro up to his temple and in the best Clint Eastwood voice I can muster, I say, "Go ahead, make my day."

I make the sound of a gun clicking. Rico snorts and sits up. I chuck the fried pastry and smile at Patrick who has been filming the whole thing. Rico grunts and grumbles as he gets up from the table to head to the restroom.

"Quick, we have maybe three minutes. Let's do this!" Patrick gives me the thumbs-up and I deliver my lines flawlessly. I rave about the tapas at Las Positas in the Basque city of San Sebastian before Rico Munster returns and ruins our perfect take.

I STARE OUT at the crashing waves as I think about Nick. He may have driven me bonkers and might have made me do ten retakes, but I miss him like crazy. I take a sip of my sangria as the sun slips into the Atlantic. If he were here with me right now, he'd be kissing my neck with his strong arms wrapped around me. We'd make love under the Spanish stars until the sun breached the horizon. I sigh as I finger the silver quarter in my pocket.

Patrick sits down next to me.

"Did Herman go back to the hotel?" I ask.

"Yeah, I told him we'd be fine without him. He just grunted so I'm assuming he understood." He bumps my shoulder. "You doing okay?"

I sigh as I look out at the churning waters. "Confused, mad...confused."

Patrick flings an arm over my shoulder. "Yeah, crazy turn of events. I always knew Nick Elliot wasn't just a film producer..."

I snort. "You had no clue he was a...I don't even know what he is."

"Ethan Hunt."

I chuckle. "Who?"

"*Mission Impossible*...Tom Cruise. He's Ethan Hunt."

I scrunch up my nose. "Tom Cruise is weird."

Patrick sighs, "I'm not saying Nick is like Tom Cruise...he's like the character he plays. You know what, never mind."

I look over at Patrick. "I sure know how to pick 'em, don't I, Trick? Do you think he's really a bad guy?"

"No, I don't think he's a bad guy, I think Simon was just trying to scare us. I can spot a bad guy a mile away. Nick Elliot was one of the good ones." We watch the waves crash. "You know he's the first one you've dated that I've actually liked."

"I wouldn't call sleeping with him dating."

Patrick shrugs. "He knew how to handle you."

"How to handle me? Geez, you make me sound like I'm some crazy fly-off-the-handle lunatic." He side-eyes me, making me laugh. "Shut up, you."

"He really liked you, you know."

"Yeah, I know," I whisper. "I liked him too."

"He'll come back for you. He just has to be his badass self, take out a bad guy and save the world."

"Ha, yeah." I sip my chilled wine. "Funny, we had a conversation about this. He said he'd choose you over me if he needed a friend to call on to help him out of a jam."

"Seriously?" Patrick puffs up with pride.

"Yeah, something about you not cutting a pink wire and me having short legs," I grumble, still annoyed by that conversation.

"I'd never cut the pink one," Patrick vows. "He'll come back for you, Lovie, just give him some time."

"Do I really want to get involved with some ex-military *Mission Impossible* dude?"

"Hell yes! It's badass. Besides, he and I are pretty close now. I could help you."

This makes me laugh. "Oh, so now you two are besties because he chose you to not cut the pretty wire?"

"Yup."

I look over my shoulder. "Patrick, shh! Do you feel what I feel?"

Patrick tenses next to me. "I feel it. It's like an STD that won't go away."

"I wouldn't know, Trick, but thanks for the heads-up."

Patrick splutters. "It's a figure of speech, Lovie. I don't have crabs or the clap."

I giggle as Rico pulls out a chair at the table next to us. "Do you think Simon inserted a tracking chip in our necks while we were asleep?"

Patrick rolls his eyes. "You've been watching too many spy movies. It's probably just in our shoe or something." I nod as we both look over at the conspicuous security detail as he picks his teeth with his nail. Eww, definitely *not* Nick Elliot.

My fingers glide along the cool metal of the quarter I've been absentmindedly flipping with my fingers. I'm not sure what to do about Nick, but he was right. Spain is the perfect place to end this journey.

I need to get back to the States and get some answers.

Chapter 35

Nick

A Gentleman Caller

Three months later

I LOOK AT my phone checking the address before I step up on to the front porch. I wipe my hands on my jeans. Jesus I'm nervous. I chuckle because I've been in far more precarious situations than this. Situations of life and death, and yet begging Lindsey Love for her forgiveness makes me feel like I'm about to go in front of a firing squad. I take a step toward the front door when a creak comes from an apartment door to my left. I spy two little beady eyes staring back at me from behind a chain.

I give whoever it is my most charming smile. "Oh, good evening. I'm—"

"State your purpose!" The woman rudely barks from behind the chain. This must be Lindsey's... grandmother? She never mentioned living with her.

"Hi there, I'm..."

The door swings open faster than I can blink causing the words to die on my tongue. She looks at me with pure hatred and disgust. Her expression wars with her appearance. She looks like someone's sweet grandmother on her way to a ladies luncheon or to a potluck dinner at church. Like she'd smell like freshly baked cookies and just got done crocheting a blanket for her soon to be grandchild. "Are you one of them *gentleman callers?*"

Her accent is very Southern and thick, so I'm not sure I heard her correctly. "Ma'am?"

"Speak up! It's rude to mutter."

She's got her hand clutched to her pearls like I'm about to lunge forward and rip them from her throat. Her other hand holds a crystal tumbler. I extend my hand to her but she rears back in repulsion. The look on her face suggests that she'd rather eat a pie made of shit then touch my hand. I quickly put my hand in my pocket and give her another smile.

"Are you Lindsey's grandmother?"

"Are you trying to sell me something? Did that two-timing, backstabbing harlot sign me up for another retirement home? Listen here, and listen good. I will call the police and they will be here in minutes! I have life alert and a taser I'm not afraid to use on you."

"Uh...Mrs..."

"It's Mrs. Dinah Lenoir Bixby, if you must know. I should spank your bottom with a paddle. It is rude to come sellin' something at dinnertime on a Thursday evening."

I look around wondering if Lindsey is secretly hiding in the bush laughing her ass off. I wait for her to jump out and yell "gotcha!" Nope, it's just me and the cantankerous Dinah Bixby. I clear my throat. "I'm not selling anything, Mrs. Bixby."

"Are you trying to sass me, boy?"

"No, ma'am."

She squints at me. "What do you want? Are you here for that tramp that lives upstairs?"

"Yes!" Now we're getting somewhere. "I mean, she's not a tramp, but yes. Is she home?"

"What do I look like, her personal social director?"

"Uh, no ma'am. Can you give her this for me?" I reach into my pocket and give her a blank card with my new number on it.

Mrs. Bixby snorts. "I'm sure she's out with one of her other gentleman callers. She's like a cat in heat that one, always bringing them around." She rattles the ice in her glass.

I stuff my hands in my pockets, at a loss for words. I'm trying to connect the Lindsey I know with the person she's describing.

"My granddaughter Elinora is single." She looks me over appraisingly like I'm a blue-ribbon steed. "You look about her age. Don't let that hussy upstairs sink her claws into you. Last week it was Brad and this week it will be someone new. Why just yesterday she made that poor sweet Roman take her to see her mother in the hospital. She just had a face transplant you know."

If Mrs. Bixby poked me with a feather I'd fall flat on my ass. Lindsey's mom had a *face transplant?* She never mentioned her mom, just her sister...*and who the fuck is Roman?* Lindsey made it seem like her dating life was dismal, but according to Mrs. Bixby it sounds like she has a parade of men coming through her door.

"Mrs. Bixby, I think we might have a mix-up. I'm looking for Lindsey Love."

"Oh, I know exactly who you're lookin' for. She's out with her boy-toys like I said. Lipstick on a pig is what she is."

I swallow my pride and slowly back away from Mrs. Bixby. "Okay, well it was nice to meet you Mrs. Bixby."

"I could call up my Elinora, she would be quite smitten with you."

I hold up my hand halting this conversation. I shudder at the thought of dating any descendent of this woman. "I'm taken, but thank you for the offer. Have a good night, Mrs. Bixby."

"Goodnight Mr..." She cranes her neck and puts her hand to her ear.

I don't want to give this woman my real name, so I say the first name that comes to mind. "Martin Scorsese."

"Well that's a peculiar name. Poor pedigree is what that is," she sniffs as she rattles the ice in her glass.

I wander back to my car feeling confused and tired. How presumptuous of me to think she would be at home waiting for me to show up—that she would *want* to see me. According to Mrs. Bixby, I was probably just another warm body to keep her company while in Europe. Just an itch needing to be scratched.

I hesitate and pull her number up, but if what the old lady said was true...perhaps this is for the best that she's moved on. This is what I wanted from the beginning isn't it? No strings, no attachments. She's safer without me around.

So why do I feel like my heart has just been flattened by a hammer?

Chapter 36

Lindsey

Satan's Lair

I LEAVE MY sister's house, my belly full with an amazing homecooked meal that Dan prepared. My sister's lucky. He's not only an amazing dad, but he helps with the housework and cooks all the meals. Even with the good food, it was a long evening of my sister peppering me with questions about how the show was doing and if I had heard from Nick.

I try to pull into the parking spot I'm allocated behind the house, but the old bat parked her car between her spot and mine, so I can't even squeeze in if I tried. I find a spot eventually down the street and quickly walk up the side alley to the front porch. I bring up my text messages stupidly hoping there might be one from him. It's been months and I still haven't heard a peep since the night of the bombing, even though I've pathetically texted him a couple hundred times to call me back. There might have been some drunken voicemails too. Jesus, I wouldn't call me back either.

"It's about time you slinked back in."

I jump a mile out of my skin, not expecting for the devil incarnate to be rocking away on the front porch at this hour.

"Hello, Mrs. Bixby," I say sourly, her name a bad aftertaste in my mouth.

"Next time you travel out of town you need to board that mangy cat so I don't have any disturbances."

I still can't believe Mrs. Bixby called the cops on Dan every time he came over to my place to feed Mac. After the fourth episode, the police department had had enough and would call Dan to verify that it indeed was him breaking and entering into my apartment.

"Maybe we should board you," I mumble under my breath. I turn and smile as I reach for my house key. "Great idea." I've been home for three months, but she makes sure to slide in a daily comment about what a pain Mac was while I was gone.

"Someone was snoopin' around here this evenin' like a dog in heat. I'm tired of the riffraff you bring round here. I told Richie that he has a street-walker living in his apartment."

I turn and look at her strangely. "Someone was looking for me?"

"A Mr. Marlin Scorzalia. Outlandish last name if you ask me."

She must be having dementia because I don't know anyone by that name. "Are you sure it wasn't an Amazon delivery guy? Did he leave a package?"

"Do I look like your personal secretary? I know what I saw," she bites out as she scrunches up her face as if she's peering at something in the distance. "Callin' me a fool."

Um… "Well, can you describe him?"

"Nondescript. Average at best. Mediocre face, short. I've already forgotten it."

"Really fucking helpful," I say under my breath as I look longingly at my door. I just want to pour myself a glass of wine and chill out, but I can't because I have Nosy Nellie here yammerin' on about how she missed a *Jeopardy* question because someone was on our porch. And now it's my fault because they were asking for me. Maybe it was Patrick, although Patrick Healy doesn't sound like Marlin Scorzalia.

She shakes a tumbler with what looks like whiskey or scotch in it and I almost fall over from shock. *Mrs. Bixby drinks?* I've never seen a glass in her hand before tonight. A microscopic part of my heart feels a little bit sorry for her. She must be lonely. It explains her crabby attitude. If I tried really hard, I could maybe be her friend. I sit down in the rocking chair next to her.

"I didn't invite you to join me! Get the hell out of my rockin' chair!"

I hop up, scared shitless that she might shank me with a whittled twig from her gardenia bush she's been saving for this exact moment.

"Okay, okay…it wouldn't hurt to be a little bit friendly, Mrs. Bixby," I grumble. "Sheesh."

"Friendly people are assholes. I don't trust them." She eyes me suspiciously. She may be an old bat, but her hearing is top notch. "He gave me this. I was going to keep it for my Elinora, but I'm hoping he's someone undercover and you'll be arrested for tax evasion or prostitution." She hands me a white card with a phone number on it. She's actually giving me something that belongs to me? Floored doesn't begin to scratch the surface of what I'm feeling.

"Goodnight, Mrs. Bixby. I hope the bedbugs bite."

"Tell that cat of yours to stop meowing or else I'm going to bury him six feet under my prize-winning roses."

"Always a pleasure, Mrs. Bixby." I roll my eyes as I unlock my door and leave Satan to rock away on the front porch. I trudge up the stairs and open my door. Mac greets me, meowing.

"You better pipe it down, Mister, or you're going to become rose food." I feed him, check my messages, and sink down onto the couch, flipping on the TV. I mindlessly flip through the channels, my mind drifting to Nick like it always does late at night.

Patrick told me he's been in touch with him through email since he had to send all the footage to him, but they never discussed me, which means Nick never asked him about me. Which means my heart is just a little more broken inside.

I never told anyone else what Simon told me about him. Only Patrick knows the truth. I feel like if I told Shannon or any of my friends I'd be hurting him somehow, damaging his trust. Which is quite laughable really since he's withheld so much from me. I mean I get national security…people could be killed, blah blah blah. But I just can't connect the two parts together. Why the hell is he producing this show with me when in reality he's agent number two twenty-five in the killer-for-hire catalogue?

It doesn't make sense, and I'm tired of thinking about it. I blow out a breath and flop my arms on the couch in frustration causing Mac to try and bite me.

"Even my cat fricking hates me," I yell out to the empty living room. A pounding noise comes through my floorboard from downstairs. I roll my eyes, get up, and grab the heaviest cooking book I have in my kitchen and slam it down hard.

"Take that, you ol' witch."

I look up and Mac is staring at me from his perch on the couch like I'm the biggest moron he's ever met. I probably am to be fighting with an eighty-year-old woman. I flop back down on the couch and he immediately attacks my messy bun.

"Agh! Shit, Mac, I can't imagine you ever did this to Mom and Dad!"

They probably aren't even on a cruise around the world. They're probably hiding in their house, Mac-free and laughing about it every day. *Oh haha that Lindsey is such a sucker for believing we needed her to take Mac while we "cruise the world."*

I lay down away from Mac's claws and pull out the card thinking about what Mrs. Bixby said. I had someone named Marlin Scorzalia stop by? Nondescript. A forgettable face…who on earth? Something niggles the edge of my brain, but stays just out of reach enough to drive me crazy. I say the name over and over in my head, who the hell is Marlin Scorzalia… Suddenly I sit straight up, my brain sorting the puzzle to make the pieces fit. Martin Scorsese? No, no, it can't be. Can it? I immediately think of a warm kitchen in Germany, the smell of schnitzel frying…me snidely calling Nick 'Martin Scorsese.'

He's far from nondescript, but Mrs. Bixby is probably just being her usual asshole self to get under my skin. She knew exactly what she was doing. She could pick him out of a lineup with a hundred other men, blindfolded, I guarantee.

Was Nick really here on my front porch? I pick up my phone and gather my courage.

His phone rings once and then his voicemail picks up.

"Hi Nick, it's…me. Were you here tonight? Call me back. I need to talk to you."

A few minutes later I receive a text asking me not to contact him for my own safety. He'll be in contact with me when he can.

I stare at my phone in disbelief. That's it? He just shrugs me off like an itchy sweater? What if I don't want to be protected? What if I want answers? What if I just want to see him and have him hold me? What if I see him and feel that spark reignite? What if I see him and hate him all over again and want to knee him in the balls?

I sigh as I plop face down onto my bed. So many what-ifs and I'm not getting any answers.

Chapter 37

Lindsey

Hotter Than a Jalapeño Coochie

Two months later

"LINDSEY LOVE! LOOK this way! What are you loving tonight?"

"Lindsey, over here dear! Who are you wearing?"

"Lindsey, are you nervous? Smile big, Miss Love!"

"Lindsey, can we just have one with you?"

Camera flashes blind me as I walk across the red carpet at *Food and Travel Network*'s Annual Awards show. Patrick squeezes my arm gently as we smile for the cameras and then an aide reaches over and quickly ushers us along. Margot meets me on the other side and quickly pulls me into an embrace, effectively loosening my grip on Patrick.

"Lindsey, you look fabulous! Spectacular, really! This red dress is stunning on you! Power color, I love it! How are you feeling?"

"I'm—"

"Oh, don't be nervous," she cuts me off as she bends her head to my ear as she shuffles us along. "Look, lots of big wigs in here tonight. I'm going to work my magic at the after parties, but hopefully I won't have to if we take home the big one, right? Oh look, there's Stephen! I'll touch base with you in a bit. Stephen, dear, marvelous to see you!" Margot sweeps away just as quickly as she came in, making my head spin.

"Wow, she's…a lot." Patrick gives me a half-smile.

"I'm sorry, she didn't give me a breath to introduce you."

"Don't worry about it. I'm just your eye candy this evening." He smiles goofily.

I snort as I look over at him. He does look pretty dashing in his tuxedo, but his red Converse offset the debonair look he was going for.

"Do you think he'll be here?"

"Relax, Lindsey. He's out of the country."

"Why is it he talks to you, but is 'too afraid' he'll get me killed to have any contact with me? Face the facts, Trick, he wants nothing to do with me."

Patrick shrugs. "He texted you when the ratings went off the charts."

"Yeah, a big ol' *congratulations on the success of the show*. A robot could have come up with that gem. Why doesn't he care about your safety?"

"He had to talk to me to put the show together so that I could convey to you what he wanted for the voiceovers and stuff. It made sense. It's not like we were hanging out having beers together. We both agreed we didn't want to put you in harm's way." He grins. "Besides, I'm his sidekick remember?"

"How can I forget. You bring it up every time you mention him," I grumble. "Oh quick, hide." I try and pull a befuddled Patrick behind a pillar, but I'm too late. "Shit, he's seen us."

"Well, well, well. If it isn't the cutesie Lindsey Love Loves. Tell me Lindsey, what are you loving tonight?"

I eye Jimmie 'The Jerkface' Russo as he approaches Patrick and me. He's been nicknamed The Pasta Boss, but really he's just a mediocre hack who thinks he can cook better than everyone else. He claims his Italian grandmother, *god bless her soul*, taught him everything he knows in a tiny kitchen in Little Italy. He's probably never even made homemade sauce in his life. Another thing that grates on my nerves is his New Jersey accent. He grew up outside of Dayton, Ohio, so it doesn't quite jive...I bet he's not even Italian. I wouldn't care one iota about any of this if he wasn't such a jerkface.

He slandered me on social media when my show aired calling me a 'ridiculous excuse for a food critic' and that 'I'd be better off washing his pasta dishes than in front of the camera.' His new show *The Pasta Pit* is up for the same award as *Lindsey Love Loves* and there's nothing more I'd love to do than to rub the win in his smug face.

He pretends to air-kiss me, but what I really want to do is put him in a choke hold and mess up his bleach blonde bouffant hair. I cling to Patrick a little tighter. He's somehow magically gotten a napkin full of appetizers.

"Well, don't you two look...charming. It's like *Pretty Woman* meets *Pretty in Pink*." He snidely looks us over. I always thought Jimmie was gay, but he's not cool enough to be. He's just a wannabe poser who can't find his own identity.

"Same to you, Jimmie. Did you get your suit from 1800-budget tux?"

"Oh haha, you're always so funny...you." He bops me

on my nose. "I brought some extra Kleenex for you when you *lose* tonight. *The Pasta Pit* is going to be the crown jewel of tonight's ceremony, *everyone* who's *anyone* is talking about it."

"So…no one is talking about it. Good to know, Jimbo." I pat his lapel dismissing him as I turn from him.

He grabs my arm. "You think you're untouchable, Ms. Love, like you mean something around here, but I've got news for you, you're a nobody," he hisses, his grip tight. "Some Podunk South Carolina girl who came out of the woodwork. Be prepared little lady, because I'm about to send you back to live with the termites."

I open my mouth to give it right back to this pansy-ass-munch when a voice behind me makes my vocal cords screech to a halt.

"Get your hands off of her."

The low deadly rumble rolls over my heart smashing it like a bowling ball into my ribs. I'd know that voice from anywhere. I've craved it. I've waited for that voice to reach out to me and bring me back home. I look over my shoulder as Jimmie releases his grip, loathing shining in his eyes.

"Well, look what the cat dragged in. Mr. big-shot producer. You should have come on board with me, Nick."

Patrick pops a canape into his mouth, his eyes darting back and forth as he watches the shit show unravel. I turn around, rubbing my arm where Jimmie's talons had dug in and face Nick head on. He strides toward us with a tall redhead linked on his arm. *He brought a date?* Not only did he bail on all the press releases to pump up the show before it aired, the hundreds of interviews and parties after, the lonely nights when I needed him most, but *now* he shows up on *Food and Travel's* biggest night with a red slinky on his arm? What. The. Fuck.

His sapphire-blues lock onto mine and I want to bury myself in his arms, hug him, and throat-punch him all in one beat. Ugh, I hate that he has this kind of confusing power over me. It renders me speechless...for a second.

"Nick Elliot. What the hell are you doing here?"

"Lindsey Love, what a warm welcome. I thought you'd be a little more excited than that to see me."

I see red is what I see. "You egotistical—"

"Oh my gosh! Lindsey Love? Nick has told me so much about you!" the redhead pipes up in a sugary, twangy accent. She shimmies over to me because her mermaid style dress is too tight to take normal steps in. Her honeysuckle perfume wafts over me as she squeezes me into a tight hug.

"Uh..."

"Honey, you need to give her some breathing room."

Honey? He calls his date sweet endearing nicknames while he called me his *Pain in the Ass?* Honey is a term of endearment you call someone when they've been with you for months. My heart feels another fissure cracking its way through as I step back from this bubbly woman who is now shaking Jimmie's hand enthusiastically. Ugh, Jimmie. Why the hell is he still standing here at my most vulnerable moment?

I look over at Patrick silently sending out my S.O.S. cues, but he's currently busy inspecting a pig in a blanket. I clear my voice loudly and wave a hand around, giving up on being subtle.

Unfortunately, Patrick doesn't get the hint and Nick's date misinterprets my hand waving. "Oh my gosh, it *is* hotter than a jalapeño coochie in here, isn't it? My makeup is melting off my face."

Patrick chokes on the canape as sweet innocent *Honey* tries to help fan me with her clutch. I give Nick a loathing stare, silently asking him where he picked up Ms. Sugar Queen from and what time does she need to get back on her parade float, when Jimmie rudely interrupts.

"Hope you guys are prepared to lose. I'll be sure to thank you in my acceptance speech." He laughs loudly like a hyena.

"The only thing you'll be accepting tonight is a participation swag bag."

He looks me over like he's plotting some nefarious plan. "Are you going to Vicky's celebration after this?"

Vicky Calhoun is a recurring judge on many of the *Food and Travel* shows. I've heard she throws fabulous parties, but sadly, I was not invited to this one. Jimmie knows it too as he gleefully smiles at me. The jerkface is making me feel like I'm in a bad after school special where the bully loudly tells the girl she's not invited to the party, her best friend is lurking behind her eating canapes, while the varsity football captain and his cheerleader homecoming queen stand by witnessing the whole pathetic scene.

"She's going," Nick's deep voice resonates across from me.

"Oh goody! I love me some part-tays! Woop woop!" his date cheers as she tries to shimmy in her dress.

I give Nick a questioning glance as Jimmie huffs. The little toad purposefully bumps into me before brushing by

Nick. "Later, losers."

"Wow, he's not very friendly." Nick's date takes tiny steps back over to him and holds onto him tightly.

"He's a con artist is what he is," I reply as I shoot killer laser beams from my eyes in Nick's direction. Nick's eyebrows draw together as he tries to determine if I'm talking about him or Jimmie. His gaze skips over to Patrick.

"Patrick, it's good to see you, bud."

Patrick nods enthusiastically as he tries to swallow the mouth full of food.

"Lindsey, can I speak to you privately for a minute? Honey, why don't you and Patrick go get a glass of wine."

"Ooh! Okay, but I can only have a little or I get *really* giggly."

"Okay, well, you know when to cut yourself off," he says turning from them.

I fold my arms across my chest as she and Patrick totter over to the bar.

"Lindsey—"

"I don't have anything to say to you."

"I'm sorry."

I throw my arms up. "You know what? Scratch that, I have a whole lot to say to you! You have some nerve coming here tonight after completely ghosting me. I've waited for your call for six months!"

"Ghosted you?" He has the audacity to look surprised. "I couldn't contact you, but I sent you flowers every week with notes."

"How convenient that I never received them or that you changed your number," I say snidely. "And then when I finally do see you, you show up with some sweet Georgia peach on your arm."

"Honey is just a friend, Lindsey." He slides his hands up my arm, his touch igniting a fire I thought had gone dormant in me.

"I don't call my friends *Honey*. Ugh! I hate that I even care!" I shrug off his hold.

"No, her name is Honey. Honey Rothschild. That's her given name." He gives me a rueful smile as he looks over at the bar.

"Oh."

"Yeah. I did send you flowers, I don't know why they didn't get to you, and my note had my new phone number. I couldn't keep the old one for obvious reasons."

Dammit, why does he have to look so fucking good in a tux tailored perfectly to his body? He's like James Bond on crack and it's distracting the hell out of me from my mission to hate on him.

"Why didn't *you* call *me*, Nick?" I look up into his eyes, pleading for him to talk to me.

"I've got me my chardy and I'm ready to party! Woo hoo!" Honey and Patrick join us.

"Apparently Honey is a woo girl." Patrick smirks. "We better go take our seats."

Nick bends to my ear. "We'll talk later, I promise. This isn't the right time or place."

"All right!" Patrick claps. "Who's ready to kick Jimmie Russo's ass and take home some accolades?"

"Woo hoo!" Honey shouts loudly.

Nick takes Honey by the hand and walks toward the

auditorium. I'm frustrated because none of my questions have been answered and now I have to pretend for the next couple hours that he is just my producer and I am just his pain in the ass, Lindsey Love.

Patrick grabs my hand. "You okay, Lovie?"

"I feel numb, Trick. I thought you said he was out of the country."

"I swear, that was his last email to me."

"Let's just get through tonight and then I'll kick someone's ass tomorrow. By the way, worst wingman ever."

"Who me? What did I do?"

"Never mind, just don't leave me alone with those two tonight, okay?"

"Got it. Don't worry, I've got your back."

Chapter 38

Nick

Funny Honey

LINDSEY KEEPS MUMBLING about Patrick being a horrible wingman and how he'd get everyone blown up as I set a drink down in front of her at Vicky's after-party. Honey is babbling on about some story, talking to anyone who will listen, and Patrick is on the dancefloor with a woman he met at the bar.

People keep coming up to Lindsey and congratulating her. She flashes them a quick smile and then scowls as soon as they leave. She should be on cloud nine, not down in the dumps. We beat out Jimmie Russo in our shared category and I couldn't be prouder of her. The show has gotten rave reviews and she's already set with *Food and Travel* to do a second season. They asked me if I wanted to produce, but I told them I had other obligations…that was until tonight, when the CEO personally asked me to head up the project.

I eye Lindsey over my glass. I know she's angry with me. She has every right to be, but I'm mad at her too. I did try and convey to her that I was still thinking about her by sending her flowers the first month she was back home. When she didn't acknowledge them, I came to see her against my better judgment...well, by that point Mrs. Bixby made it clear she had moved on.

What was I supposed to do? I was trying to protect her. After a treacherous meeting in Morocco I had to disassociate with her. I couldn't put her in any more danger.

"How's your mom, Lindsey?"

She eyes me curiously. "She's good, why do you ask?"

I raise my eyebrows surprised about how casual she sounds. "Having a face transplant is a pretty big deal."

Lindsey spits out her martini on the table and then immediately starts apologizing profusely to Honey and some other people next to our table. "What are you talking about?"

"Oh my God, your mom had a face transplant? I've always wondered what that would be like...you know, if I had to have someone else's face on me. I'd probably pick Giselle. She's got great bone structure." Honey takes a big gulp of chardonnay and starts to giggle. "If I picked Ellen, I wonder if that would make me funny..." She gasps. "Do you think that would make me gay?"

Okay, so it was a bad idea bringing Honey along. I see that now.

"You can't turn gay from a face transplant, Honey." Lindsey pats her shoulder as she looks over at me with a quizzical look, probably wondering where I found her. "Where did you come up with the idea my mom got a face transplant?"

"When I came to see you. I stopped by and talked to your neighbor, Mrs. Bixby. She told me you had just visited your mom in the hospital with your boyfriend Roman because she had just had a face transplant."

"What? I don't know anyone named Roman…"

"Oh my gosh, this sounds just like an episode of *Days of our Lives!*" Honey cries.

The problem with my brain is that I have a photographic memory. I can remember every single detail from years before. I remember every conversation, every feeling, even the temperature and time that conversation took place. Some days, I wish I could erase my brain and start over, like right now.

I watch Lindsey chew her bottom lip in confusion as she tries to figure out what I'm referring to. The party is loud, Honey is incessantly chatting and giggling in my ear, while the music plays some hip-hop beat. I wish I could start over with Lindsey from the very first time we met and be a different guy. A guy that doesn't have secrets. A guy that wasn't using her to get a mission done. A guy that she could fall in love with.

I remember Lindsey's sopping wet hair and large evergreen eyes as she stared at me across the booth at the diner. I remember the waitress Mary taking her order and The Four Tops were playing "When She Was My Girl" while it poured outside. I remember being a total dick to her and yet, she still sat there smiling at me. I remember thinking this woman was going to turn my world upside down.

"Honestly, I have no idea what you're talking about. You must be confused."

"Well, see that's the problem. I'm never confused."

Lindsey rolls her eyes. "Oh really? Because I'm pretty sure you got *us* confused."

"Oh, did the two of you used to be an item?" Honey pipes up.

"No," we both say at the same time. Lindsey glares at me.

"Honey, would you mind getting me another whiskey? Thanks." I gulp my drink and hand it to her, turning my attention back to Lindsey. "How did I get us confused?"

"You came in here tonight looking all sexy in your tuxedo, bringing Honey with you hoping it would make me so jealous that I wouldn't be able to see straight because you meant something to me. You were hoping I'd tell you I've missed you, that I can't live without you. But I don't miss you. I don't even *think* about you. And when I saw you tonight it wasn't with longing, it was with loathing. What happened in Paris was just sex, Nick."

"Really, so that was all an act? You didn't feel anything for me?"

She swallows thickly and lifts her chin. "Yes, it was all an act."

"That's bullshit and you know it."

"Well, you won't have to worry about whether it's bullshit or not. After tonight, you'll never have to see me again."

"Lindsey..." I scramble trying to fix this broken rollercoaster we're on. Every time we're about to get to the top it stalls. "I've accepted the offer to be your producer on the next round of *Lindsey Love Loves...*" I hadn't signed papers, but she didn't need to know that.

"What?" she splutters as she looks around the room in panic. "No! No, no, no."

"Yes. I was approached again by the head of *Food and*

Travel tonight. After the awards we took home, they don't want anyone else. I agreed. Don't you get it? This is the big time for you."

"And I thought that didn't matter to you!" She gulps her drink as her eyes crazily race around the room.

A polished black-haired woman steps up to our table. "Well hello, Mr. Elliot, we've never officially met. My name is Margot Reed." She offers her hand to me, which I politely shake. "I'm Lindsey's publicist."

"You can call me Nick." I flash her a smile not letting on that Lindsey and I were just quietly arguing.

"Where is Simon, is he around?"

"Ah, I'm afraid he's no longer with *Food and Travel*." Lindsey arches an eyebrow at me as she takes a sip of her martini.

"That's a shame." Margo pouts. "Lindsey, there's someone I want to introduce you to if I'm not interrupting anything."

Lindsey pops out of her chair. "Nope, I'd love to meet someone, but first Margo, maybe you can settle something Nick and I were discussing."

"Oh, I'd be happy to." Margot gives me a friendly wink.

"Is it true Nick will be producing my second season?"

Margot smiles confidently as she holds her two fingers behind her ear. "That's the word on the street. You both did so great the first round. There's even talk of an Emmy," she whispers excitedly. "I was actually going to introduce you to Dan Turner. He's the CEO of *Food and Travel Network*."

Lindsey gives me one last grim look as she walks away with Margot. Honey huffs down next to me and starts uncontrollably giggling. I don't want to give her the satisfaction of asking her what she finds so funny, but maybe it will make her stop.

"What's so funny, Honey?"

"Huh? Oh, I don't know, I've already forgotten. But that rhymes! That should be my new nickname, Funny Honey!" She bursts into peals of laughter and the sound rubs my nerves raw. I shouldn't have brought her. Lindsey's right, I did want to make her jealous after Mrs. Bixby told me she had a parade of men in and out. I assumed she'd bring a date, not Patrick. But that plan backfired big time because Lindsey didn't care, and now I have a blitzed Honey to take care of. I'm going to kill my sister Kelsey for setting me up with her.

"I think I should take you home, Honey."

"Why?" She hiccups. "Some guy over at the bar invited me to another party after this." She starts to giggle and hiccup and it's all I can do to stay seated and remain calm.

"Honey, you are under no obligation to stay with me here tonight, but I'm leaving early because I need to head to my parents' house in the morning."

"Aw! Are you asking me to meet your parents? That's so sweet, I'd love to!" she gushes as she wraps her arms around my neck.

"No, Honey." I gently extract her from me. Shit, how do I get myself in these situations? I scrub my hands down my face. "No, I'm not inviting you along. I'm just telling you that I need to leave here soon."

Honey hunches forward and starts to cry. "You don't like me?" People walk by our table and give me horrible looks because I'm a dick for making his date cry.

"Honey, shh, listen to me. You've had too much to drink. I'm going to take you home now."

"But the guy at the bar wants to take me out," she whines and for a split second, I almost welcome the idea, but she's had too much to drink and I'm not about to send her off with a total stranger. Besides, my sister would have my balls cut off.

Honey slowly slides out of her chair and slinks down to the floor, like her body just went boneless and she melted.

"Honey? Honey are you okay?" I try to heft her back up, but her damn dress is slippery. She starts to giggle again and it reminds me of a dolphin when it chatters. "Honey, can you please get off the floor? You're embarrassing me."

"It's sleepy time, Nick." She lays her head down on the floor.

"Oh, for fuck's sake."

Patrick walks up. "Wow, is she okay?"

"Yeah, just too much chardonnay." Thank god Lindsey isn't witnessing this. "Hey Patrick, can you help me lift her up and then I can get it her to the limo."

"Yeah sure, no problem, man. Where's Lindsey?"

"She's walking around with Margot."

Patrick and I manage to get Honey on her seat. She's thin but gangly and her tight satin mermaid dress doesn't help. There's nothing to grab onto. Honey's head lolls forward and *thunks* on the table.

"She's out, dude."

"Thanks for that keen observation."

"I don't think there's a way to discreetly get her out of

here."

"Nope." I eye the distance from the table to the door. I'll have to walk right by the bar which is ten people deep. I turn back to Patrick.

"By the way, I'm producing season two of Lindsey's show. I want you filming. We'll be heading to Africa."

"Seriously?" Patrick's voice cracks in excitement. "Yes! I'm in! Does Lindsey know?"

"Not the details. I figure you can fill her in. I'll see you soon."

Patrick's face falls in disappointment. "Why do I have to break it to her?"

"Because you're my sidekick."

"I knew it!" He fist-pumps the air. I lift Honey up and heft her over my shoulder. The crowd at the bar cheers as I walk her through. This night couldn't have been more of a nightmare.

Chapter 39

Lindsey

I'm Not His Girlfriend

I SWALLOW BACK my nerves as I pull up to Nick's cabin in Upstate New York. Dan Turner wanted me to stay back in the city for a few days to talk about the second season and where he sees this show going. I wasn't expecting it to go to Africa, that's for sure. I'm angry with Nick. I'm pissed he's inserting himself back into my life...into my career, and there's not a damn thing I can do about it. Patrick told me he was at the cabin, so I decided to come up here and convince him to back out. Yeah, I'm annoyed Patrick knows where he is and I don't.

There are several cars in the driveway that weren't here the last time I was. I wipe my sweaty palms on my jeans and ring the doorbell. I can hear voices from inside and I'm about to say screw it and hightail it back to my car when the front door swings open. A woman, I'm guessing to be in her mid-thirties, smiles at me. "Hi, can I help you?"

"Uh, hi yes...is Nick home by chance?"

"Who is it, Arden?" Another woman pops up behind her and smiles.

"I don't know, Kelsey, back up so I can let her in. I'm so

sorry, please come in, I didn't catch your name."

"Oh, it's—"

"Oh my God, it's Lindsey Love!" A third woman pops up from the sectional in the living room to join the other two who are curiously eyeing me over. They all have Nick's same shade of blue eyes. "What are you doing here? Are you lost? Are we on some new show where you pop into people's houses and see what they're cooking? This is so awesome!"

"Bridget, Jesus, take a breath and give the poor woman a chance to talk," Arden yells over her shoulder. "Besides, she's looking for Nick."

"Our Nick? Little dick Nick?"

I cough into my hand trying to cover the laugh that bubbles up. These women must be Nick's sisters. They pull me farther into the house not giving me a chance to run. I look around the living room, and nod my head hello to two men watching a golf on the television, but there's no sign of Nick.

The three sisters steer me toward the kitchen where two women are cooking. Kids are running in and out from the back porch. It's a lot more chaotic than the last time I was here.

"Mom, Mary Katherine, look who just rang our doorbell! It's Lindsey Love from *Food and Travel Network!*" Bridget bounces on her toes in excitement causing me to blush.

"Yeah, and you won't believe who she's looking for…Nick!" Arden smiles widely.

"Oh, well welcome, Lindsey!" Mrs. Elliot wipes her hands on a dish towel. "I'm a hugger. My name is Anne." She gives me a light hug and then looks at me worriedly.

"Did Nick tell you to meet him here? He's out right now…"
She looks at her daughters.

"Oh, um…" Shit this is awkward. "I'm actually here
because—"

"Oh! You have to join us for dinner. MK is making her
lemon chicken which is insanely good." Bridget drags me
over to a stool at the kitchen island and pushes me down
onto it.

"Jesus, Bridget, give the poor girl some room. Sorry, she's
obsessed with your show."

I smile weakly. "Oh it's no prob—"

"Oh my God, I died over that episode when you were in
London. That was freaking hilarious. Did you really eat
scorpion? You could hear it crunching and the look on your
face, I nearly peed in my pants. Oh, and when you hit Rico
with the churro." She snorts. "But my favorite is still Paul's
balls, so funny. Did he really get tasered?"

"I'm going to taser you if you don't give her some space.
Lindsey, just ignore her. I'm Mary Katherine, but you can
call me MK. That's Arden, Bridget, and Kelsey. Can we get
you something to drink?"

"I'm…" A glass of chardonnay gets shoved in my hand
before I can blink. "Oh okay, this is great. Thank you."

Geez, these four are like Shannon on crack. No wonder
Nick is always so quiet and reserved. They just railroad right
over you.

"So is Nick going to be here soon?" The sooner I can talk
to him and convince him to drop the show, the sooner I can
go back to the city and get out of this mess.

"So how do you know Nick, Lindsey?" MK asks as she

slices lemons.

"He was my producer on my last show."

"Shut the front door! Nick produced *Lindsey Love Loves...Europe*? I swear he never tells us anything!"

I look up at five sets of curious eyes looking me over. Yikes. "Yeah, we were in Europe last fall for it."

"Oh, I knew Nick was over in Europe for work, but I didn't know he was producing a cooking show." Anne flashes me a genuine smile.

"There's a lot Nick doesn't reveal apparently," I murmur into my glass. "Where's Sasha?" I look around curiously.

"Oh, have you met her?" Arden smiles knowingly at Mary Katherine.

"Uh...yes. Nick and I stayed here before we left for Europe."

"Oh, wait a minute!" Bridget snaps her fingers.

"She's the pukey underwear girl," Kelsey and Bridget say in unison.

"Uh..." Shit, I had forgotten Sasha had puked my underwear on the couch. "Oh my goodness, I'm so sorry about that." I can feel my cheeks fire up.

"Dear, don't give it another thought," Anne says kindly. "Kelsey and Bridget, mind your manners please."

I take a large gulp of wine. "Anyway, he wanted me to try Betty's Fish Camp as a practice run before we went abroad."

"Did he now?" Kelsey smiles at her sisters.

"Yes, but it was closed. I'm sorry, I thought you all knew I had stayed here."

"Nonsense. We love having the kids' friends stay here.

Such a shame about Betty's. It's been there forever. But she was ready to retire and her kids didn't want to take it over." Anne dries a dish while she surreptitiously looks over at me. "Are you staying the night?"

"Oh, I was going to head back into the city after I talked to Nick."

"But you just got here. No need to drive hours back tonight, besides we have plenty of room here."

"Oh no, I couldn't impose."

"Any friend of Nick's is a friend of ours." Arden smiles, but it makes me feel uneasy. Like I'm a part of some joke, but I don't know the punchline. Anne excuses herself as she steps out on the back porch to go in search of Mr. Elliot.

"So Lindsey, have you and my brother had sexual relations?"

"Oh my God, Kelsey! You can't ask her that!" Bridget chastises her.

"What? Just trying to assess the situation." Four pairs of eyes turn to me.

"Uh..." I can feel my cheeks burn.

"Don't answer that, Lindsey. Look, Nick may be cute on the outside, but he's a pain in the ass," MK says as she slices carrots.

"I'm aware," I say under my breathe.

"Did you know he wet his bed up until freshman year of high school?" Arden raises her eyebrows at me, so I do the same in return.

"That's...um..."

"Don't give him bean burritos. He'll have diarrhea for days. Remember that time he sharted in his pants out on the lake?" Kelsey laughs as the other three join in with her.

"Oh…uh…"

"Oh! Remember the time he had to go to the emergency room when he got his peewee stuck in his zipper?" The four of them start laughing hysterically and I can't help but giggle along with them.

"Wait! Wait, no! Remember the time he got caught by Nana Kay jerking off in the pantry when he was twelve?"

"Jesus fucking Christ! Are you fucking kidding me right now?" Thunderous blue eyes sweep across the five of us effectively shutting everyone up. Sasha trots up to my side and nudges my hand.

"Aw look, Sasha likes Nick's girlfriend."

"She's not my girlfriend."

"I'm not his girlfriend."

"Seriously, is it your mission in life to embarrass me?" Nick growls at his sisters.

The four sisters smile at each other and in unison answer a resounding *yes*.

His gaze makes me want to crawl under the nearest rock. "What are you doing here?"

"Nicholas James Elliot! Is that any way to speak to a guest in my home?" Anne screeches from the back door.

Nick ducks his head. "No, ma'am."

"It's an hour until dinnertime. Why don't you grab Lindsey's bag and take it to your room? Make sure there are fresh sheets on your bed."

Nick grinds his teeth, his hard-blue eyes raking over me briefly leaving me feeling like a squished bug. "Let's go."

I drain my glass of chardonnay needing all the liquid

encouragement as his sisters start whispering and giggling. Let's be honest, I'd much rather stay and hear more embarrassing stories about Nick than be alone with him. He kisses his mom's cheek and bangs out the back door.

"Good luck with that one, sweetie." Anne gently squeezes my shoulder as I reluctantly follow Nick. Only the kids are on the back porch playing board games so I look out over the rail and spy Nick down by the dock. I quickly gather my courage and jog down to the dock.

"What are you doing here, Lindsey?" His attitude and clipped voice scream *I don't want you here* as he unties a rope attached to the dock. He jumps into a small boat and reaches a hand out to me.

"What…what are you doing?"

"Get in the boat."

"Wh…why are we taking out this small dingy instead of that nice sailboat on the other side of the dock?"

"Because I'm not in the mood to go sailing."

"I'm not getting in that canoe."

"It's a bass fishing boat."

"No."

"Get. In. The. God. Damn. Boat, Lindsey." He impatiently waggles his hand at me.

"Aren't we supposed to be changing sheets? What's your sudden obsession with boating? Are you going to take me out into the middle of the lake and drown me?"

His nostrils flare. "Pretty fucking tempted now that you mention it."

"It would never work. Too many witnesses."

"I used to plan 'accidents' for a living."

I gulp. "Are you serious?"

"A pain in the ass as always. No, I'm not serious." Before I can process what he's doing, he grabs my arm and yanks me into the boat, catching me so I don't stumble. He shoves me into a chair and plunks a life preserver in my lap. "If I were going to kill you, I wouldn't give you a life preserver."

I swallow. "Well how the hell am I supposed to know if you're kidding? I don't know anything about you! Are you going to tell me who you really are?"

"You know the real me."

"I don't think I do."

"You do."

"Goddamn it, Nick! If that's even your real name…tell me the truth!"

"You don't want to know my truths…my demons."

I ignore his dark statement. "I think you owe me that, don't you? After putting Patrick and me right in the line of your bullshit, you owe me at least that. I want answers." I clutch the life preserver tightly to my chest and look over the side at the water churning.

"I wouldn't jump in if I were you. It's chilly."

He's right of course. It's spring and the air is chilly, so the water is undoubtedly cold. "Why again do we have to sneak off in a boat?"

"Because there are eyes and ears everywhere at the house."

"Oh my god, your house is *bugged*? Is your family in danger? Is that even your real family?"

Nick snorts and looks at me quizzically. "Look up at the back porch."

I look up to see his four sisters passing binoculars back and forth as they watch us in the boat.

"The only danger we're in is from those four gossip mongers."

"Oh," I say, waving to them and feeling stupid for letting my limited spy knowledge get the best of me.

He steers the boat away from the house out into the middle of the lake. The late-afternoon sunshine on my face is welcome, and if I didn't want to strangle the man across from me, I might actually enjoy myself.

He cuts the engine and turns in his chair to look at me, mulling something over. We sit in silence, bobbing with the small waves. I hug the preserver and drink him in. I've missed him. He's so fucking sexy as he sits there in his joggers and a black t-shirt pulled tight across his chest. His jaw ticks as we stare at each other.

"What are you doing here, Lindsey?"

I flip him the quarter I've had clenched in my hand since I walked in to the house. He deftly catches it out of the air. If I weren't so nervous, I'd be impressed. "I'm phoning a friend."

"I'm not your friend."

I tilt my head as I stare at him. If that's not a punch in the gut, I don't know what is. *What happened to the nice guy from the other night?* "I guess we finally agree on something."

He silently stares at me and it makes me fidget. "Did you really get your penis caught in your zipper?"

"What? No." He runs his fingers through his hair. "Don't believe anything those four tell you. Jesus, that was from *Something About Mary*."

"So...you didn't get caught by your grandmother spanking off in the pantry?"

He shakes his head and blushes. "I have a hard time believing you came all this way to ask me if I got caught jerking off by my nana."

I take a deep breath. "You're right. I came to ask if you would let someone else produce the show. I reall—"

"No."

"What? Why not?"

"Because the ink is already dry on the papers. I explained to Dan that I would be in Africa during that time filming the rhinos, but we could work in some shows along with it. He thought it was brilliant. Sorry, Lindsey, but you don't get a say in this."

Fury bubbles up like acid burning my throat. "The hell I don't! This is *my* show! I'll just refuse to do it then." I pout as I fold my arms over my chest.

"I figured you say that. You're under contract, Lindsey. Those contracts you signed with Simon say in the fine print that you are obligated for a second season if the show is successful. To be honest, you're not in a position to say no. Get a second season under your belt and then you can tell them where you want to go. Trust Margot, she has your best interests at heart."

"And what about you? Do you have my best interests at heart?" I narrow my eyes at him, something not quite adding up. "What happened to Simon Blake anyway? He just...disappeared? When I mentioned him to Dan he implied that Simon worked for you, not the other way around."

Nick sighs and looks out over the water. "It's a long story."

I drum my fingers on my leg. "I'm in the middle of a lake on a boat. I've got time."

"It could get you killed."

I huff out an annoyed breath. "I'll take my chances. I've already survived a bombing."

He flinches, but quickly recovers as he ties a small thin rope in different knots in his hand. "Simon recruited me after the SEALs to work with a group called the Syndicate. We were an elite security team that no one could touch. CIA, FBI...no one could touch us because we had protection from a very influential senator."

"Oh my god, you *are* Jason Bourne. Do you have an imbedded tracking chip?"

He snorts and shakes his head. "No, that's just Hollywood stuff. I have a photographic memory and I can speak up to eight languages fluently. I was the guy that would go in, meet with the informant and collect information. I'm trained to kill, but that rarely ever has to happen. The first mission I went on, I did for Mike. I thought if I could help get the bad guys, it would make his death seem"—he scrubs his face—"like his death wasn't for nothing.

"Anyway, one mission turned into more. Simon knew I wanted to get into directing and producing and called in some favors. The senator loved the idea of using television documentaries as a good cover for my role in the Syndicate. I did a few small documentaries and then I was approached by E&N network to do *Naked in the Wild*. It was a huge success, but it almost cost me my life."

"Why?"

"Because I had an undercover mission I was doing for the Syndicate at the same time between a Colombian drug lord and the Russians. It didn't end well. That's when I said enough, but Simon needed one more, and I was already involved with *Food and Travel Network* at the time, so I agreed, one more and I'm out."

He looks at me and gives me a sad smile. "Simon found out Margot was actively looking for a show for you and I was in talks with *Food and Travel* to work on *The Pasta Pit.*"

"No!" I gasp. "You were going to produce that dumpster fire?"

He chuckles. "Yeah, but then Simon saw an opportunity to use your show as a cover to go unnoticed around Europe. I was working a double assignment—producing your show and gathering some intel that the senator needed desperately, but as you know, things went awry. Claudine turned out to be a traitor and tried to have me killed."

"Wait...Russian Barbie is a spy?" I screech. "Why would she try and kill her summer childhood fling?"

"I never lived in Germany as a teenager, that was just a cover." He grimaces as he looks up from his knot tying. "Simon had set up our meeting. It...didn't go as expected. She was very upset when you tried to bring that guy along."

"John from Florida...Oh my God, you mean I sat there and made an ass out of myself in front of a *spy?*"

He chuffs out a laugh. "What am I, minced meat?"

I wave a hand dismissing his fragile ego. "Do you think John from Florida was a spy too?"

"No, I think he was an idiot that placed himself in a

precarious situation."

"So, I'm confused…how did Simon tie into *Food And Travel?*"

"He didn't. He posed as an executive producer, but it was just to get me tied to you. I was already in with *Food and Travel*, so it just made sense. To *Food and Travel* execs, he was my personal assistant."

"Shut up," I say in wonder as I look at him. "Why involve Simon? Why didn't you just approach Margot yourself?"

"Because it was Simon's idea. To be honest, I didn't really want to get involved with your show. He introduced himself first so that he could assess the situation."

"Assess the situation…" Hurt burns like a wildfire in my chest, spreading fast and furious, but I don't let it show. "Is your name really Nick Elliot?"

Nick gives me a sexy half grin. "Yeah, it is. Sometimes it's Nick Scar, but this last time I used my real name."

"Is the Syndicate a bad group? Or are you one of the good guys?" *Please be a good guy, please.*

"The Syndicate members are good guys. They are ex-military who want to protect our country. Sometimes we get a bad apple in the bunch, but they get dealt with in due time."

I shake my head squeezing the life jacket to me as my brain tries to keep up. He waves to a passing boat like we aren't having the most intense conversation of my life out here in the middle of a lake. "I got out."

"What do you mean you 'got out'?"

"I told Simon after Paris that I was done with the Syndicate. I went into it thinking I'd do one or two missions…five years later here we are."

"On a boat in the middle of a lake."

He laughs. "Something like that. Me wanting out didn't go down too favorably. There's a situation going on that I can't tell you about…I'm trying to tie up all the loose ends before we can go to Africa. I'm hoping it will be done soon, but I still need you to be careful."

I look at him dubiously. "They'll never let you go, Nick. You know too much. They'll kill you."

He shakes his head. "Again, Hollywood. The only way they would kill me is if I betrayed them and turned. I've taken an oath to my country. I want my simple life. I'm sorry for what happened in Paris, that you and Patrick were put in harm's way. I've been beating myself up the last few months telling myself to just forget you."

"Yeah." I look down and fidget with the buckle on my life vest. He's told me a lot and I can't quite fully process it all. I'm understanding things a little better now. "What about Honey?"

Nick shakes his head. "Honey was a friend of Kelsey's. You were correct in your assumption that I brought her to make you jealous."

"Why the hell would you want to make me jealous?"

"Because Mrs. Bixby said you were dating a new guy every night."

I groan. *Fucking Mrs. Bixby, of course she would say that to him.*

"And you believed that old bat? And by the way, who the fuck do you know that gets a face transplant like it's no biggie? That senile devil's spawn was probably retelling a soap opera episode like Honey said."

He rubs his jaw looking chagrined. "I thought it was strange, but I didn't know."

"Pretty sure I would have mentioned that to you."

He shakes his head. "I don't know, she scared me."

I snort out a laugh. "*You* were scared of Mrs. Bixby? Damn I wish I could have been a fly on the wall for that one."

"So...you weren't dating other men when you got back from Europe?"

I look away, my cheeks heating. "No. I told you dating never exactly worked out for me. Case in point." I gesture between us.

"Hmm...it's probably for the best...you and me. You know...having to have a working relationship and all."

My heart sinks further than I thought was possible. I want to reach out and grab him, beg him to let me back in, but I don't. This tattered heart knows when it's had enough. "Probably so." I shift in my seat. "So, you're not going to step down and let me go my own way with *Lindsey Love Loves?*"

"And miss out on the chance to see you eat snails again? They are like the size of tennis balls in Africa." He winks at me and I cringe just thinking about it. "Not a chance. You're stuck with me."

We sit in silence for a moment not sure where to go from here. "Hey, Lindsey?" he says eventually.

"Yes?"

"Can we have a do-over?"

I sigh, feeling worn out. All the fire I had built up on the way here has slowly petered out. I should have just called him. It's torturous having to look at his handsome face as he gently friend-zones me. But even so, I'd always give him do-over. "Yeah."

He smiles at me as he starts the boat up again and heads back to his house.

Now I have to sit through dinner with his family when all I really want to do is curl up in a ball and cry my heart out.

Chapter 40

Lindsey

Get Down

A NOISE WAKES me from a dreamless sleep. I can't believe this. I knew I should have stayed at a hotel. I'm practically hanging off the bed trying to get as far away as possible from Nick, not daring to move a muscle. His mom and sisters insisted I stay. Nick never said a word one way or the other. When he crawled into bed tonight just wearing his boxer briefs my heart went into a lust driven cardiac arrest. I had a difficult time tearing my eyes away from him as he got into his side of the bed.

He was the last man I had sex with and I can remember every hard edge of muscle on his body vividly. He's stayed true to his 'let's just be friends' policy and hasn't tried to kiss or snuggle with me during the night. It probably doesn't help that his sister let me borrow some sleepwear—an oversized plaid nightshirt that makes me look like I'm fourteen and Amish. It screams the opposite of sexy.

All the kids are upstairs on the sectional "camping out" and the sisters and their husbands are in the spare rooms while his parents have the master bedroom upstairs. Nick has the master suite downstairs which I didn't even realize existed until tonight. Thankfully we're in a king-sized bed with plenty of room to keep our distance.

Heavy panting in my face causes my nose to scrunch in disgust. Why is Nick breathing so heavily? He's in serious need of a breath mint. I can't sleep with his hot stinky breath on my face. I pop one eye open and yelp in surprise. A big black bear is staring me right in the face...wait, not a bear...just Sasha. I reach out and stroke her head.

"What's up, friend?" I ask groggily. "We need to have a serious talk about your dental hygiene." I look over my shoulder at Nick's silhouette in the dark as he steadily breathes in and out, quiet as a mouse. My bladder is about to explode, so I gingerly get out of bed and head to the ensuite bathroom.

I fumble in the dark as I make my way back to my side of the bed. I gently pull back the covers not wanting to wake up Nick. I slip into bed but collide with a mass of fur.

"Sasha! Get out of bed," I hiss. Sasha stretches but makes no move to leave. "Sasha, get down!" I whisper harshly. Ugh, she probably only listens to foreign commands.

"Sasha! *Nein!* No, get down! What the hell is the Afghan-istan word for no?" I cry out as I shove her, but she's like trying to move a moose, or what I imagine it would be like to move a moose. I haven't actually tried as moose aren't rampant in South Carolina, but it's safe to say, she ain't budging. I check the time on my phone, three-thirty a.m. Ugh, it's not like I can even get up early and start my day. I'd wake the whole house up if I went upstairs. How the hell is Nick sleeping through this?

I pace the bedroom just wanting to go back to bed.

Should I wake Nick up? We didn't exactly go to bed on the best of terms last night. I was cranky and snappy and he was quiet after his sisters peppered me with ninety-nine thousand questions over dinner.

I walk back over to my side and squeeze in next to Sasha. She stretches and kicks her leg into my back. I shove in to her with my butt determined to get some space on the bed. A low growl has me freezing. I cling to the edge of the bed and pull the thin sheet up to my chin. Okay, okay...I can hang like this...no big deal.

Sasha pushes her feet against my back shoving me off the side of the bed. I fall to the floor with an oomph. Maybe I'll just sleep here. Hardwood floors are good for achy backs, right? I think about the soft bed with fluffy blankets and Nick's warm body. The sheets smell like Downy and him. The hardwood floor smells like Murphy's oil soap. Okay, it sucks and I don't want to sleep down here.

I stand up and assess the situation. All one hundred and twenty pounds of Sasha is lying diagonal across the bed with her head on my pillow. That little shit. I get on my knees at the end of the bed and try to roll her but she's not budging. I crawl over to Nick's side of the bed.

"Nick," I whisper. "Nick, wake up."

I'm scared to wake him. What if he does some reflexive karate chop move to my face? I sit back on my haunches in case he does strike out. "Niiiick!"

Nothing. *What the hell?* I thought he was supposed to be alert at all times? I stand up, fidgeting as I ponder what to do. Hopefully the kids upstairs don't hear me. "Nick!" I shout in his ear and then run to the bathroom. I sneak a peek around the corner. Nick is sitting up in bed rubbing a hand down his face.

"Oh good, you're up," I say cheerfully.

"What time is it?" His voice is low, gruff, and sexy as hell.

"Oh, not too early...just a nice rooster cocka-doodle-doo three forty-five a.m."

Nick looks at me like I'm deranged. I don't blame him. "Why the hell are you up at three forty-five?"

"Ha, well, truly I was up at three-thirty. Funny story actually..." Nick doesn't look like he's in the mood for a laugh so I cut right to the chase. "Sasha stole my side of the bed."

"How did she kick you out of bed?" Nick looks over and pushes her. "Sasha, down."

Sasha immediately gets down off the bed. "How the hell did you do that?" I ask with my hands on my hips. "I told her to get down."

"No, the command is just *down*."

"Oh, for Pete's sake."

"You better get in bed before she changes her mind." He sexily smirks.

I scramble over to my side of the bed and get in under the covers. I feel Nick turn toward me. Strong arms reach out and pull me into him.

"Pain in my ass, come here." He spoons my back to his front.

I freeze in his arms, confusion making me unsure of what to do. Do friends snuggle like this in bed? I mean, I'm not going to turn down being his snuggle buddy. I relax a fraction as his heat envelopes me. I breathe in his masculine scent that's uniquely Nick and sigh in contentment. *So good.*

"Lindsey?"

"Yeah?"

"Did you just smell me?"

"Yeah." I sigh, not caring anymore what a weirdo I am for Nick Elliot. His chest vibrates with laughter against my back. He runs his fingers through my hair and I purr in contentment. If this is what friends do, then I like being his friend. I try to picture Patrick doing this to me and I grimace in revulsion. Ugh, that would just be awkward and weird, but it's not with Nick.

"I tried to forget you, but I can't. You're like a drug that lingers in my system. I need the adrenalin kick you give me. I'm addicted to your taste, your smell…I'm addicted to you and I don't want to get clean."

My eyes pop open. Holy shit, did I just hear him correctly? "What are you trying to say?" I rasp out.

He rolls me toward him and I let him, loose like a ragdoll. "I was lying earlier when I thought we could just be friends." He caresses my cheek with his fingertips. "I want more."

More…what does that even mean? A higher degree than what we hope to have? I want this elusive more too, but his definition might be slightly skewed from mine. It's a slippery slope and I'm scared to hand over my heart for him to pick apart.

"What do you mean by more?" I whisper.

He kisses me gently, softly coaxing my lips apart. I sigh as I taste him, wanting so much more too. He deepens the kiss and I moan as I run my hands down his muscular back. He breaks the kiss, both of us panting with want and need. "I've missed you so much," he murmurs as he looks into my eyes. "I want all of you. I want to be your twenty-five-cent call and for you to be mine. I'm tired of trying to stay away, trying to convince myself it's for the best. I don't want to anymore."

I reach up and kiss his lips, sealing my fate to his, swallowing his words because I want it too.

I lean up as he peels off my nightgown. "God, that thing was hideous." He smiles down at me as he captures a nipple in his mouth. I arch into him, wanting more.

"I think your sisters were trying to protect my virtue."

"I think my sisters were just being assholes."

I laugh as I quickly shimmy out of my panties and we're finally skin to skin. My fingers touch every hard ridge, every bunched muscle I've fantasized about as he holds himself over me. He smiles down at me and it takes my breath away, he's so handsome and he's *mine*. I trace my finger over his brows, his straight nose, and full lips.

He bends his head and kisses me as if it will be our last time. He blazes a path from my lips down to my breast, his tongue lavishing my other nipple as zinging heat explodes right to my core. He inserts a finger into my slick heat causing me to bow off the bed with need. "So wet for me, *meine schöne*."

"Only for you," I whisper back.

"I don't have a condom."

"I'm on the Pill."

"I'm clean."

"Me too."

He enters me slowly allowing me to adjust to his size. I wrap my legs around him and arch, taking him fully. He groans as he pumps in and out. "God, you feel so fucking good, Lindsey." He sits up on his knees, grabbing my hips for leverage as he pounds into me, rubbing his thumb in circles against my clit. My orgasm builds quickly and I want to hang on...to make this last longer, but I can't. Stars dance across my closed eyes as I luxuriate in the incredible high he has me flying on.

"God, yes Lindsey, so fucking good," he whispers as he pulls me up into his arms so that I'm straddling him. He sucks on my nipple as he bounces me on him and the second wave catches me by surprise as it crashes roughly over me. "I've missed you so much."

Nick quickly comes with me, spilling into me as I ride the wave of pure bliss, washing me away right along with him.

He takes more from me than I knew I wanted to give. He takes everything my heart can offer as we make love into the early morning light.

Chapter 41

Nick

Noodles and Other Little Things

HEAVY SNORING STARTLES me awake. I sit up in bed and smile down at the sleeping beauty and my dog next to me. When did Sasha get back on the bed? Lindsey's arm is thrown over Sasha's side as she spoons the dog that's almost as big as she is. Her mouth slightly open as she snores along with the dog. I get out my phone and take a picture because I know she'll deny it.

"Sasha, down," I say quietly. She immediately jumps off the bed and slinks out of the room. I pull Lindsey to me and nuzzle my nose into her warm neck. She smells like vanilla and baked goods, it almost makes me want to eat her. *Oh wait, I already did that.* I smirk as I think back to the mind-blowing sex we had last night. Feeling her without the barrier of a condom was incredible. I feel such an emotional connection with her that I've never felt with anyone else.

I nibble her neck causing her to squirm.

"Mmm...noodles," she murmurs.

"Noodles?" I chuckle. "What are you dreaming about?"

"Tie me up, bad boy." She smiles sleepily, her eyes closed. "Oh yeah...noodles."

"Do you want udon or rice noodles?" I smirk.

"Spank me with that noodle." She giggles.

"That better be dream Nick you're asking to spank you." I gently bite her earlobe.

She sighs. "Me likey noodles."

I laugh as I try to shake her awake, but she starts to snore again. I get up and head into the bathroom to take a shower before the whole house wakes up and takes all the hot water. I was hoping Lindsey would have joined me in the shower, but when I walk back into the bedroom she's sprawled out across the bed diagonally, drooling on my pillow.

I jog upstairs and run into my sister Arden in the kitchen. She gives me an all-knowing smile over her coffee cup as I take two coffee mugs down.

"What?"

She shrugs. "I didn't say anything."

"You're saying it with your eyes."

"Morning, sleepyheads." Kelsey strolls into the kitchen in her PJs. "Coffee stat."

I pour her a cup and reach up to get another mug.

"Where's Lindsey?" Bridget bounces into the kitchen having just come back from a run. She gulps down some water as she waits for my answer. "Ooh! Thanks. Just need some cream." She takes the cup I just poured from my hands like I'm her fucking personal barista. I grab another cup down and turn around, folding my arms across my chest.

"Why's he so moody?" Bridget looks over at Arden.

"I don't know, he scowled at me as soon as he walked into the kitchen."

"I'm not moody, I'm just waiting for the fourth to ap-

271

pear so I don't have to repeat myself ten times."

"Maybe you should have some coffee first, you're being a dick," Kelsey says as she passes the cream to Bridget.

I sigh and pinch my nose wishing I could be back downstairs wrapped around Lindsey. Sure enough, MK walks in with a big smile. "Oh good! It's just like when we were kids."

She takes the mug out of my hands and pours herself some coffee. "Nick, you need to make more coffee."

I hang my head and grumble in annoyance as I reach up and get the ground coffee bag down. I busy myself with making coffee while my four sisters have a silent conversation behind my back. They aren't saying anything, but I can just *feel* it.

I turn back around while the coffee percolates. "Who's first? Come on, just get it over with."

"What are you talking about, Nick?" Arden plays dumb.

"Yeah, paranoid much?" Kelsey smiles at her from behind her mug.

"Leave Nick alone, you guys." Bridget smiles at me. "He can't help it he's in loooove."

It's times like these where I wish I were an only child, or had a brother instead of four obnoxious immature sisters.

"When's the wedding, Nick?" MK winks.

"Does she know about your reoccurring case of the crabs?" Kelsey actually has the audacity to look concerned.

"Remember when he had jock itch at summer camp and kept rubbing himself against the pine tree? So gross." Arden smirks.

"I wasn't rubbing—"

"Aw, can I plan your wedding?" Bridget sighs happily.

"Ooh! I get to choose the bridesmaids dresses." Kelsey jumps with her hand in the air.

"Does she know you have that weird toe thing where your pinky points the other way?" Arden looks down at my feet. "That would be a dealbreaker for me."

My four-year-old nephew zooms into the kitchen. "Mommy, I'm hungry." He spies me and starts to jump up and down cheering, "Uncle Nick! Uncle Nick has a little dick! Look Uncle Nick it's almost as big as mine!"

I run a hand over my scruff and try not to laugh as I look up at the ceiling.

"Oh my god, Charlie, no! Go in the other room baby, I'll get you some cereal. Jesus, Kelsey, what else did you teach him?" MK shoos Charlie out of the kitchen before he pulls his pants down.

Kelsey snorts. "I'm sorry, I was singing it the other day. I forgot he was in the car with me."

"Uh…" The five of us turn to see Lindsey standing at the kitchen screen door with a horrified look on her face. "I was just going to grab some coffee, but I can come back later or drive to a Starbucks…somewhere…far."

"No, hold on a sec." I quickly pour two cups of coffee. "I'm coming with you." I give my sisters a scathing glare that would have anyone else wilting, but the four of them just smile back and wave. I hand the cup to Lindsey. "Don't pay attention to whatever you heard. It's all bullshit." We sit down at the deck table.

"The song was…catchy. How the hell does your pinkie toe do that anyway?"

I look down suddenly embarrassed by my pinkie toe that

curves out a little. You would never notice unless you were closely examining it. I'm going to kill my sisters.

"What's up with noodles?" I ask, quickly changing the subject.

She side-eyes me. "Um…they're good with sauce?"

"Do you have a noodle fetish?"

She snorts. "What on earth are you talking about?"

I smile at her. "You were talking in your sleep about being tied up and spanked with noodles."

She chokes on her coffee as a blush blossoms on her cheeks. "Uh…I don't recall having a dream about noodles…"

"Must be some subconscious thing." I smirk. "I'll keep that in mind next time I make you dinner."

"We're quite a pair, huh? Little dicks and noodles." She takes a sip of coffee as she tries to cover up her embarrassment.

I chuckle as I lean back and put her legs in my lap. "Can you stay another day?"

"No. My flight leaves out of JFK tonight. I'll need to leave here shortly."

I run my palm up her smooth thigh. "I wish you could stay longer."

She looks up at me, her big green eyes shining. "Me too. I'll text you when I land in Charleston tonight."

"Give me your hand." She gives me a curious look as she places it in mine. I place the quarter she tossed at me yesterday on her palm. "Hang onto this. It makes me feel better knowing you have it on you."

She smiles. "You're so sure I'll call you?"

I wink at her. "I'm counting on it."

She closes her fingers around the quarter and pockets it. "Okay. Wanna go back downstairs?" She moves her eyebrows up and down suggestively.

"Yes, but we can't."

"Why not?"

"We have an audience." We turn around to see my four sisters and my mom drinking coffee and staring out the family room window watching us like we're some new exhibit at the zoo. They smile and wave.

Chapter 42

Lindsey

The Pink Wire

THE UBER DROPS me off at home. I check my phone and it's nine p.m. I shoot my sister and Nick a generic text letting them know I landed and I'll call them tomorrow. I heft my roller bag up the stairs of the front porch. I'm expecting Mrs. Bixby to open her door and start griping about the racket I'm making, but she never does. This is odd considering she accosts me every time I come home. I pause on the porch as I look and see an Amazon package sitting by one of the rocking chairs. Now I know Mrs. Bixby would blow her panty hose off her toes if she saw that sitting there.

I walk over to Mrs. Bixby's door and lightly knock on it. The door creaks open. The hairs on the back of my neck stand on end. I feel like this is a pink wire moment, wishing Nick were with me right now. He would know what to do. I don't really want to walk into her apartment and discover something awful. Maybe Mrs. Bixby fell or passed out drunk. Maybe she's dead and her body has been decomposing for days. Shit, the last thing I want to do is come across a dead Mrs. Bixby! As much as she drives me insane, I don't really want the old bat to die.

"Mrs. Bixby?" I say tentatively as I open her door wider. "Are you in here?"

I cautiously walk into her pristine apartment. I was expecting musty, old outdated dark furniture with doilies on every surface and a scary-ass porcelain doll collection, but it's actually quite elegant. I'm scared she'll taser me if she suspects I'm trespassing in her apartment.

"Mrs. Bixby? It's me...Lindsey Love. The trampy harlot from upstairs? That one..." I reach into my purse and get out my phone. "Mrs. Bixby? Are you home? I'm going to call Rich...your Richie, okay?" I hear a gameshow on in the living room so I walk in that direction.

Her crumpled body is on the floor by the couch. There's a drink sweating on a coaster on her sideboard. I rush over to her.

"Shit, Mrs. Bixby, please don't be dead." I start to cry as I kneel next to her. I pick up her wrist and feel a thready pulse. "I'm going to call an ambulance, Mrs. Bixby. Don't worry, help is on the way."

I call 911. "Hi yes, I need an ambulance over at 642 Meeting Street Apt A. My neighbor has passed out. She's breathing, but...I don't know." My voice shakes and I start to cry. The operator informs me they are sending help and asks if I want her to stay on the line. "No, I'll be okay."

I back away from Mrs. Bixby. I'm looking up Rich's number when radial pain shoots down my neck and everything goes black.

Chapter 43

Nick

Sidekick

"SIMON, SHE HASN'T called. I'm worried. Patrick hasn't heard from her; her sister is blowing up both our phones. No one has seen her."

"What do you want me to do, Nick?"

"I'm asking for your help, dammit!"

"Oh, so *now* you need me. What are you going to do for me?"

I breathe through my nose trying to not blow up and smash my phone against my desk.

I'm hoping she still has the tracking device I put in the quarter I gave her. I watched her put it in her pocket, so I'm praying to God it's still on her. "I need your help finding her. I know this has to do with whatever went down in Paris."

"What if you're too late?" Simon says quietly.

"I can't think about that right now. Please, Simon, can you help me get to her or not?"

"Meet me at the Syndicate in thirty minutes."

I hang up on him with my plan in place. I'm going crazy out of my mind with worry. It's been two days since she got back. When I first called Patrick, I was worried that maybe she had changed her mind about us, but he hadn't heard from her either. They were supposed to meet for coffee this morning and she never showed. When she didn't answer her phone, he called her sister who's on spring break in the Bahamas and has been trying to reach her as well. Patrick is on his way to her place as we speak to make sure she didn't fall or anything. But I know the truth. This is payback for Paris and Morocco.

My phone buzzes and I immediately pick it up. "Hey man what you got."

"Well, it's weird. She hasn't been home. Her cat Mac was going crazy meowing. It's not like her to not feed him. So I looked around her place. The note for her cat sitter is still on the table. Lindsey is a lot messier than this. She doesn't even have dirty laundry in the hamper."

"Shit." I run my fingers through my hair. "Have you talked to her neighbor, Mrs. Bixby?"

"She wasn't home."

"I don't have a good feeling about this. Patrick, do me a favor and go check the dumpster out back."

"No problem, just give me a sec." I hear a gate opening and Patrick jostling the phone as he jogs. "Ugh gross it smells back here. Ugh...Nick? This is bad. Shit this is so bad. Oh Jesus, Lovie."

I tighten my grip on the phone, my heart pounding in my chest. "Patrick, just tell me!" I bark, fearing for the worst.

"It's Lindsey's suitcase and her purse."

"Don't touch it. I'm sending help. Don't call the police. Don't do anything," I say desperately.

"Is Lovie going to be okay?"

I can hear the panic in Patrick's voice. "Yeah bud, we're going to get her back."

"Who has her?"

"I can't tell you that but I'm going to need you up here. Ready to be my sidekick?"

"Shit, shit, shit."

"Patrick, get it together. Lindsey needs us right now, and she needs you to stay calm. I'm booking you a flight to New York for this afternoon."

I hang up on him and gather a duffle bag of clothes, money, my passport, and a few weapons. I'm going back to Europe and those fuckers are going to pay.

I pull out my cell phone and dial. "Hey, I just made contact with Simon. Any word?"

"She's in Paris. The device is still on her."

I hang up and breathe a sigh of relief. Let's just hope I'm not too late.

Chapter 44

Nick

Parlez-Vous Français

I TRACKED LINDSEY to an old church in Paris, France. I'm just so grateful she still had the coin on her. I knew if I had told her what it really was she would have tossed into the lake. My initial instinct to protect her was the right one. Simon said his contacts in Paris told him they wanted me, and they knew I'd come after her. He wanted to send his guys with me, but I couldn't chance anyone making a wrong move. He also warned me that if the mission was unsuccessful and they got me, he would have to blow the church up. I guess Lindsey was right, I know too much.

But what Simon doesn't know, is that I know the truth. I know that he's been secretly dealing with the Russians, selling the Syndicate's secrets. He's a traitor, and this whole plot to kidnap Lindsey was his idea. But I can't let him know that I'm on to him, or else he'll kill all of us. He needs something from me and I have to play along until I figure out what it is.

I look over at Patrick as he stares out the private jet's window, a closed Harry Potter book on his lap. I know he's worried and anxious, because I am too. I'm not sure why I brought him with me, he's one more body that I have to worry about and keep alive. But he's part of the plan, and I need him to distract Simon.

I get up and walk over to Simon as he lounges in his seat like he doesn't have a care in the world. I wish he wasn't here, but I didn't have a choice in the matter, I needed his help to get to Paris quickly. It would have caused red flags if I hadn't asked for his help.

"Let's go over the plan again."

Simon looks up. "Are you sure he's up for this?" He nods in Patrick's direction.

"Yeah, he's really smart, he knows what to do. Luckily, Claudine's never seen him."

"Okay, we'll have ground support for you. Remember, we want Claudine alive."

I nod, aware of what this means to the Syndicate if we can turn Claudine over to the CIA.

I worry my bottom lip as I think over everything that could go wrong. Claudine is my insurance ticket to surviving this. I'm not naïve enough to think Simon would just let us go scot free...still the plan is risky and I not only have Lindsey and Patrick to worry about, but Claudine as well.

I ADJUST MY ear mic and speak. "Patrick testing one, two, three...can you hear me?"

"Copy, copy. One, two, three."

"Alright, you know what to do bud."

"Yep." Patrick's voice cracks.

It's a warm dusky evening as I take position on a side street across from the entrance. The church where we tracked her is small in comparison to some of the cathedrals around here. It's currently under renovation, so it's hard to see around the scaffolding. Patrick walks across the street jumping when a motorbike speeds by. Sirens can be heard in the distance.

"Take it easy, bud. Remember, you're an American tourist out taking pictures."

"Yeah, yeah, I got it."

"You need to tell me how many people you see."

He lifts his camera and starts to take pictures. He tests the front door of the church, but there's a chain around it. He turns to take another pic when a man comes from the side of the building. This is when I move.

"Hors d'ici!" the man shouts for Patrick to get out of here. I quickly run around the back to see how many guys she has stationed around the church. I'm surprised to find that she only has one other guy. I quickly knock him out and tie him up. I run back up the side.

"Uh…par-le vu fran-say?" Patrick says in a heavy Southern accent. The man looks at him strangely. "Ha, of course you speak French. You're French. Ha ha, I meant, par-le vu in-glaze?"

The man grunts, clearly irritated with Patrick. "Go."

"Sure, sure, I understand with all the construction. If you could just help me out." Patrick unfolds a large map. "I'm looking for Les Deux Magots."

"Ugh." The man takes the map from Patrick and concentrates on the tiny intersecting streets. I sneak up behind him and stab him in the neck with a syringe helping him go night-night. Patrick helps me drag him into the shadows where I tie him up.

"I almost shit my pants when he came around the corner yelling."

I shake my head as I quickly get out bolt cutters and snap apart the lock. "I'm going to go in first and make sure it's clear, but then you're on your own."

Patrick nods as I slip quietly into the dim church. Candles are lit on the side by a statue of Mary, and some lowlights are on by the chapel, but it's otherwise empty and dark. Where the hell are they? Patrick slides in behind me and nervously looks around. I place the bolt cutters in my backpack and slip it off. With a gun in hand, I quietly slip down the side aisle of the church in the shadows.

Patrick starts to take pictures of the church as he hums nervously. I freeze as the *click-clack* of high heels comes toward me.

Chapter 45

Lindsey

Mother Mary

THE VOICES ECHO down to where I'm tied up. I almost peed in my pants when I saw Nick and Patrick walk in. At first I thought I was hallucinating from the drugs they used to keep me knocked out. My body still feels funny from whatever they used on me at Mrs. Bixby's apartment. I'm so relieved they found me, but that relief quickly dissipates as anxiety washes over me. I try to shimmy out of the chair they have me tied to on the side of the church in the dark. That damn henchman she has attached at her hip tied the ropes really tight and they're cutting into my skin.

"What the hell are you doing here?" Claudine shouts causing me to jump, but I quickly realize she's addressing Patrick. "Ivan, check him for weapons."

"Oh hi, there. I'm taking pictures for the magazine article I'm doing on European churches."

What the hell is he talking about?

"How did you get in here? The front door is locked." Claudine strides toward the front door.

"Oh, really? It was open for me. Funny, it's kind of empty in here. Are you in charge of the church? Hi, Patrick

285

Rod..."

"Patrick Rod?"

"Rod...rigo. Patrick Rodrigo."

If I were able to move my hands I'd slap them to my face and groan. Worst made-up name ever. *Did he even practice that?*

Patrick sticks out his hands so that she can't get by him. "I'm a hugger, come here you." He picks Claudine up in a big bear hug before she can protest. "Ooh, you smell nice, like a breezy ocean...breeze. Anyhoo, I was just taking some shots for our local paper."

"I thought you said it was for a magazine," she says irritably as she straightens her jacket and hair.

Oh god, Patrick is going to get us all killed.

"Have you ever seen the movie *Harry Potter and the Philosopher's Stone*? No? Shame. Ivan here looks just like Voldemort in the scene when Professor Quirrell was speaking in the Mirror of Erised and his face pops out of the back of his head." Patrick shivers. "I was on a date and it was really embarrassing because I accidentally threw popcorn all over her."

Jesus, here we go. I knew he'd spout Harry Potter trivia during a time of crisis.

"Fun fact for you all, did you know that the Mirror of Erised is actually desire spelled backwards? I know, crazy! It shows us our deepest desires of the heart. Ivan, what is your deepest darkest desire? Don't worry Miss, you're next." He winks at Claudine like she's dying to let him know. I'm pretty sure she's ten seconds away from clobbering him.

A hand wraps around my leg and I let out a barely audible scream. My mouth is bound so tight, I can only make a throaty noise.

"Shh, Lindsey. Fuck, thank god you're alive and okay," Nick whispers. "I'm going to get you out of here, okay? But I need you to run. I'll find you. Just run." I nod my head in understanding. "I'll meet you at Les Deux Magots."

"And did you know written on the mirror in what appears to be ancient language it says, 'I show not your face, but your heart's desire' backwards? Wild, right?"

"Jesus, you weren't kidding about his Harry Potter fun facts." Nick quickly cuts the ropes. "You're going to have to tear the tape off your mouth once you get out of here, okay? I can't take the chance of you screaming." He kisses my temple and holds my head. "I love you so much," he says fiercely.

I nod, blinking back tears, my heart pounding in my chest. I wish I could tell him that I love him back. "Go run, she was lazy and only had two guys covering the place. They've both been taken out."

"I'm guessing if you looked in the mirror, you would see a cheeseburger," Patrick continues. "I feel like you could really...ow Ivan, what the hell? Watch the camera equipment dude. Do you really need to handcuff me?" Patrick's voice goes up an octave.

"That's my cue." Nick winks at me and takes off into the shadows, but not before kissing me one more time on the nose and then he's gone. It's all I can do not to reach out and hold him to me, but I know Patrick needs his help more than me. I repeat what he told me over and over in my head. Meet him at what sounded like Le Doo Magoo. I go the opposite way of Nick and stay in the shadows.

I stop in my tracks when I hear Ivan go down with a thump, Claudine's voice making me shiver.

"He shouldn't have cuffed you."

"Holy shit, Nick, she just took out her own guy!" Patrick shouts hysterically in confusion.

I don't blame you, Trick, I'm confused too. What the hell is going on? Claudine looks around the room as she keeps a gun pointed at Patrick. I slowly peel the masking tape off my mouth. It hurts like a bitch and I have to go really slow so that I don't scream in pain.

"Come on out, Nicky." Ugh, that nickname she uses grates on my nerves. "He's on his way."

"Uh, I don't think she wants to help you, Nick."

"Your little friend is annoyingly chatty, Nicky." She turns away from Patrick. "I was right about Simon. He wants you and your little girlfriend dead."

"He wants me to turn you in alive." Nick steps out of the shadows holding a gun.

"Da... He wants to leave the Syndicate. He wants to frame us—kill you and have me take the fall." Whoa, I didn't see *that* coming.

"How am I supposed to trust you, Claudine? You tried to have me killed in Paris."

"I know, I'm sorry about that." She pouts. "Honestly, I didn't want to, I didn't have a choice."

"Are you all having a party without me?" Simon steps in through the front door. My eyes widen in disbelief as he walks down the aisle pointing a gun at Nick. "Darling, just shoot them and let's be done with this." he says casually like Nick and Patrick are disposable garbage. "Did Ivan take care of Lindsey?"

"Da. No one will find her for a while."

"Good. Take care of this one too."

Claudine raises her arm and shoots Patrick with a silencer. He crumples like a sack of potatoes and I have to cover my mouth and silently scream.

"No!" Nick shouts as he rushes toward Patrick and kneels next to him.

"He's a liability, Nick." Claudine gently kicks him with her Louis Vuitton.

Oh my God, not Trick! *No!* I drop my head to the floor as tears stream down my cheeks. You can still save him Lindsey. You can get an ambulance. Think! I start to crawl to the front of the church.

"I can't believe you would betray me this way, Simon. That you would betray your country," Nick says quietly.

"I wanted out and the money was too good."

"So, it's true what Boris said, you've been selling intel to the Russians."

"Like handing candy to a baby. The senator is such a lazy prick. He's going to get everyone in the Syndicate killed."

"Why kill me? Why drag Lindsey and Patrick into this?"

"Friend, you dragged them into this, not me."

"I'm not your friend. I never was."

"Yeah, I know. You always blamed me for Mikey's death. Maybe it *was* my fault for not watching his back like I was supposed to, but he was a fucking cowboy. He should have been more careful. No one ever forgave me for it, including you."

Nick growls as he stands up, fists clenched. "I didn't think I could fucking hate you more than I already do, but you just confirmed my suspicions."

Simon shrugs. "Well, I'm tired of this party, I think it's time for me to depart." He turns to Claudine. "Ready, lover?"

Bile rises in my throat.

"Da." Claudine looks over at Nick with remorse as Simon raises his gun to Nick's head.

"No!" I scream causing the three to turn toward me. Nick immediately jumps on Simon and takes him by surprise. They wrestle as Nick tries to gain the upper hand. Simon's gun clatters to the ground. Claudine kicks it away from them and tosses something next to Patrick before quickly running to the front door. She gives me one last look over her shoulder and winks before she slips out into the night. I run toward Patrick on the floor.

"Lindsey, get the hell out of here," Nick grits out as Simon and him wrestle on the floor. Simon pulls a knife and holds it over Nick's throat. Nick uses his legs to twist Simon away from him, but Simon still has the upper hand.

I can see the strain on Nick's face. Without thinking I run over to the side of the church and grab the two-foot statue of Mary. *I'm so sorry, Mother Mary.* I raise the statue over my head, and pure adrenalin has me swinging it down on top of Simon's head. The clay statue shatters into several pieces as he immediately collapses on top of Nick, the knife clattering to the floor.

Nick rolls him off and checks for a pulse. I rush over to Patrick and try to staunch the blood. I run my fingers over his chest. Wait, why isn't there any blood? Why isn't there a bullet hole? His shirt looks perfectly fine.

I pat his chest several times, wondering what the hell is

going on. I saw Claudine shoot him with my own eyes. My gaze races around his body when something glitters next to Patrick. I pick up the large diamond solitaire necklace Claudine was wearing the night we had dinner and I pocket it.

Patrick's eyes flutter open. "Lovie? Is that really you?"

I burst into tears. "Yes! Are you okay?"

"Why is your mouth so swollen?" Patrick rubs his eyes. I touch my puffy mouth as I look over my shoulder at Nick. He's tying Simon to a column with ropes. Now that I know Patrick is okay, I rush over to him. He stands up and catches me as I jump into his arms. I pepper his face with kisses. "Oh, thank god. I love you, I love you, I love you."

Nick smiles and it takes my breath away. "I love you, too, Lindsey Love." He kisses me. "Guess what?"

"What?"

"You cut the right wire."

I grin like a loon at him. "I did?"

He nods as he kisses me again. "You can be my sidekick anytime."

"Right back at ya, Nick Elliot."

"Hey guys, glad you're back together, but uh, can we get the hell out of here? I've had enough Harry Potter creepy vibes for one evening." Patrick gingerly sits up, rubbing his back.

I pull the necklace out of my pocket. "I think she left this for you?" I ask quizzically as I hold the necklace out to him.

"Thank god, my insurance." He kisses me again and pockets the necklace.

"Come on, I'll explain everything after I call the senator. Let's get out of here."

Chapter 46

Nick

The Traitor

WE NURSE OUR beers at a small outdoor café, still shaken from the turn of events. I hold Lindsey's hand, I can't seem to let it go. I don't ever want to let it go.

"Are you sure you don't want to go back to the hotel?" I dip my head and sweep a kiss on her jaw.

"I'm okay. The fresh air feels good, and I just need to decompress for a moment with all the normal activity surrounding us."

I nod, understanding exactly how she's feeling. Sometimes normal things like sitting at a little café bar and watching people walk by doesn't make the events of what just happened seem so overwhelming. Her face is looking a little better from where the tape had marred it.

"I just…I'm so confused. What did Claudine use on me? Did she try and kill me?" Patrick holds his head in his hands.

"She saved you bud." I take a sip of my beer mulling over everything that happened. "She must have some kind of weapon that knocks you out but doesn't kill you."

"Like a stun gun, but it doesn't touch you? That is so insane!" Patrick says with wonder as he starts looking up guns on his browser.

"I doubt you'll find it on there."

Lindsey shakes her head. "I still can't wrap my head around the fact that Simon was behind this thing the whole time."

"I just got off the phone with the Senator and told him everything. He's sending someone in to take care of Simon. I don't think we'll be hearing from him again."

I filled the senator in on everything that had happened. He thanked me for my loyalty to the Syndicate and to my country. He was disappointed Claudine disappeared into the night, but I wasn't going to force her to stay. Maybe subconsciously I felt I owed her that freedom since she spared me mine. Realistically, she could have killed everyone involved if she wanted to and washed her hands of it all.

"I still don't get it. Why involve you and me? Why this whole elaborate scheme to get you to Paris?"

I sigh, not wanting to share too much information with them that could compromise their lives, but feeling that I owe it to them after dragging them into this.

"What I tell you stays between us, got it?"

They both look at each other and then at me with wide eyes and nod.

"While shooting *Naked in the Wild* my mission was to come to a meeting as an interpreter for a deal between a Colombian drug lord and a Russian arms dealer living in London named Boris Slavanko. The deal went south and I found myself in the middle of a shootout between the Russians and the Colombians. I managed to apprehend Boris, who begged me to spare his life in trade for some intel that he assured me I'd want to know. I agreed and he told me that there was an American selling information and weapons to him. He was connected to a very influential senator."

"Simon…" Lindsey breathes out.

I nod. "I left Boris tied up for the FBI to find. Boris is a very powerful man in Russia. Even from prison, he helps fund a private arms group based in London."

"So, Simon is selling the Syndicate's secrets to Boris?" Patrick raises his eyebrows.

"Yes, not only secrets and weapons, but undercover agents as well. The more information Simon sold, the richer he became. I immediately went to the senator with this news and started working with him privately on a plan to gather evidence against Simon."

I take a sip of my beer making sure Patrick and Lindsey were still following. "But I couldn't do it alone. Claudine is KGB and was already working undercover in Boris Slavanko's group. I needed evidence on Simon's nefarious dealings and reached out to her for help. I asked her to establish a relationship with him so that he would trust her within the group and I could get evidence that he was trading secrets.

"Simon needed an excuse to be over in Europe, which is why he wanted to do your show. It gave him the freedom to meet with Claudine without the Senator questioning what he was doing. Little did he know I was one step ahead of him. The show was the perfect cover for both of us, like a present Simon dropped right in my lap."

"I can't believe I hugged a Russian spy," Patrick says in

wonder.

"This is crazy," Lindsey whispers. "Why would Claudine help you if she was undercover?"

"Uh…we had history together."

"I knew it," Lindsey grumbles.

I squeeze her hand. "It was a long time ago. My plan started to fall apart when we were in Germany. Claudine told me that Simon wanted out of the Syndicate and wanted protection from the Russians. He was going to use me as the fall guy. He sent Claudine to meet me, to get pictures of us together so that he could frame me as the one leaking secrets." I pause as the waitress brings fresh beers.

"This is so complicated. So Simon had Claudine meet you so that he could photograph you two together and send it to the senator framing you for selling info to Slavanko's gang to cover his own ass."

"Correct. Simon thought if the Russians would kill me, then he could tell the senator I was working with them and show him the pictures he had from dinner. Claudine was starting to get paranoid as well. She couldn't afford to have her cover blown, so she offered to kill me. She planned the bombing in Paris to prove her allegiance to Simon and to keep her cover in Slavanko's group." I scrub my hands down my face. "Simon told me the Russians wanted to kill me for having Boris arrested and Claudine was behind it."

"Why couldn't you just kill Simon and be done with it?"

"Because we needed to know what intel Simon was giving the Russians. Was he selling guns or nuclear warfare? We needed evidence. Was he alone, or were there other members involved? We didn't know. We needed him alive."

"Jesus." Patrick shakes his head. "This is intense."

"After Paris, Simon sent me on a mission to Morocco to gather some intel on an arms deal about to take place. Claudine got word to me that it was a fluff mission, he was trying to set me up again. Simon sent one of Slavanko's guys to try and kill me, but obviously, he was unsuccessful. He failed in Paris and again in Morocco."

Patrick and Lindsey's mouths hang open in shock. "Why couldn't you just go straight to the senator?" Patrick asks.

"I was waiting on Claudine to deliver the evidence. The senator couldn't do anything without it. At this point it was my word against Simon's. I knew Simon was going to try a third time, I just didn't know when. He was watching me, waiting for me to make a wrong move. For a couple months I laid low and things went silent. That's why I couldn't contact you, Lindsey. I had to pretend I was just working with Patrick and producing the show. I feared for your life. I cut off all contact with Claudine...I didn't trust her either. It was a mistake for me to go to that awards show, but I had to see you for my own eyes and make sure you were okay. I was expected there and Simon was waiting patiently.

"I was discreetly working with a trusted friend and Syndicate member. You might remember him—Lukas, the schnitzel maker."

"What? Lukas is a spy too? Is everyone a fucking spy? Seriously...mind blown." Patrick makes the 'mind blown' gesture with his hands.

I smile and cross my arms over my chest. "He runs his grandmother's restaurant. He told me Simon had evidence that I was the mole and he had a plan to lure me back to

Europe."

"Kidnapping me."

I nod. "Simon knew you were my Achilles heel and was just waiting for the right opportunity. I just didn't realize it would happen so quickly, he must have been getting desperate."

"So why call Simon to help you if you knew he planned the whole thing?" Patrick asks incredulously.

"I needed Simon to think I was clueless, that I believed the Russians were behind it. Claudine was my insurance and I was counting on her to deliver. That's why they discarded her bags in the dumpster. There are cameras in the alley way. He wanted it to be easy for me to find out she had been kidnapped by the Russians."

"Oh god, my favorite Chanel bag is in the dumpster?" Lindsey sits back in her seat in shock.

I smirk at her. "I think you should just feel lucky to be alive at this point."

"Ha, yeah…but it was so pretty…and expensive," she murmurs.

"And Claudine, was she a good guy or a bad guy?" Patrick shoves some bread into his mouth.

"I suspect Claudine was working both sides. She had her own agenda; she had to deliver whatever she needed back to the KGB."

"I don't understand why Simon needed to bring you to Paris…"

"He needed to make it look like a deal gone bad between the Russians and me. The Russians kidnapped you, I went in to rescue you…I suspect he was planning on killing Claudine along with me."

"Did Claudine ever give you evidence on Simon?"

I hold up the diamond necklace. "There's a chip behind the diamond."

"So…she *was* a good guy?" Patrick looks back and forth between Lindsey and me. "I'm so confused!"

"I think in the end, she was helping out an old friend. She knew Simon wasn't going to keep her around. She saw her chance and she ran. She's probably been planning this for a while."

"She winked at me right before she left."

I gently squeeze Lindsey's fingers. "She liked you. She thought you were funny."

"Hmph, funny way of showing it by kidnapping me."

I gently run my thumb along her brow. "Sorry, babe, she had to. She had to follow the plan to keep herself in the game. I am forever grateful to her for keeping you and Patrick alive."

Lindsey smiles. "Yeah."

"What intel was Simon selling to the Russians?" Patrick's eyes widen.

I smirk. "That's classified."

"What about you? Won't there be repercussions?"

"Nah, I struck a deal with the senator. My 'death' for Simon. Word will get back to the Russians that I died in a church bombing in Paris."

"But wait, your name is all over television."

"The Russians know me as Nicholas Scar, aka Scar." I give Lindsey a wry smile.

Just at that moment sirens race down the street making

us all jump.

"Jesus, this is…this is insane! This is like Hollywood *Mission Impossible* crazy! I don't think I could make it in the spy business. Cheers to coming out alive." Patrick shakily raises his beer. We clink our glasses together.

"Cheers for coming out alive," Lindsey and I murmur as we smile at each other.

"Hey, Trick, this is going to give you major street cred with the ladies." Lindsey winks at him.

"Ah, sorry bud. Remember we can never discuss what happened tonight, or what has taken place with Simon and Claudine."

"I guess I'll just have to woo them with my sparkling personality." He smiles.

"So, what's going to happen to Simon?" Lindsey asks as she worries her bottom lip.

"I don't know." I squeeze her hand. "That's for the Syndicate to decide. I'll have to give Lukas the necklace and let him decode the info."

"And what about you?"

"Me?" I smile at her. "I'm going to Africa to save some rhinos and eat some South African cuisine with my girl and her best friend."

"Best damn sidekick around!" Patrick preens.

Lindsey snorts as she sets her glass on the table. "That's debatable."

"What? Lovie, I'm hurt. I saved your life tonight!"

"You're right. Who knew Harry Potter trivia would come in handy?" She playfully rolls her eyes.

"I did." Patrick nods his head with a self-satisfied grin.

"So, what happened when I was passed out anyway?"

Lindsey and I look at each other and grin. "Not much," we say in unison.

Lindsey lifts her almost-empty glass. "Cheers to my twenty-five-cent call." She places the quarter with the tracking device I gave her on the table.

"So about that..." I grin as I chuck the quarter out into the street.

Chapter 47

Lindsey

Superpowers

Two months later

"IF YOU COULD have a superpower, what would it be?"

I can feel Nick's body move as he breathes in deeply. "Really? We're doing this right now?" he whispers as he looks through his night-vision goggles.

"I'm sooo bored right now, just amuse me."

"I know mine!" Patrick whispers loudly on the other side of Nick.

"Will you guys shut up?" Nick hisses.

"What is it, Trick?" I ask causing Nick to grunt in annoyance. "It can only be one."

"If I had one superpower, I'd want to read everyone's thoughts."

"Really? Like that Mel Gibson movie...what was it called? I can't remember, but he hated it. Like everyone's voices chiming in his head. It drove him crazy in the movie. That would drive me bananas."

"Kind of like you're driving me? The movie was *What Women Want*. Now, shut up, you two," Nick whispers.

"I didn't think about that," Patrick continues, completely ignoring Nick. "But I'd finally know for sure if you really like Harry Potter or not."

I roll my eyes. "Of course I like Harry Potter, who doesn't? I just don't need a fun fact about the movie or the book every time we meet."

"See? You don't need a magic power, just ask her. Now be quiet," Nick hisses.

"Geez, Lovie, I didn't realize I was such a Debbie Downer." Patrick sounds hurt.

"I'm sorry, Trick, I love you just the way you are. Tell me Harry Potter trivia whenever the mood strikes you."

"Wait, wait, maybe I want heat laser vision, or even better, x-ray vision." Patrick waggles his eyebrows.

I roll my eyes. "X-ray vision would just allow you to see everyone's bones, not boobs. Heat vision would melt things. What's the point of that?"

"Maybe I could have a dial on my x-ray vision where I can adjust to the level of degree I want to see. If I'm at a bar I want to see boobs, if I'm looking for weapons, bones."

"This is the dumbest conversation I've ever had to sit through," Nick grumbles, making me giggle.

"Hmm...what would my superpower be..." I tap my finger to my lips.

"Jesus Christ, woman."

I smile at him and pinch his firm tush. "I think I would like the ability to be invisible. Then we wouldn't have to sit here twiddling our thumbs. We could just walk right up to the guy and be done with it."

"Good one, Lovie! Just like the cloak of invisibility."

"Exactly, see? I don't hate Harry. Okay, Nick Elliot, spill

it. What would your one superpower be? Besides the obvious one of making us shut up."

"That would take superhuman strength for you, Lovie."

Nick shifts on his belly totally annoyed with us and it makes me smile. I love it when I get under his skin and get him all revved up. It's like sexual foreplay for us.

"Oh wait, I change my mind again. I would want to time travel. Okay, done. Sorry Nick, you're turn, bud." Patrick nods his head. "Or maybe I'd rather teleport..."

"Like Nightcrawler," Patrick and I say in unison.

"Jinx, you owe me a Coke!" we both shout.

"For fuck's sake will you two shut up!" Nick hisses.

It takes monumental effort not to squeeze his butt again. "If I answer, will you two please just shut up?"

"Uh...sure," I hesitate. "I mean, at least for a few minutes."

"I knew bringing you two would be a bad idea."

"Sidekicks, remember?" Patrick gives me a high-five over Nick's back.

Nick shakes his head and grumbles. "Flying. That would be my superpower."

"So you can be with the birds? That's poetic, Nick." I smile as I inspect my nails.

He shakes his head and chuckles. "I love to fly and jump out of airplanes, so how cool would it be to not have to rely on an instrument, just shoot up in the air."

"Of course he knows how to fly an airplane," I mumble. "Why did you sign up with the SEALs then? Aren't they Navy?"

Nick shrugs. "I wasn't into planes at the time." Nick's

body tenses. "Don't say a word."

He adjusts a dial on his Cheyenne Tactical M-200 Intervention, looks into his scope again, and pulls the trigger. The bullet hits the man's leg and he goes down.

"Did you kill him?" I ask, burying my head in my arms.

"Whoa, that was unbelievable," Patrick whispers next to Nick.

"No, remember, no more killing, just maiming until the authorities can get him."

Nick walkie-talkies the Game Reserve police as I look into the night vision goggles and watch the rhino and her baby peacefully eating on the prairie. Another asshole bites the dust.

I've learned a lot these past few weeks on the reserve. Not only about South African cuisine, but also the importance of protecting our wildlife. Nick's documentary on rhino and elephant poaching has been incredible to take part in. I even got to help grind down a rhino tusk. I was afraid it was hurting the animal, but Nick's friend J.D., the veterinarian, assured me it doesn't, and that the rhino doesn't need his tusk to survive. Poachers have killed them almost to the brink of extinction just for their ivory tusks and it makes my heart bleed. What have these poor innocent animals ever done to us?

Chapter 48

Nick

The Wise Woman

WE GATHER OUR things as we head back to camp. Patrick is replaying his video.

"Man, that shot was perfect, Nick. I got it all."

"I hope you got that stimulating conversation as well," I say sarcastically. I swear I was about to throttle those two. Luckily, I'm able to block everything out around me when necessary.

"Hey, it's important to know these things about each other. We're a team now." Lindsey links her arm in mine as we stumble along the path back to the Jeep.

"Oh we are, are we?" I raise one eyebrow and smirk down at her.

"Of course, we're a team, silly. We've been one from day one." She winks at me.

"Okay Snow White, whatever you say." I kiss the top of her head.

"Hey, Nick?"

"Yes, Lindsey?"

"Thanks for giving me a do-over."

"There was never a question."

She sighs happily, stopping me on the trail back to camp. "Patrick we'll be right there, just give us a sec," she hollers to him. I give her a puzzled look as she reaches up on her tippy toes and softly kisses my lips. "Lindsey Love loves…Nick Elliot," she breathes against my lips.

I wrap her tightly in my arms and whisper against her lips. "I love you so much. Thank you for always being my twenty-five-cent call."

"Even when I cut the pink wire?"

"Especially when you cut the pink one." I kiss her cute little nose.

"I'm glad you said that." She steps back from me. "Because I think I might have cut it again." She takes a white stick out of her pocket and hands it to me. I take the stick and look at the two pink lines quizzically.

"Is this…are you?"

She's hesitant, gauging my reaction. "I'm pregnant…it's yours."

I laugh. "Well I should fucking hope so." My smile is so big it hurts my face. "Wait, how did this happen?"

"Well, Nick, when a man and a woman have sexual—"

I huffily interrupt her, "I know *how*, but I thought you were on the Pill?"

"Yeah…I've been wracking my brain all day. The only thing I can think of is the herbal tea that wise medicine woman gave me when we first arrived welcoming us. She told me to drink it every night…"

"And you did? You follow instructions from some old tribal woman but if I tell you to go right, you veer left?"

"She's a *wise* woman, Nick. She *knows* things."

I grin stupidly. "Yeah, she knows I'm going to have you in my bed every night." I pick her up in one swoop and kiss her lips.

"Does this mean you're happy? I mean I know it wasn't exactly planned...we're not even engaged, but sometimes unexpected gifts are the best things in life, right?"

I kiss her lips, shutting her up. I look into her large green eyes. "Beyond happy, Pain in My Ass. You are my world and so is this little life growing inside of you. I promise to always protect you both until the day I die." I wipe the tears from her cheeks and kiss her lips. "I love you."

"I love you too. Oh god, wait until we tell our sisters." She smirks. "Shannon is going to go in mother-hen doctor mode."

"Let's just enjoy the moment while we can. Okay?" I grimace thinking about what's going to happen when mine find out. I can just picture Kelsey asking Lindsey how my little dick could even produce offspring. Arden will be right behind her asking if she had heard about the time I had a black and purple rash on my balls and dick, and how everyone was positive I wouldn't be able to reproduce. *Not a true story by the way.* Bridget will smother her with hugs and start rubbing her belly and MK will smirk and give me a slow clap.

She beams at me. "Well, we have to go tell Trick he's going to be an uncle!"

"How long have you been keeping this to yourself?"

She thinks for a second and quickly looks at her watch. "Uh, thirteen hours, thirty-two minutes, and forty seconds. Thankfully Shannon packed a safe sex kit in my bag that happened to include a pregnancy test. She doesn't leave anything to chance."

"I'm impressed you've kept it to yourself this long."

"Well, I had a complete meltdown this morning. Thank god you and Patrick were busy helping J.D. Then I went into nesting mode."

I chuckle. "Nesting mode? Isn't that at the end of pregnancy?"

She waves her hand. "I need to be prepared. I ordered a bunch of items off Amazon." Her face goes slack. "Oh my god. Oh no…"

"What's wrong, are you okay?"

"I think I already have pregnancy brain. I've read about this, but how could I forget? Shit!"

"Lindsey, you're starting to scare me. What's wrong?"

"Oh sorry, it's just…I ordered over a thousand dollars' worth of stuff."

I choke, "Uh, don't you think you should wait until we see a doctor?"

She smiles. "Yeah probably, but I got nervous, then excited, then worried. But I forgot about Mrs. Bixby."

"What about her?"

"She of course blames me for her break in, even though I tried to save her life. She's out of the hospital and meaner than ever. She's going to blow her control-top panties when she sees the boxes."

"It will be fine. Just have your sister go get them. We'll be home next week."

Lindsey huffs out a laugh. "Yeah, okay."

I kiss her lips and smooth her worried brow. I love this woman more than I thought was possible. "Come on, Snow White. Uncle Trick is probably pacing."

Epilogue

Lindsey

Dessert

YOU KNOW THE best thing about being a food critic? The dessert at the end of a meal. I have very rarely in my career ever experienced a bad dessert. Okay, okay—the scorpion ice cream was disgusting, and an exception. But no matter how bad your meal is, the dessert always comes to the rescue. It's rich and decadent and always makes you feel happy. Whether you're a chocolate cake kind of girl, a sorbet lover, or an elegant mixed berry fruit cup, it's not going to let you down. I will never pass up on dessert.

It's our last night in South Africa and Nick wants to film a final segment for *Lindsey Love Loves...South Africa* at our camp. Friends are all gathered around the large round table outside looking over the reserve. Giraffes and zebras dot the landscape as the sun begins its nightly descent over the savannah. It's breathtaking and I'm really going to miss it. We have Dr. J.D. Evans and his crew, our guide Radu and some camp staff. I'm glowing with happiness, and have been careful not to eat anything that might upset my stomach. I leave the weird stuff to Patrick.

Ruby, one of the chefs, comes out of the house with

what looks like a tray of mini chocolate cakes. She places the one with a lit sparkler in front of me. They all start to sing "Happy Birthday" which makes me blush with all the attention. I smile at everyone as I get teary-eyed.

"Thank you, everyone." I look over at Nick and his devastating dimpled smile makes my heart quicken. "I can't imagine a more perfect birthday celebration."

Ruby clears her throat. "This is a South African Malva pudding. My specialty." She winks at me.

Everyone digs in, myself included, and I moan in appreciation. "Oh my god, this is amazing…"

"Cut. Do it again."

"What? Why? The whole thing? Ruby is going to have to get everyone new puddings."

Of course, Nick decides to pull this shit. I give him an annoyed glare and he returns it with a level look. "We'll keep the first part, just another take of your first bite."

"What was wrong with the first time?" I look at Patrick who just shrugs.

"Why do you always have to argue with me? Do it again, with a little more oomph."

I roll my eyes and apologize to the table. "Sorry guys, apparently I wasn't *enthusiastic* enough." J.D. smirks as he licks his spoon. I wish I could enjoy mine like that.

Patrick gives me the signal to go and I scoop up a big bite with my spoon. I put the concoction in my mouth and groan in appreciation. "So incredible, it's moist, chocolatey…"

Nick gives me his infamous death glare, the one that makes me want to pee in my pants. "What?"

"Again."

I jam my spoon into my pudding, my blood pressure rising as I glare at Nick. He takes a bite of his pudding and smiles sweetly back at me which pisses me off even more. I take a bite and my tongue feels something like metal. What the...? My brain registers the shape as I slowly spit it back on to my spoon. "Oh my God..."

On my spoon is a square-cut platinum diamond ring covered in chocolate pudding cake. I look up at Nick in shock as he gets down on one knee next to my chair. Ruby reaches over me, plucks the ring from my spoon, and dunks it in my water then dries it off with her dishrag, handing it to Nick. I watch this all transpire with my mouth hanging open unable to speak.

"Lindsey Love, pain in my ass, my snail-eating Snow White queen, mama to our little miracle..." He pauses as he swallows. "My eternal love, will you do me the honor of making my life complicated and crazy? Will you be my forever twenty-five-cent call?"

I nod as tears stream down my cheeks. "Yes!" I croak out. "Yes, I will be your forever twenty-five-cent call. Sorry, Patrick." I sniffle and giggle at the same time as Nick slips the ring on my finger.

"There's no one else I want to have my back, but you. For always."

"For always." I kiss him and everyone claps and whistles.

"How did you...when...did you just get this?"

"I've been carrying it around with me since we left the States."

"You have?" Tears track down my cheeks. He gently

311

swipes them away before looking over his shoulder.

"Hit it, Patrick."

All of a sudden Whitney Houston's "How Will I Know" starts blasting from the outdoor speakers, cracking me up. I cover my face with my hands as he drags me from the table and envelops me in his arms, swaying me to the music. "Oh god, you remember?"

"How could I forget? It was the moment I was a goner."

This knocks me on my ass. "But you hated me…"

"Never. I guess I just needed a couple do-overs." He winks and I kiss him. *How will I know if he really loves me, Whitney?* Because he loves all of my crazy and it turns out he doesn't really want to kill me.

"Thank God for those do-overs." We kiss as the stars over the savannah twinkle and bless us in love.

Post Epilogue

Lindsey

The Perfect Ending

"NO WAY!" I seethe as I watch the footage Nick obtained from the security cameras in the back alley. "That lying evil old bat!"

"She's pretty spry for being in her eighties." Nick smirks as we watch Mrs. Bixby toss a bouquet of flowers Nick had sent me over her shoulder into the dumpster.

"See? I told you I never got flowers. That's the reason, right there. Why is she so hateful?"

Nick shakes his head as he fast-forwards. He had a friend go through and cut down the thousands of hours of security tape from the restaurant that butts up to our garbage in the back alley. "Wait, stop!"

Nick pauses the video and presses play. "Oh my god, she tried to put Mac in the dumpster?" We watch as Mac lithely manages to jump right back out. "She's insane!"

Nick shakes his head. We watch Mrs. Bixby drag a step ladder she keeps hidden behind an azalea bush next to our gate. She sets it up next to the dumpster and then leaves.

"This is odd." I look at Nick who is watching with an amused smile.

She walks back into the frame, tugging a garden wagon behind her filled to the brim with Amazon boxes. "I knew it." I boil with anger. "Can we have her arrested?"

Nick gives me the side-eye as we continue to watch Mrs. Bixby throw thousands of dollars' worth of baby merchandise into the dumpster. "You're really going to arrest an eighty-year-old woman?"

"She stole from me!" I say indignantly. "She threw my cat in the dumpster! Imagine the emotional turmoil he went through!"

"He jumped right out."

I nod furiously. "Because it was so stinky! He's not an alley cat. He's used to the life of a pampered cat."

Nick sighs. "No you can't arrest Mrs. Bixby."

"Can't you have one of your Syndicate buddies take her out?"

Nick chuckles. "Lindsey..."

"What? I was just asking in case you hopefully said yes."

Nick closes the laptop. "Well, it's a good thing then that you can finally say *au revoir*, Mrs. Bixby."

"Hmph, she deserves retribution." We get up from the kitchen table and look around at the empty apartment. In a way, I'm kind of sad to leave 656 Meeting Street. It was a good apartment. I look over at Nick as he smiles and holds his hand out to me. Oh, who the hell am I kidding, I was miserable here. My life started the day I sat down across from Nick Elliot in that coffee shop in New York City.

We bought a cute little four-bedroom beach bungalow over on Isle of Palms. My sister is super excited that we are staying in South Carolina. The perks of being a food critic and a producer, you can live wherever you want.

"Let's go, we've got to catch our flight."

"I'm coming, I'm coming. I guess Staci is running late. Let me just text her and tell her I'm leaving the key in the door."

Meeting Staci was pure serendipity. I sat down next to her at the vet hospital while waiting for Mac's annual appointment. I wonder how many times he got tossed in the dumpster...it's no wonder he's such an ornery asshole cat. He's been secretly recovering from dumpster PTSD.

Anyway, Staci and I started chatting and she revealed that she was new to town and looking for a place that was pet friendly. I told her I had just the apartment if she didn't mind living over an elderly person. She said she loved the elderly and used to volunteer at a retirement home. I talked to Rich and Staci is now renting my apartment.

My phone buzzes. "Gah, Margot won't stop blowing up my phone. God, I hope I don't look like a Macy's Day Parade float at the Emmys tomorrow night."

Lindsey Love Loves...Europe is up for an Emmy against a couple other food shows. Guess who didn't get a nomination? That's right, *The Pasta Pit*. I sent Jimmie a year supply of Kleenex with a note attached that read, *Saving you a seat at the Emmys!*

I know, it was petty, but he totally deserved it.

Nick kisses my lips and rubs my little beach ball as we lock the door behind us. "You're gorgeous."

We walk down the narrow steps and out on to the front porch. Mrs. Bixby's door opens a crack. "Oh Jesus, here we go."

"I'm just going to wait in the car...turn the A/C on."

"Chicken." I laugh.

The door opens wide and Mrs. Bixby glares at me. "Back in my day pregnant girls went to live at the convent if they weren't married."

"That's nice, Mrs. Bixby," I say, waggling my ring finger at her. I might have accidentally flipped her off as well.

Her eyes narrow. "Your cat peed on my gardenias again. I put rat poison down to keep the critters at bay."

"Mrs. Bixby, my cat hasn't been here for over two weeks. Remember? I moved out."

"Then what are you doing on my front porch? Don't think I won't taser a pregnant hussy."

I roll my eyes. "Listen you Satan's spawn—"

"Hi, Lindsey!" Staci waves to me as she crosses the street with her three chihuahuas. They start yapping like crazy when they see me. "Turbo, Mikey, Louie, hush! Ugh! They are *so* loud!" Staci shouts over the barking. I can't keep the smile from spreading across my face as I look over at Mrs. Bixby.

"Mrs. Bixby, meet your new apartment mate, Staci! Oh, she has three dogs. Aren't they cute? I bet they don't pee on anything."

"Oh my gawd, I think they stopped on every planter on the way over here! Doggies, hush! Do you mind holding their leashes?"

She hands me two and then picks up the little black one. "Louie's an ankle-biter. Will take your finger right off!" She wipes her hand down her dress and holds it out to Mrs. Bixby. "Hi, I'm Staci! It's sooo nice to meet you!" she shouts in Mrs. Bixby's face thinking she's hard of hearing.

Louie growls at Mrs. Bixby and shows his teeth. "Oh Louie, we don't growls at the kind old woman. That's a no-nos," Staci says in a baby voice. Mrs. Bixby grimaces.

"*Seasons by the Bay* is looking pretty damn good right about now, huh, Mrs. Bixby?" I wink at her and hand Staci the dogs back, but not before one pees on the planted pot by the rocking chair.

"She must not have heard you." Staci steps closer to her. "MRS. BIXBY, I'M GOING TO TAKE YOU TO SALSA DANCING AT THE RETIREMENT CENTER! YOU AND I ARE GOING TO MAKE CRAFTS TOO!"

Mrs. Bixby looks like she's about to pass out as Staci smiles winningly at me over her shoulder. I wave goodbye to her and Staci and quickly get in the car.

"That was entertaining." Nick smiles at me.

"The perfect ending for Mrs. Bixby. I feel like chocolate cake. The lava cake kind that you have to order before dinner because it takes an insane amount of time to cook. But oh god, when it's done, it's perfection…"

"Uh, okay, random craving, but we'll get one when we get to Los Angeles."

I smile as we pull away from the apartment. Chocolate cake after all is *the perfect ending*.

The End

Thank you so much for reading *Lindsey Love Loves*!
If you enjoyed it, please leave a review on Amazon,
BookBub, or Goodreads!
J.D. and Patrick's books will be coming in 2021.

Author's Note

When my oldest daughter was five, we started a family charity to give back to the community. We asked her who she would like to support and without hesitation, she said, "The elephants." She had heard that they were being killed for their tusks and she didn't understand why someone could kill such a majestic creature. She held a lemonade stand at a golf event and raised $1,200 and we donated it to the Sheldrick Wildlife Trust.

The following year, she raised money for the rhinos. For the last five years we have raised money to help protect, and it's an important cause to my family. If you would like to donate to the rhinos' preservation, whose numbers are dwindling at an incredibly alarming rate, please go to www.rhinopride foundation.org/donate or www.sheldrickwildlifetrust.org.

Please help protect these magnificent creatures.

Thank you,
Sophie Sinclair

Acknowledgments

A big thank-you to Allisson for going over the plot with me repeatedly. I think we got it...can you read it one more time? Thank you to Lisa and Heather for being the very first readers and loving Lindsey and Nick like I do. Your support means the world to me. Thank you to my super important beta readers, Rachel and Brittni, your input was invaluable as always. Thank you to my ARC readers who were so excited for this book. Your support means so much to me! To my loyal bookstagrammers, thank you for always voicing your love and pushing my books. I wouldn't be here without you. I love each and every one of you. To Michelle, for having to read and edit yet another crazy book of mine. I'm sure when you see my emails come in you're thinking oh great, here we go again. My writing wouldn't shine without you. I promise to work on blond vs blonde and lots of other things. Thank you to Stephany for tying up all the loose ends. To my family, for their support and insisting on reading my books, thank you and I love you. To my husband and kids for putting up with my: just give me one more paragraph, one more minute, one more second! Your patience made this book happen. To Josephine and Richard, thank you from the bottom of my heart for all your love and support.

Other Books by Sophie Sinclair

The Coffee Book Series
Coffee Girl – Coffee Book 1
The Makeup Artist – Coffee Book 2
The Social Hour – Coffee Book 3

About the Author

Sophie Sinclair lives with her husband, two daughters, and a gaggle of animals in Davidson, NC.